THE INTENTIONS BOOK

THE INTENTIONS BOOK

Gigi Fenster

Victoria University Press

TE WHARE WĀNANGA O TE ŪPOKO O TE IKA A MĀUI

VICTORIA
UNIVERSITY OF WELLINGTON

VICTORIA UNIVERSITY PRESS
Victoria University of Wellington
PO Box 600 Wellington
http://www.victoria.ac.nz/vup

National Library of New Zealand Cataloguing-in-Publication Data

Fenster, Gigi.
The intentions book / Gigi Fenster.
ISBN 978-0-86473-823-3
I. Title.
NZ823.3—dc 23

Published with the assistance of a grant from

creative
nz
ARTS COUNCIL OF NEW ZEALAND TOI AOTEAROA

Printed by Printstop, Wellington

For my father who told stories and my mother who reads them.

Acknowledgements

Thank you to Abby, Anna, Craig, Emma, Kate, Lucy, Mary, Sue and Tom, who read and reread. To Bill who taught me and Eirlys who reminded me what I'd learned. Thank you to Damien who championed. To Fergus and Jane who gently guided. And, of course, to Ruth, Hannah, Dirk, Pnina, David, Jonathan, Rahla and Nici, without whom not.

I

What's the definition of a schmuck, I mean a schlemiel. No, no, a schmuck. What's the definition?

Of which one? A schmuck or a schlemiel?

Schmuck. Schlemiel. Doesn't matter. What's the definition?

But I don't know what I'm defining.

Come on. This is a joke. Not a Yiddish test. All you have to say is, 'I don't know, what?'

What?

Damn. Now I have to start at the beginning. I'll choose one if it makes you happy. What's the definition of a schmuck?

I don't know. What?

When he leaves a room you think someone's arrived and when he enters you think someone's left . . . You can smile, you know. I told you it's a joke.

And what, Morris wonders if the schmuck lives alone? Does he drag all the air out of the house as he moves from room to room? A man in a vacuum.

He shakes his head slightly. This is no time for forgotten conversations. There is something he needs to do. He must email his client at the Securities Commission. He must warn him that tomorrow's deadline might be missed. Something has happened.

He will email his client. Then he will put on his jacket and collect his keys. Then he will drive to David's, where he will await further instructions.

Morris sits in front of his computer, composing the email in his head. The opening is simple enough: Dear James, thank you for the data sent yesterday. I now have all the information I need.

But from there things get difficult.

Morris is aware that postponing a deadline, like calling in sick, is probably not something you do by email. You're probably supposed to front up and use the phone so the other person can say how sorry they are and ask if there's anything they can do. Then you thank them for the offer and say that the police are working with Search and Rescue, they're doing all they can, thus freeing the other person to put the phone down and tell everyone in the office that Morris's daughter has gone missing on a tramping trip. And the new guy can ask, 'Who's Morris? Do I know Morris?' and someone else can say, 'He's that consultant who does the computer stuff. He works from home.'

'You mean that old tall man who always wears a tie?'

'Yeah, yeah, the tall kind of bulky guy with glasses.'

'I thought he was an accountant. How embarrassing.'

'Don't worry, you're not the first. It's 'cause we don't imagine such an old guy doing computer stuff.'

'And he looks like an accountant.'

Then they'll turn to talking about people who go missing on tramping trips. Someone will ask where the daughter was and, on hearing she was in the Tararuas, will give a whistle full of exaggerated worry. Of course they'll discuss the man who died in the Tararuas a few months ago. It was all over the news, the body being airlifted out, the man's father thanking the searchers in faltering, accented English.

Some people in the office will think, What if the computer guy's daughter has died? Who will work on the insider trading matter then? It's hard to find computer forensics people at short notice.

Morris writes an email: Due to a family matter the report may be delayed.

He does not specify how long a delay.

There's a moment, just before Morris instructs his

computer to shut down, when he feels something like panic. The computer doesn't like being shut down. It delays its death with questions about saving or not saving and is he absolutely sure he wants to shut it down? Has he thought about the email that will slip in seconds after the screen has gone blank?

Normally he would leave it on, allowing it to put itself to sleep and then to sit dozing on his desk, hibernating.

But not today.

Today he must rush through the answers. He must shut down the computer and go to his bedroom and—

Morris stands at his bedroom door and wonders what he's doing there. He gazes at the neatly made bed, the laptop on the bedside table, the dumb valet holding his jacket. He's looking for clues.

Stupid idiot, he thinks, you stupid, stupid idiot.

Sadie would have been impatient with this self-reproach. She always was.

Give yourself a break. Everyone has the experience of walking into a room and wondering what they're doing there. You're distracted. You're worrying about Rachel.

Which is why I need to be less distracted, not more. Anyway, most people don't walk into a room and then forget what they're doing there.

Everyone does it. Young, old, everyone. Just last week you heard a funny story about someone doing it. At David's party.

Morris had not wanted to go to his son's party. He'd tried pleading work, a previous engagement, even (this he was slightly ashamed of) grief over Sadie's death. But David had been short with his excuses, the grief one most of all.

'C'mon Dad, it's been over a year and, let's face it, it's not like you were . . . it's not like you were . . . Please come.'

And then as a final sweetener: 'Rachel is coming. You two can look after each other.'

And so he'd agreed to go. To keep his daughter company and to keep his son happy, though he couldn't imagine why David wanted him there. Perhaps David didn't desire his father's presence so much as feel discomfort at the thought of his absence.

Rachel arrived at the party late—too late to spend much time with Morris—but he had, despite her late arrival, enjoyed himself. David's wife Debbie was a good cook, and David a thoughtful host. He moved amongst his guests, one hand offering canapés, the other steering someone towards someone else who had just that second found himself alone. A benign conductor who noticed every empty drink, every awkward silence. Who had only to wave his baton to make it right.

'Dad, come here.' David led Morris towards a small group among whom a bald man was holding court. 'You must hear the funny story Simon is telling.'

The bald man paused in his story, and five faces turned to stare at Morris.

'I'm sorry to interrupt. I . . .'

'Welcome, dear sir.'

'Thanks, I'll . . .'

'Come. Join our little soirée. You'll soon get the gist of what is, I assure you, a most amusing story.'

Did he always talk like an English actor? Or was he putting on an accent for added entertainment?

'Now, where was I?' said Simon, 'Ah, yes. I march into the spare room, all purpose and direction.' He stood up to demonstrate, arms swinging, grin widening. 'I turn on the light.' His hand shot out and mimed switching on a light switch, then he paused, his hand hanging in the air, paralysed.

Someone in the group let out a small sigh of pleasure.

'I look around the room.'

Another little mime followed, of Simon smacking his bald head and blinking—a fool who has suddenly found himself questioning his place in the world.

'There's a pile of clothes on the spare bed. Was I supposed to collect them? For washing maybe? I contemplate the clothes. Contemplate and cogitate and, and . . . I don't know what the hell I'm doing there.'

Forget about the accent. Focus on the words.

'If I'd had a long pole I would have poked it at the clothes. But, being pole-less, so to speak . . .'

A woman giggled loudly. Simon wagged his finger at her. 'You dirty-minded wench, you.'

The woman giggled louder and raised her glass to him.

'As I was saying,' said Simon, 'before being so charmingly interrupted, there was nothing for it but to turn the light off, back out of the room and close the door. Now I'm standing in the passage. I'm too embarrassed to go into the kitchen and risk being caught by my long-suffering wife who will no doubt ask me whether I've done whatever it was I was supposed to do.' He gestured towards a woman in a red dress. She looked indulgent rather than long-suffering. Like she was enjoying the story. She probably enjoyed all of his stories.

He's revelling in his own folly, Morris thought, exaggerating it, playing it up. He has turned his mistake into a party trick.

Sadie used to do that. She'd come home, off-load the parcels (were there always so many parcels?), turn to whoever happened to be closest and say something like, 'You'll never believe what a silly thing I did today.'

If she'd done something really embarrassing, she'd repeat it over and over, and with each telling it became more exaggerated, more ridiculous and, if audience reactions were to be trusted, funnier.

There was, for example, the toilet paper incident. Sadie must have told that story a hundred times. Every time she'd laughed till tears rolled down her face. The listeners laughed too—at the image of Sadie walking through a fancy hotel, trailing toilet paper out of her handbag. Was that all there was to it? Sadie, in a fancy hotel, trailing toilet paper? There must have been more. Everyone had laughed so hard. Could she have been stealing the toilet paper? Surely not.

Morris remembered to smile at Simon, but what he really wanted was to move away from the group, draw David or Rachel into a corner and ask why their mother had been trailing toilet paper around a fancy hotel. What was she doing there and why was it all so very funny? But David was busy and Rachel hadn't arrived yet. Morris forced his attention back to Simon and his story.

'Well, you can imagine what a bloody ass I felt, standing in the dark in the passage. My wife—' another gesture towards the woman in the red dress—'at one end of the corridor. A pile of dirty clothes in the spare room, and me, stuck in the middle, pole-less and cogitating.

'What to do? What to do? I could stand there all day, but that would be too much—even for a man such as me. And my lovely wife would catch me sooner or later.'

Simon's wife, right on cue, gave a mock little curtsey.

'And then it hits me. Simple.' Simon smacked his forehead, rather hard, Morris thought. Everyone laughed. 'All I need to do is to retrace my steps, go back to where I've come from and I'll remember. So I do. I walk back to the kitchen door, stand just outside it, and . . . and . . .'

'You remembered,' someone called out, giving Simon's wife her cue.

'No he didn't. I came out of the kitchen and asked him

whether he'd woken my father yet.'

'It wasn't a pile of dirty old clothes.' Simon's voice boomed over the laughter. 'It was my father-in-law.'

Morris tried to laugh. Everyone else was.

'The moral of the story,' said Simon, 'is that retracing your steps really does work. Well, that and having a very clever wife.' He winked across at her.

'Clever, lovely and long-suffering,' she said, and winked back.

Everyone was smiling and laughing, and Morris was wondering why Simon didn't knock before entering the room. Isn't that what you do? Especially if you've got your father-in-law staying.

Simon should have knocked. That would have been the right thing to do.

Morris looks into his bedroom, half-expecting the bed to contain a pile of clothes or an old man sleeping. But if there ever was an old man, or even the ghost of an old man, he's been chased away by the schmuck who now stands steadying himself on the doorframe and wondering what he's doing there.

Smack your forehead. Retrace your steps.

He's halfway down the passage before he remembers: his jacket and car keys.

It's cold in the car. Morris turns the heater on, the radio louder. It's almost time for the news and, after that, the weather.

Sadie used to get irritated by his interest in the weather. 'It doesn't matter what the weather is,' she'd say, 'we'll get on with things.' Or, if she was talking to the children, 'Never mind the weather, as long as we're together.'

But this time she would understand. If Sadie were here, she too would be leaning towards the car's single speaker. She too would be squinting up at the clouds, trying to work out whether they were getting heavier or lighter.

The news starts with a report about the opening of the Arctic Sea Route. The European Space Agency has formally announced that the shortest route between Europe and Asia is, for the first time since records began, fully clear of ice, and navigable.

The newsreader's voice is deep, composed. Morris is grateful for his measured pace as he advises of the political battles which the new route may create. Measured is the correct pace for such news.

Excitement is not correct, but excitement is what Morris had felt that morning at breakfast when he'd read in the newspaper about the opening of the route. He'd known, as soon as he felt it, that he shouldn't allow himself even the slightest thrill at the thought of the earth's layers stripping away, ice floe by ice floe. Global warming was not something to be thrilled about. But still—all that stripping away! It made him think of ancient artefacts coming to the surface, of new worlds opening up. Tall men wearing heavy coats and fur-covered boots were captaining ships, forging forwards. They grew their beards long to keep out the cold.

At breakfast he'd tried to imagine the melting of the Arctic ice. He'd told himself what to picture: a white expanse, nothing but white, and then, through the middle of it, shaped like a series of lightning bolts, grey cracks which widened and grew, fracturing the ice on either side.

You need to close your eyes to imagine it, he'd told himself. There's no one here to see you. Just close them and try to picture it. First there's nothing . . .

Had it been a black nothing, it would have been as simple as closing his eyes and seeing what he saw. But to imagine white—that was too hard. Maybe Sadie could have done that.

He'd run his hands over the toast crumbs on the table, embarrassed himself with the thought that he was like a blind man reading Braille, and opened his eyes to wipe the crumbs into his cupped hand.

Perhaps his mistake had been in trying first to imagine nothing. Ice isn't nothing. There's never really nothing. He knows that.

As a boy Morris had a Bible Studies teacher with a huge black beard and deep booming voice.

'Before the creation, what was there?'

Hands flew up. 'Nothing.' 'Nothing.' 'Nothing.'

The black beard shook from side to side. 'Now I will teach you something. There wasn't nothing. There was something worse.'

He paused. The room was silent.

'I'll tell you what there was—there was chaos.'

Chaos. Morris felt the word catch in the back of his mouth.

'Chaos,' boomed the black beard. 'Chaos and disorder. A muddle of wild and waste.'

Some teachers would have joked about things being as chaotic as the playground at lunch time. One teacher would have made jokes about Morris's handwriting. 'Quite a chaotic jumble of letters we have here. Or am I the confused one and is this actually a drawing? Yes, yes, I see it now. This isn't handwriting. It's a picture of an aeroplane. I'm right, aren't I? An aeroplane flying upside down with its wing on fire.'

Black Beard did not make jokes. He knew that muddle was not to be taken lightly.

He made them close their eyes to try to imagine. 'Screw them up tightly. We're not having an afternoon nap. We're trying to imagine something horrible. Tighter. Tighter. So tightly you can hear it in your ears.'

Morris screwed his eyes tighter. He listened to his ears.

'When you first close your eyes, you think you're seeing only darkness.' Black Beard lowered his voice. 'But look closer. There are imperfections in the dark. There's wildness and disorder. See those creases and particles in front of your eyes?'

Morris pressed his hands over his eyes, and the darkness started creasing.

'Imagine that each one of those imperfections is huge, gigantic. Monstrous and constantly changing. The imperfections bump into each other, splinter, re-form. Now focus on one of those monstrous heaps of matter. One minute it looks like liquid, and the next it's a thin strand wrapped around blackness which is moving and changing, and now it's a hard sharp light changed into wet cotton wool which is pulling apart into a blur of chaos and movement and grating energy going nowhere. There's nothing for your mind to hold on to. You don't know up from down.'

You don't know up from down. There's nothing for your mind to hold on to.

Morris pulled his hands away from his eyes. He was gazing into his lap when Black Beard said, 'Before you open your eyes, I want you to remind yourselves that you have not even begun to imagine the horror of the chaos that was before the creation.'

The room was quite silent.

'That,' said the teacher, 'is the real miracle of creation. God gave us something to hold on to. He brought order. Form and matter. Direction to our energy.'

Order, thought Morris. Direction to our energy.

A few days later, when his Uncle Norman asked how his lessons were going, Morris didn't say, 'Fine thank you.' He told him about the teacher with the black beard and how God brought order where previously there was only chaos.

'Is that so?' said Norman. 'My. My.'

'Yes, and once things were ordered, God could see what was missing. My teacher didn't actually say so, but that's how God knew what to create next, I think.'

'Well I never,' said Norman. 'Aren't you a clever boy?'

Morris's daughter is missing and he sits in his car outside his son's house, daydreaming about long-dead teachers.

Order, thinks Morris. Something for the mind to hold on to. You are in your car. You have driven to David's house. The radio is on. You have allowed yourself to be distracted.

He unbuckles his seatbelt, leaving the key turned so he can hear the radio till the last minute. The weather report comes on just as he's about to remove the key. The car door is open. His body has shifted. He sits, neither inside nor out, uncomfortable.

The whole country washes over him.

David's head sticks out through an upstairs window. 'The front door's open. Come in. I'll be down in two minutes.'

Morris stands in the entrance hall for a moment before heading left, to the lounge. He sits on the sofa with his hands in his lap, his watch face pointing towards him, and waits. It's almost ten minutes before there's a noise from above and footsteps coming down the stairs.

David's hair is standing up in front, giving him a surprised, frightened look. Morris half-rises from the sofa to greet him just as his son turns to close the door.

Faced with David's back, Morris looks down at his own hovering hands and wonders what he'd been intending to do with them.

He catches himself on the arms of the sofa to stop from falling.

David says, 'You won't fucking believe this,' and Morris sinks into the sofa.

David's been on the phone to the police. The police have been on the phone to Search and Rescue. Search and Rescue have spoken to the park warden. The park warden said Rachel's not due out yet.

Not due out yet.

'According to them she's only due out at four. Four o'clock. So according to them she's not even missing.'

Rachel's not missing and David is furious.

He says, 'Honestly, I could kill her. Why did she do that? Why the two different times?'

'Two different times. I don't understand.'

David runs his hands through his hair, takes a deep breath. Is he counting to ten in his head before he speaks?

'Okay Dad, so here's the thing. Rachel told us—me and Debs—that she'd be finished her tramp around twelve. We made her promise to phone us when she got out. And we made her type out her plans—where she was going, when she'd be out, that sort of thing. We didn't want her rushing off without anyone knowing where she was going.'

'She would have . . .'

Stop right there.
Stop?
You were going to tell David that she would have let someone know her plans anyway, even without him telling her to.
I . . .
Oh Morris, for crying out. Give the boy a bit of comfort. Let him think he did the right thing. For crying out, Morris.

'What did you say, Dad?'

'Nothing. It was good of you to get her to type that all out.'

David's face softens for a moment. 'Thanks.' He pauses, as if to recover both his train of thought and his anger. 'We wouldn't have even known she was going tramping, but Debs bumped into her at the gym and convinced her to come for dinner. That's when she told us she was going and we made her type up her plans.'

'Type up her plans.'

'Yeah, where she was going and stuff. So anyway, she said she'd be out around twelve, so at about half past I tried calling her cell phone. It went straight to voicemail. I kept trying her, then I called the cops. And you. Debs also thought I should.'

If David would pause again, Morris could tell him that

he did the right thing when he called the police, but David keeps on speaking. 'So the cops called Search and Rescue and they called the warden. So the warden checked the book they keep at the entrance to the park.'

'The Intentions Book.'

'And that said she'd be out at four. So, according to them, she's not late until then.'

'Four o'clock.'

'Panic time. They call it panic time. Can you believe they call it panic time? They even put it in the Intentions Book. What is your panic time? Four—that's what Rachel wrote. Her panic time is four. They reckon four is the correct time to be getting out of there anyway, 'cause the last day's hike is quite long.'

'Did you ask about the weather?'

'The weather's fine. It's been fine for days. Of course I asked.'

They look at each other for a moment then David says, 'Bottom line, Dad. Bottom line is she's not even late. She's got us worrying for nothing. And now what do we do? Now we wait. And what are we waiting for? We're waiting to start worrying. Man, I could kill her.'

Panic time is more than two hours away. The last day's hike is long. The weather's fine. Rachel's not even missing yet. There's just been some confusion. The Tararuas aren't that bad really.

Morris can ignore the tightness in his throat. He can go home.

He says, 'Well, if there's nothing to do, I guess I should—'

'Nothing to do until three. The cop said we should call again round three to check in.'

'Round three.'

'Yeah, and Wendy's on her way.'

'Wendy.'

'She knows about the later time but she said she'd come here anyway. To wait with us.'

'Wendy.'

'Yes, Wendy. I guess she'll be here soon.'

They both look at their watches.

David says, 'We can all wait together.'

'Together.'

'Yeah, but not my kids. Debs will take them to her mum.'

Morris says, 'Is it necessary, I mean Wendy coming and the children going? Is it all necessary?'

'No, Dad, it's not necessary. But here we are, in this situation. What are we going to do? Not bloody business as usual. We've got Rachel to thank for that.' He gives a soft snort. 'Look, Dad, I don't mean to be harsh, but let's face it, she really stuffed up this time.'

David's face starts to crease, like Sadie's did when she was about to cry.

Maybe he's not angry. Maybe he's confused.

'David, I—'

Then Debbie's in the room. She's holding a briefcase in one hand and Benjy in the other. She says, 'Oh, hi Morris.'

Morris wants to look at the baby, but Debbie hands him directly to David, who buries his face in the soft blueness and says, 'Ben Bon a Bullabay.'

'I thought you might want this,' she says, and puts the briefcase on the floor. When she straightens she puts her hand on her back like an old lady. She gives Morris a weak smile. 'What a mix-up.'

She looks tired.

Morris could get up and hug her, take the opportunity he'd missed with David, but the sofa is so damned low, Emma's shouting for her mother, Debbie's calling, 'I'm coming sweetheart,' and turning on her heel. Morris slumps back into the sofa just as Debbie turns back into the room.

'Gosh, I nearly forgot Benjy. I guess I'd better take him with me.'

Once more Morris tries to lift himself from the sofa and once more he's thwarted by its soft sag. From over Debbie's shoulder the baby peers accusingly.

David gives a wave before bending down to open the briefcase. He finds the document he's looking for, rests it on his knee, strokes it.

'So, this is what Rachel left with us.' He reads aloud— 'Due out at twelve p.m. on Tuesday fifteenth of August'— then puts the paper back on his lap. 'She means twelve noon. Twelve noon.'

Morris wants to take the paper. He wants to stroke it. He wants to hold it up to the light, to search between its words. He wants to study the words 'twelve p.m.'. Did she press harder on the keys when typing them? Or did her fingers falter, uncertain?

David says, 'So she probably forgot she'd told us twelve. And left her cell phone off or forgot to charge it. She keeps her phone off half the time. It's like she . . . like she . . . And we all know how forgetful she is. She left her phone and her purse here when she came for my party. She would have forgotten to come at all if Debbie hadn't reminded her. She's so forgetful.'

Is Rachel forgetful? She'd seemed such a well-organised child, her room always tidy, her desk so ordered.

Morris says, 'D'you remember how she used to line her coloured pencils up along her desk?'

David looks up from his papers. 'Coloured pencils? No, I don't remember. But it wouldn't surprise me. She's a big one for lining things up.'

I know that, thinks Morris. Rachel was ordered as a child.

'Tidy room. Messy mind,' David says. 'Don't tell her I

said that, but honestly, she can be so . . . so . . .' He returns to his reading.

'Um, David.'

'Yes Dad.'

'She doesn't mean to forget things. She wouldn't do this on purpose. I don't think.'

David's face is creasing again.

Now look what you've done.

David has gone to help Debbie with the baby. He's left Morris with Rachel's typed sheet and a map printed from the internet.

Morris turns the map face down. He doesn't want to look at the Tararua Ranges. He hates the Tararuas. The Tararuas are his mulberries.

The children were at primary school when Sadie bought the mulberries. She came rushing into the house, rustling shopping bags and jangling keys, calling, 'Children, Morris, come quickly. Come and taste something. Quickly.'

Groceries on the kitchen table and Sadie's face bent over a bag.

'Come, the taste of my childhood.'

Then her face lifting, shining. She's holding a small plastic container.

'Right, you lot. Stand in front of me. Eyes closed. Mouths open. You too, Morris. Leave the milk. It can wait.'

They lined up, closed their eyes, opened their mouths.

Sadie said, 'Behold. The taste of my childhood,' and put something in each waiting mouth.

Rachel swallowed her berry, then scowled and said, 'Eeugh'.

David spat his into his hand.

Sadie said, 'It's not your fault,' and left the room.

Morris put away the shopping. A dollar fifty for a few berries that no one wanted to eat.

Later, when it was just the two of them, Sadie said, 'It wasn't the price that upset me. It was the way they messed with my memories. I'd stopped missing those berries years ago. I'd forgotten about them. Until today. In the supermarket. There they were—jumping up at me, saying, 'Remember remember.' So I bloody remembered and then I craved them and now . . . now I hate them. I crave them and I hate them. How unfair is that? They should have jumped up saying, 'I've been frozen and shipped halfway across the world. I'm bruised and battered and I taste bloody awful.' That's what they should have said. That's what.'

Her face started creasing. 'It would have been better if they tasted nothing like the ones I remembered, but they were almost there. Close enough to mess up my memories for good.'

And crying.

Morris didn't understand. Until she said, 'Now I can't be sure that my childhood mulberries were as nice as I remember them. It's like they've made me doubt my happy memories.'

He thought about how something could make you doubt your happy memories. He thought about the Wellington Tramping Club and the Tararuas. Maybe he had his own mulberries.

Wendy is Sadie's sister. Morris hasn't seen her in weeks.

She's bent over the boot of her car, passing things behind her to David. He's talking to her back, and when she straightens they move to hug each other, plastic bags, Tupperware containers and all.

Morris watches from the front door.

Wendy doesn't look like Sadie. She's shorter, even in her high heels, and her hair is dark. She's really nothing like Sadie. And yet the sight of her, turning to face him, the sound of the car boot slamming behind her, the way she helps David carry her parcels. The parcels themselves.

These things are paralysing.

That's Wendy coming from her car, Morris tells himself. It's Wendy.

But the light is behind her, blotting out her features, so that all he sees is a silhouette, a shadow wearing Sadie's shawl.

It's only Wendy, his head instructs his limbs. But they won't listen. They're too deeply frozen.

Suddenly Emma comes crashing past him, through the gap between his rigid body and the door, crying, 'Bendy Wendy. They never told me you were coming.'

Wendy picks Emma up and twirls round with her, and asks who is the greatest, grandest great-niece in the whole wide world?

Morris just manages to remove himself from the doorway before the two of them stagger in together.

Later, when Debbie has prised Emma from her aunt's side, and they've all been through the complicated task of getting Emma and the baby strapped into the car and waved off to their nana, David sits opposite Wendy and tells her everything.

She says it's all some silly mistake. They'll laugh about it later. Rachel got the times mixed up. She forgot to charge her phone. Everyone knows how forgetful she is.

Wendy instructs David to stand up immediately and give her a hug.

Oh for goodness sakes, Morris thinks, he's not five years old any more.

David stands and allows himself to fall into Wendy's arms. She reaches up to smooth his hair. When he finally lets go, she says, 'I'll kill her when she gets home. I wonder—will I kill her first or hug her first?'

David says, 'You hug her. I'll kill her.' He smiles, but his eyes are shining and he leaves the room.

Wendy says, 'Come outside with me.'

Even her voice can paralyse. Especially the voice. If you close your eyes you can imagine.

'Come outside and keep me company while I have a cigarette.'

But that line—that keep-me-company-while-I-have-a-cigarette—is Wendy's line. Entirely.

There was a time when Wendy used to smoke in the house. So did Sadie. If Sadie invited guests or the two sisters sat up talking, the smell of cigarette smoke would linger for days. Morris found it repulsive and dirty, though he occasionally smoked himself.

He didn't say anything, but Sadie must have guessed. One day she said, 'How about we make this house smoke free? Shall we draw straws for who gets to tell Wendy?'

Sadie told her sister and Wendy took it surprisingly well.

'Outside it is. Now come and keep me company while I have a cigarette.'

How many hours did Sadie spend outside keeping Wendy company? How many smoky conversations and slow secrets passed with the drags on cigarettes that Sadie, and later David, took on the deck? Even Rachel, who never smoked, did her time outside with Wendy, waving away the smoke and complaining that it was bad for them all, but still outside, still keeping company. Morris would watch them through the window and wonder what Rachel was telling Wendy. Would Wendy repeat it to Sadie? Would Sadie repeat it to him?

Morris gave up smoking completely when the ashtrays moved outside. 'No commitment,' Sadie teased. 'One hint of a cold wind and you give up altogether. Where's your staying power, Morris Goldberg?'

Sadie gave up or pretended to give up more times than Morris can remember. He'd smell it on her after Wendy or certain friends had visited. 'You don't have to hide it from me,' he once said. 'I don't mind.'

'But that's half the fun,' was her reply.

He started smoking again when she was in hospital the first time. He didn't hide it from her but he didn't tell her either.

After she died, he stopped again. Completely.

Wendy says, 'Come keep me company.'

'That shawl,' Morris manages once they're outside.

'You recognise it. Of course you do. Sadie gave it to me not long before she died. She said she didn't want it to end up at the Sallies.'

Does Wendy know that Morris bought the shawl for Sadie? He'd gone on a business trip to Sydney, and with time to kill at the airport found himself gazing at a pile of neatly folded shawls.

The shop assistant came and stood right up close to him. 'Aren't they pretty? They're so soft. Merino. Feel it. Bury your hands in them.'

Morris patted the top one.

The woman said, 'Where are you from? New Zealand. I hear it's cold there. Are you married? Your wife will love this.'

She'd wrapped it in tissue paper.

Now Wendy runs her hands along the fabric. 'I guess I shouldn't have worn it. I didn't mean to upset you.'

'Upset me? No, I don't mind at all.' It would be silly to mind. It was just a shawl.

Once, watching people at a crowded bus stop, Morris had seen a man reach over and stroke a woman's jacket. He was watching the couple as the bus pulled into the terminus. No—not watching exactly, rather gazing at them through the window in a tired, unfocused way. They were standing close but not touching. They might have been strangers, but as the bus pulled in the woman turned towards the man and said something. Then turned away.

They didn't touch before she walked away, her face towards her bag, looking, perhaps, for her ticket. But then, as she was about to merge with the queue, almost beyond reach, the man did it, raised his arm, lifted his hand and stroked the back of her jacket.

The jacket was padded nylon, puffed beyond the woman's body. Morris watched the woman's face, really watched, and saw no satisfaction. She is numb to his touch, he thought. Did the man not know it? Did he know that his hand would not make its way beyond the stuffed coat?

Morris stroked the arm of his own jacket tentatively, aware that he was surrounded and that while stroking the jacket of another may be quite acceptable, caressing one's own on a crowded bus might draw attention. The fabric was rough and warm, not unpleasant, but not so it was hard to return his hand once more to his lap. No, it was not the feel of the fabric—surely.

Morris had heard that a bereaved person might bury his face in the clothes of a loved one, trying, he supposed, to sense that which was lost. He had not done that. Even when the guests were gone, taking their pity and their sorrow with them. Even when the house was silent and ticking, he had not once thought to open Sadie's closet and forget in the feel of her fabric. Not once.

And then the clothes were gone. Rachel saw to it. It was done in a day. Morris could have gone in and kept her company that day. He could have offered to help and then, when Rachel left the room, perhaps, lifted a dress off a hanger, a jersey off a shelf, put it to his face and breathed in the stuff of Sadie. But Morris left Rachel and the room and the clothes well alone. I'll only get in the way, he thought, and he sat in his study, eyes to the computer, back to the door, and listened to the clacking of hangers, the closing of drawers, the sighs of clothes settling themselves in the depths of dustbin bags.

Then the dragging of the bags out of the room, down the passage to the door, his door, the study door where the bags were silenced. And in that silence stood Rachel, clenched fists holding the bags closed. Or perhaps her hands were hanging at her sides, the bags sufficiently well packed to stand alone. One on either side of her. Like stakes. Perhaps the bags were propped against each other. Balancing just so. What do we two do now? wondered Morris. What now? He could have turned from the screen. He could have faced the silence or risen from his chair. He could have walked to the door and turned the handle and held her hard and tight, and stroked her hair and murmured that she was a motherless child and he a sorry old widower. They could have sat together on those dustbin bags and cried.

On the computer the image of a window flew into a window flew into a window. Morris sat and stared at the relentless windows, stared and waited for Rachel to stand in the doorway and say that she was done, would see him tomorrow. And Morris, still gazing at the moving windows, raised his hand, 'See you tomorrow then,' and listened as the dustbin bags heaved their heavy way out of the house.

Some weeks later Morris stood at a traffic light and there, on the other side of the road, looking directly at him, was a young woman wearing what was once, could it be, a dress of Sadie's? The young woman looked good in it. Morris could have told her so. He could have waited at that crossing and watched her as she approached, and then, when she was just close enough, he could have smiled and said, 'You look good in that dress.' Or he could have crossed her path, come close and glanced the fabric, skimmed the skirt as it breathed on the breeze of a young spring woman. But Morris did none of those things. People do not go around complimenting strangers on their dress. And a glance could become a touch, could be felt through the fabric.

The man had not kissed the woman or stroked her hair or touched her hand before she turned to the bus. He had not hugged her or patted her cheek or even, Morris suspected, muttered a goodbye. But he had reached out, when she was beyond his compass, and stroked the back of her departing jacket. People do that, Morris had thought. People do that.

Sadie had loved the Australian shawl. She said it was exactly the right colours for her. She wrapped it around herself, around him, playful, happy to have him home. Glowing with the softness of her gift. She didn't want it to end up with the Sallies.

He could have gone in when Rachel was packing up the clothes and taken the shawl. He could have made up some excuse about using it to keep his legs warm while he was working at the computer. But Sadie had already given the shawl to Wendy.

Take it now, Wends. It'll end up with the Sallies if I leave it up to Morris.

Morris wonders whether merino requires particular attention, whether Wendy knows how to look after it.

He could ask her to let him feel it. Instead, he says he wouldn't mind a cigarette.

Wendy doesn't raise her eyebrows. She just warns him that they're menthol and hands one over.

He lights the cigarette and braces himself for a sore chest, but there's no pain. Only a thin, watery mist which leaves him faintly nauseous.

Wendy takes a deep drag on her cigarette. 'It's the catapult feeling that's making you want to smoke.'

'Catapult feeling?'

'It's like I've had catapult elastic round my waist ever since David phoned. Every minute it's being stretched further and further and if Rachel doesn't turn up by four . . .'

'Panic time.'

'Panic time. Who thought up that term? At four o'clock the bugger who thought up the term panic time is going to let go of the elastic and I'll be shot out of the catapult. All hell will break loose and I'll . . . I'll . . . I'll fucking panic.'

'Wendy, I—'

'Thank goodness you're a calm force. We need at least one non-panicker in the house. You're our man. Morris Goldberg, the man-who-never-panics. And you're right. You're right. There's no need to panic. She's not even missing yet and here I am with the catapult feeling. It's ridiculous of me, I know.'

Morris had forgotten how much he dislikes menthol cigarettes. He inhales again. Deeper this time.

Wendy says, 'Poor David. This is just awful for him. He feels so responsible for Rachel.'

'Mmm.'

'He's blaming himself.'

'David blaming himself? For what?'

'I don't know. For letting her go on her own, for not double-checking where she was going or what time she'd be out. For phoning the police before panic time. I don't know.'

'But he hasn't . . . nobody has . . . It's no one's fault. She's not even missing yet. He knows that.'

'Yes, but knowing something in your head and believing it to be true are, of course, two different things.'

Morris nods. There's nothing to be gained by challenging Wendy. She speaks with such conviction, such certainty that she's correct.

Just like Sadie: Every child must have a pet. David Lynch is an appalling film maker. Rachel must carry the lollies in her own school bag. You absolutely cannot substitute parmesan for feta cheese. That teacher of Rachel's is thick as a brick. David blames himself. Knowing something in your head and believing it to be true are incompatible. These are truths. Indisputable.

Like Sadie, Wendy would be able to give examples, cite research. She would have read about it in a book or seen a documentary on exactly this topic.

Morris taps his cigarette on the ashtray, though he hasn't smoked enough for the ash to build up.

'It's especially hard for David,' Wendy continues. 'He's always been so protective of Rachel.' She takes a sharp pull on her cigarette. 'It's a good thing none of his friends ever tried dating her. He would not have taken that kindly.'

She rests her cigarette in the ashtray, strokes the shawl.

She'll make it smell of cigarette smoke.

'Mind you,' she says, 'one or two of them could at least have tried their luck with her. Sadie and I used to wonder why none of them ever did.'

She was too young for them, thinks Morris. She wasn't interested in them. They were too loud, too rough.

'She would have been the same age as some of their girlfriends,' says Wendy. 'And pretty. I guess they never looked at her in that way—her being David's sister and all.'

That was how Rachel wanted it. That was what she chose.

'Sadie used to worry about her,' says Wendy.

Once, when the children were teenagers, Morris drove them to a social event at the school.

Some time before they were due to leave, David started banging on Rachel's door, calling, 'Get a move on. My friends are waiting for me.'

When Rachel finally came out she had her arms folded tightly across her chest and a thick stripe of blue eye shadow on each of her eyelids.

It was a good thing Sadie wasn't there. She would have made a fuss of Rachel and gone on and on about how pretty she looked. Rachel wouldn't have wanted that. She also wouldn't have wanted Morris telling her that her blue eyelids made him want to cry.

Sadie would've phoned Wendy the minute they were out of the door. They would have laughed about the blue eye shadow.

David didn't notice the eye shadow. Or didn't care. 'About time too,' was all he said.

He sat in front and fiddled with the car radio. Morris looked at Rachel in his rear-view mirror. She stared out of her window.

The car filled with teenage music, loud and heavy, and David started drumming his hands on the dashboard. Rachel kept looking outside and Morris found himself wondering what would happen if he swerved suddenly, or started weaving the car across the road, dancing this way and that in time to the music. The road before him was empty and open. The music was loud. He could turn the wheel sharply to one side, then spin it back. What would the children think if he did that? David might like it. Rachel would not.

He turned the music off. He didn't need the distraction while driving.

When they got close to the school they passed groups of teenagers. David opened his window and shouted at some of them, waved, grinned. Rachel kept her window closed. Morris wondered whether she wanted to go to the dance. Was it compulsory? Had Sadie insisted she go? Couldn't he write her a note of excuse and take her somewhere—to a movie maybe, or the beach. They could buy ice cream. They could sit in the car and watch the people walking past.

David said, 'Rache, I'll keep an eye out for you and you can always come and find me. If you want money for a cold drink or you can't find your friends.'

Rachel swore at him.

The next day Sadie said, 'I hear Rachel and David had an argument on the way to the dance. Why didn't you tell me?'

'Tell you?'

'Yes, tell me. Tell me that the kids went mental at each other on the way to the dance.'

Why hadn't Morris told Sadie? Because it wasn't much more than the usual arguing and he knew she'd hear about it soon enough from David?

Or maybe because it wasn't the argument itself which stayed with him but rather what happened after. David bursting from the car—'I was just trying to be nice but if that's the way you want it, fine!'—to be swallowed up by a group of laughing, punching boys. Rachel, small and alone, with all those people swirling around her. Teenagers crashing and colliding, grouping and re-forming. No one she could latch on to. David searching his sister out, peeling himself off from the crowd to go to her, and she, seeing him approach, lifting her chin high and walking away from him. Putting one foot in front of the other.

'Sadie used to worry about her,' Wendy says again, and Morris feels a wave of dislike for his sister-in-law. It was vulgar of her and Sadie to have talked about Rachel in that way. It did a disservice to the blue eye shadow, the brave chin, those feet moving forwards.

He puts out the cigarette and excuses himself to go inside.

Wendy and David are talking about strobe lights. Wendy can't believe that Rachel managed to work with strobes, to see strobes every day.

David says the strobes didn't seem to bother her at the gym. She seemed to turn them off.

'Well,' says Wendy, 'not so turned off that she didn't keep turning them on again, off and on again, off and on.' Her tone is tart.

David says it didn't do either of them any good, all that turning off and on.

'No good at all,' says Wendy.

Morris has no idea what they're talking about.

'Strobelight Stewart. He's off and he's on. He's off and he's on.'

'Mum had another nickname for him—The Wagon—'cause—'

'Rachel was off him then on him. I prefer Strobelight.'

'Well, the lights are off for good now. Finito completo.'

'I've heard that before.'

'This time it's for real. He's got a new girlfriend, and—'

'Since when did one of them dating someone else stop them from getting back together again?'

'Since the girlfriend got pregnant.'

That Bible Studies teacher with the black beard said there was a time when everyone in the world understood everyone else. A time when there was only one language and few words. There were no misunderstandings.

But the people got proud. They thought themselves very

important. So important that they could build a tower to heaven. A tower to God! Who did they think they were?

Black Beard got his students to imagine the highest building they could—higher than the Empire State Building, much higher. He made them close their eyes. Tight enough that you can hear it in your ears. He told them to imagine the building getting higher and higher. Breaking through the clouds.

'Right, you can open your eyes again. Now tell me, will that building ever get to heaven? Will it ever get high enough to reach God?'

Morris glanced around the classroom. What was the correct answer?

'Say there was a special machine that allowed you to keep on building higher and higher and higher. Layer after layer. Storey after storey. Where would you get?'

'To the moon?' hazarded someone.

'To the stars?'

'The sun?'

'The atmosphere!'

The black beard shook from side to side. 'Say you went past all of those things. Would you ever . . . ever, ever get to God?'

A girl near the front said, 'You would get to infinity.'

'Which is the same,' said Black Beard, 'as getting nowhere. You would just keep on going because no matter how high you go, you can never get to God.' He paused to glare down at the class. 'Now, I want you to close your eyes again and think. Think. Why could you never reach God?'

Morris closed his eyes and thought about infinity, about going further and further and getting nowhere.

'I will tell you why you wouldn't reach God—because God is not sitting in a seat somewhere in the sky. God is everywhere. And nowhere.'

Everywhere and nowhere.

'But those tower-builders thought themselves so important. They thought themselves equal to God.' He glared down at his class as if every child there had thought to himself, I am equal to God. 'And that,' he finally boomed, 'was their great sin.'

Morris thought, I am not equal to God. I don't think myself equal to God.

Black Beard perched on the teacher's desk. 'Well, you can imagine what God thought when He saw this tower. He thought, Who do they think they are? And He punished them.' He looked around the room. 'Does anyone know how God punished them? Can anyone think?'

A hand shot up. 'He made it so they couldn't understand each other.'

'Yes. Yes. They couldn't understand each other. He gave them different languages. He gave them misunderstandings.' A sudden smile broke through the beard. 'Isn't that a clever punishment for people who think they can reach the heavens? You take away their ability to talk to each other. You take them one step closer to animals. Blathering turkeys. That tower was called the Tower of Babel. And now I will tell you what Babel means and you will understand what we have those tower-builders to thank for.'

Black Beard waited. The class was silent.

'Babel means . . . confusion. Man tried to reach God and in return we got misunderstanding. Mistakes and mix-ups. Ambiguity. Confusion. We will always struggle to understand each other. For ever more.'

It wasn't fair. Morris had never tried to build a tower to God.

'Gabbling away at each other like turkeys.'

Gabbling away at each other like David and Wendy.

'Pregnant. Does Rachel know? She must know.'

'Debbie doesn't know if Rachel knows. I don't know if Rachel knows.'

'Debbie knows and you know. How could Rachel not know? D'you think she knows?'

'I have no way of knowing if she knows. It's not like she would have discussed it with me. Or Debbie. She certainly didn't mention it when she came for dinner on Wednesday.'

'Did Debbie raise it with her?'

'No, Debbie didn't raise it with her, but then Debbie didn't know at the time. She only found out on Saturday. Someone at the gym told her.'

'D'you think Rachel would've known before everyone else?'

'I bet Strobelight would have told her. He owed her that. At least.'

'At least. And he's a nice guy. He would have done the right thing.'

'Yes, but it wasn't only his news to tell, was it? There's the girlfriend to think of. She probably feels threatened by Rachel. She might not have wanted Rachel to know.'

'You can't keep a thing like that secret. Wellington's a small town. Debbie knew. You knew. Rachel must have known.'

'She must have known.'

'Or maybe she didn't know. Maybe the news only broke after she left to go tramping.'

'Maybe that's right. Debbie only found out on Saturday.'

'And Debbie's on to things.'

On and on, blathering away. Morris can't get a hold on their conversation. He knows it's important but he can't find his way in. His path is blocked by gabbling turkeys.

Morris knows exactly what those misguided tower-builders sounded like. They sounded like David wondering whether they should call Stewart and tell him what's going on, and Wendy saying that it's none of his business and, anyway, nothing's going on.

Like Wendy asking how Rachel seemed on Wednesday when David saw her, and David saying, 'Even keel. You know Rachel. Even keel.'

Like Sadie's silent voice saying, 'How can you be even keel when you've taken yourself off to the Tararuas. Alone. In August?'

Morris went to the Tararuas with the Wellington Tramping Club on returning to Wellington after university. All indications were that things would go well with the club. He'd written to their president from Christchurch, enclosing a testimonial from the president of his own club. He'd received a reply: they'd be glad to have him. Was he one of those southern madmen who used old-fashioned heavy backpacks? Would he like to join their next tramp in the Tararuas?

The Wellington Tramping Club promised to provide him with everything he had got from his university tramping club in Christchurch. It promised long planning sessions with maps and lists, evenings at someone's kitchen table where there was only one topic of conversation—tramping. It promised a Christmas tramp he could use to silence his Aunt Joan's requests that he spend the holidays with them, and colourful characters he could tell her about when she asked, with elaborate tact, about his friends. It might even throw up a tramping buddy.

The Wellington Tramping Club sent Morris into the Tararuas with fifteen other people who all knew each other. They started walking in the evening. Eyes on the ground, torches to avoid tripping up roots. When Morris woke the next morning, he had no idea where he was. Then the mist came and the rain came, and they spent two nights in a hut intended for six people. They spoke about people Morris didn't know. They spoke about the Tararuas.

They called themselves 'Tongue and Meats'. Their president was short. He spoke about girls and the 'rugged Tararuas'. Morris took this as an attack on the southern lakes. The president made jokes about southern men who used overly macho backpacks. Morris didn't find them funny.

Morris hated that short president. He thought night tramping absurd. He couldn't see more than ten feet in front of him in the Tararuas. He never got his bearings.

After six months of pretending to laugh at in-jokes he didn't get, Morris began to wonder whether his memories of fitting in at his old university tramping club were reliable. Maybe he was just some schmuck there too.

David brings his laptop into the kitchen so they can check the weather on the internet. They gaze in silence at the swirling arrows and moving colours until Wendy says, 'I have no idea what I'm looking at.' David says, 'Me neither,' and they both turn to look at Morris.

'Um, it looks fine at the moment.'

'That's something,' says David. Neither he nor Wendy asks what 'at the moment' is supposed to mean. David pulls the laptop closer. 'Let me show you the gym website. It's got a spiel on Rachel. I checked it earlier to see if she had any classes today.'

'And?' says Wendy.

'And she doesn't. I would have told you if she did.' He stretches over to draw Wendy closer to the screen. 'But the website's still worth a look. You can learn a lot about our Rachel from this website. Or should I say, you can learn a lot about Rache, aka Goldie, personal trainer and group fitness instructor.'

There's a photo of Rachel, and next to it (David taps the screen over the words) *Rache Goldberg, aka Goldie.*

Aka Goldie? Morris has never heard his daughter referred to as Goldie, though he has heard plenty of other nicknames for her. Sadie, self-proclaimed nickname queen of the known world, saw to that. But Goldie doesn't sound like one of hers. It's too brassy, too common and conventional. Too much a nickname that a kindergarten teacher could have thought up. No, it's definitely not one of Sadie's. Sadie's nicknames were cutting. They clawed at the heart of the person.

Sadie's scratchy nicknames followed her about like a family of fluffy chickens, soft, cute, cuddly, but capable, if turned in the right direction, of pecking their way through your eyes.

Take Sadie's one and only nickname for Morris. Morris, the one person whom the nickname queen spared, or overlooked, or found herself stumped by. Until that joke. A joke told by a banker with shoulder-length hair and a pink tie.

'Goldberg,' the banker had roared, clapping Morris on the back. 'Have I got a joke for you. Something to lighten this meeting up before I tell everyone how your brain and my brawn are going to make us all seriously rich.'

Lighten the meeting up? Did business meetings call for lightness? Morris had not prepared for lightness.

'So, a Chinaman and a Jew get into an argument in a bar.

'"You people," says the Jew, "you bombed Pearl Harbour."

'"Nonsense," says the Chinaman. "The Chinese didn't bomb Pearl Harbour—that was the Japanese."

'"Chinese, Japanese. What's the difference?"

'"Anyway," says the Chinaman, "you Yids have got a lot to answer for. Let's not forget who sank the *Titanic*."

'"What are you talking about? The Jews didn't sink the *Titanic*. It was an iceberg."

'"Iceberg, Goldberg—what's the difference?"'

Morris had looked down at the open notebook in front of him. His clicking pen rang out in the silence that followed what he thought was genuine laughter at the joke. His business partner said something. The banker laughed loudly. Cups rattled as the tea trolley rolled into the meeting room.

'Gazing out of the window, you were, for the whole meeting,' Morris's partner complained later. 'I just spent half an hour in the lobby with him, convincing him you're some kind of savant genius thing. From now on I'll deal with the meetings, you come up with the systems. And Morris, please, Morris, try to explain them in a language that ordinary people can understand.'

Morris looked up from his desk. 'It's just . . . He pulled the rug out from under me—that joke.'

'Yes, well, couldn't you just laugh?'

The banker never did make Morris rich and the business partner left soon after to go into business on his own, but the nickname stuck because Morris told the joke to his wife.

He had not planned on telling Sadie the joke. But she asked him how the meeting went. He started at the beginning, and at the beginning was the joke. He got as far as Iceberg, Goldberg, when Sadie leapt up, shouting, 'What's the difference?' and ran off to call her sister.

'Bendy Wendy,' she laughed into the phone, 'have I got a joke for you! You'll laugh like a drain.'

Sadie tended to cry when she laughed hard, and later, when Morris picked up the phone, he found the receiver still wet from her tears. He had to walk to the kitchen to get a tea towel to wipe off the handset before making his call.

Sadie had laughed till she cried. And Wendy had laughed, and by the time Sadie put the phone down Morris Goldberg had become the Iceberg.

Later that night, when he came to bed, Sadie turned to him. 'You forgot to tell me how the meeting went.'

'Fine. It was fine.'

She propped herself up. 'I'm sorry I rushed off like that. You know how I get with a good joke. Tell me. I want to know. Were you pleased with how it went . . . Iceberg?'

Sadie's nicknames didn't have a long lifespan. At least not in their original form. They tended to mutate over a period of months. David, for example, had been variously King David, Prince David, the Little Prince, Davy Crockett, Crocker, Docker, King of the Wild Frontier and, when Sadie was complaining about him to Wendy, Focker.

But Iceberg was different. Iceberg stuck in its original

47

form, immutable for at least—what was it? Three, four, five years even. It was still around at David's bar mitzvah. Morris can remember Sadie's whispered comment to Wendy on his speech: 'It's not for nothing that we call him the Iceberg.'

That nickname was a burden to Morris, and Sadie's whispered aside (was he intended to hear it?) hurt him.

Rachel must have had a stream of nicknames imposed on her. Were they a burden to her?

They seemed not to bother David. He'd made up a few nicknames of his own—for Rachel, but especially for Sadie. Queenie, which Sadie said was because of her English accent, David said was because of her attitude, and Wendy said was actually the nickname she'd had for Sadie as a child. 'I started calling you Queenie after you played Queen Esther in the Purim play.'

David said, 'You played Queen Esther in the Purim play? I thought they always chose the cute kid.'

And Sadie said, 'Actually, they chose the blond kid. How's that for bizarre?' She threw back her hair with a model's flick. 'And I happen to have a touch of the blond.'

For a while David had called Sadie 'Little Miss S', which Morris thought came from some song. And there was that other song David used to sing—'You're once, twice, three times a Sadie.'

Rachel saying, 'It's *lady*. You're once twice three times a *lady*.'

Morris finds himself humming the tune.

Pull yourself together, man. This is no time for silly songs, and David's face will crease if he hears that particular song. Look at the computer. Focus on the website. Look at the photo of Rachel who is, according to the website, also known as Goldie.

Rachel smiles up at her father. Her hair is as gold as Queen Esther's.

She is beautiful.

But you wouldn't think so to look at her.
To look at her?
Well, she always hid it, didn't she? Fringes and ridiculous haircuts, like she was trying to make herself look ugly.

Even when she grew her fringe right down over her eyes. Even when her skin broke out in pimples and she refused to use the lotions that Sadie bought for her. Through all of Sadie's 'My God, why can't she just enjoy her beauty?' and all of Rachel's small rebellions, she remained for Morris wonderfully, surprisingly beautiful.

Sadie would have liked the Rachel of the photo. Her hair is swept away from her face. Her brow is clear, her skin shining. She's glossy. Like someone dressed her up. Immediately before the photo was taken, she would have pulled a red lipstick from her bag, carefully touched up her lips, then clicked her pocket mirror closed and slipped it back in the bag.

David says, 'But wait, there's more,' and clicks on the photo. Morris leans forwards to read the words on the screen: *Rache (aka Goldie) is hugely proud to be certified to teach Impetus! Strike! Control! and Step-Up! She is passionate about spreading the word on fitness training and believes that anything is possible in physical fitness if we only commit to it. This belief has made her a strong motivating presence and popular instructor. She considers herself lucky to be paid for doing what she loves best.* And at the bottom in a smaller, less flamboyant, somehow apologetic font: *Goldie has a National Certificate in Exercise Science and a Teaching Certificate from the Royal Academy of Dance. She is a Registered Teacher of the RAD. When she is not getting down with the gym members she runs a ballet school for children.*

A ballet school for children. That's more like it.

Rachel the ballerina, solemn in her leotard and tights. Rachel rising above the other girls, holding her arms straighter, her legs higher. Morris forgetting the camera on his lap. Beside him, Sadie, glowing at the stage as if she'd never complained that she hated the ballet teacher, detested the ballet mothers and all in all believed that ballet was 'not entirely for the Jews'.

For the Jews or not, they all went to those recitals. Wendy too.

She was the first one Rachel ran to after the performance, to be grabbed in a hug that lifted her off the ground and be told that she was the greatest, the most elegant, most gorgeous, stunning, marvellous dancer of the lot. Then Wendy would put Rachel down and, still holding her hand, lift her arms high in the air. 'Wasn't she wonderful? Aren't you so proud?'

How had he replied to that? Had he also grabbed Rachel and hugged her? Had he taken his turn? Perhaps not in front of all those people. But he would have done so afterwards. He would have found a quiet time when no one was around, and he would have told her that she made him proud. He would have.

David moves away from the screen and Morris bends closer. Impetus! Strike! Control! Step-Up! Her classes exclaim their names.

'How did it come to this?' he asks aloud.

Wendy shoots him a look. 'It's no one's fault. Mix-ups happen. Shit happens.'

'No, no, I mean this.' Morris points to the computer. 'All these classes. How did Rachel come to be teaching all these exercise classes?'

Wendy's eyes stop shooting. 'Oh my God! I remember

when she first started teaching. Sadie and I went to one of her classes. It must have been about four years ago. Just before . . . Anyway, we thought it would be fun. We'd show our support. We thought we'd surprise Rachel. Well, she came in, saw us at the front of the class, came over and, believe it or not, she asked us to leave. She said that having us there would put her off her stride.'

Wendy straightens the shawl on her shoulders. 'There we were, all tarted up in our tracksuits, and she kicks us out. Talk about all dressed up and no place to go. We hung around a bit and watched the class from outside the room. We hid so she wouldn't see us. And, d'you know, she was really very good. Really dynamic and enthusiastic. Like one of those eighties aerobics teachers.'

'I know,' says David. 'Debbie goes to some of her classes. She says that Rachel whoops and sings and gets everyone clapping and cheering.'

'Your mum and I couldn't believe our eyes. It was such a transformation. I think that's why she didn't want us there. She didn't want us seeing her like that.'

'Did you know that story?' David asks Morris. 'Mum never told me. I wonder how it made her feel, to have Rachel kicking her out like that.'

'All these exclamation marks,' says Morris.

Wendy gives a little shriek. 'Oh my God, the exclamation marks. They drove Sadie nuts. They really burned her, those exclamation marks.'

Morris remembers Sadie standing in the kitchen. Holding a flier. She's angry, laughing, burning, healthy. 'Our daughter has chosen a career with exclamation marks. An exclamation-mark career. I never thought I'd see the day.' She thrust the flier towards Morris. 'Look at it. Look at those words. Strike! Impetus! They're so uncompromising. Quite aggressive, don't you think? All these years I've been

51

thinking I'd brought up a withdrawn, shy, almost cold little fish. But put her in a room with loud disco music, throw in a couple of exclamation marks and she turns into Jane Bloody Fonda. Jekyll Jane. I gave birth to Jekyll Jane.'

Rachel wants to make herself someone new, Morris had thought. She'll probably succeed. She's that disciplined.

'I wonder how long she'll keep it up for,' Sadie said. 'I mean honestly, surely at some point something's gotta give.'

Morris thinks it must be tiring dealing with all those exclamation marks, putting on the lipstick day after day. It must be exhausting keeping that up.

At five to three the phone rings. David answers. 'Thanks for calling, I was just going to call you. Yes, I've been trying her phone all afternoon. Yes, it's still off.' He says, 'Okay, we'll do that,' and, 'Forewarned is forearmed.'

He puts the phone down. 'That was the cop. Rachel's car's still in the parking lot. He says we may as well start getting information together. Just in case.'

Wendy says, 'Just in case,' and stands up.

David says, 'Though it probably won't be necessary,' and Wendy says, 'Definitely won't be necessary, but you know . . .'

'Forewarned is forearmed,' they say together.

Like they're going to battle—only not yet.

David says, 'They'll want information about her gear and her skills, that sort of thing. We may as well start with the gear.'

They sit at the kitchen table. David has a pen and paper. He says, 'So, what do we know about Rachel's gear?'

Wendy and David both look at Morris. After a while David says, 'So Dad, this is your cue.'

'My cue?'

'Well, you're the one who knows about tramping stuff. Tramping was always your thing. Yours and Rachel's.'

It was their thing. Always had been. David was busy, even from an early age, with social events that Morris had no part of. And as for Sadie: 'A day's walk on a nice track maybe. One of those trips where they carry your bag and there's a lovely lodge at the end with a restaurant I'll consider. But to spend three days grappling over loose stones with a ten-ton pack on my back only to spend the nights in some stinking hut surrounded by people who've eaten nothing but baked beans for three bath-less days sounds like bloody hell to me.'

No, it was not for Sadie, though she encouraged him and Rachel to go: 'Morris, Morris, why don't you get Rachel out of the house for a few days? These holidays are endless and there's no ballet until next term. I've tried to arrange some friends to come and play with Rachel but . . . It's like she's hermetically sealed herself in the house. Please, Morris, take her tramping. The sooner the better.'

Sometimes Rachel suggested it herself. She'd bring out the map and lay it on the table. They'd consider it together, then Morris would point to a spot and say something like, 'How about . . . there? We've never been there. I could leave work early and we could go on the ferry.'

He'd buy a more precise map of the area and they'd lay that on the table. 'We can leave the car . . . here, and sleep the first night in the tent . . . here. If we get there too late, we could stop earlier, put the tent up . . . there.'

Rachel would watch his pointing finger, solemnly considering his suggestions. Sometimes she'd ask about time or distances, but mostly she listened and nodded.

Then Morris would pull out his tramping notebook, the one he kept his lists in, and they'd write a shopping list together.

A day or two before a tramp, they'd lay everything out on the lounge floor and stand looking down on it for a while before Morris asked, Do we have everything? Is that the lot? More looking down, more running through lists in the head before she nodded, Yes, I think that's the lot, and he nodded, Yes, I can't think of anything else. And then, only then, would he pull out his notebook.

'Torch.'

'Check.'

'Gas cooker with extra cylinder.'

'Check and check.'

Once, Rachel suggested that they didn't really need the list since they remembered everything anyway. Morris sat down on the floor beside her and pointed out how every single item was essential. 'We take only what we really need and we need every single thing we take. If we forget one thing we're . . . we're, well, we're buggered.'

She didn't laugh at her father saying buggered. She thought about what he'd said and she understood.

They kept up the tramping through Rachel's childhood and well into her teenage years. When Rachel was about thirteen or fourteen, Sadie told Morris she was pleased the two of them were still going together, that they'd managed to 'navigate their way around Rachel's adolescence and the difficulties it presents'. There hadn't been any navigation necessary. One day Morris felt more discomfort at the thought of sleeping face to face with his growing daughter than he did at the thought of a hut full of strangers. He suggested to Rachel that they try out the huts, and she said, 'Sure.' Morris never slept in a tent again.

With the huts and Rachel's maturity came longer, more difficult tramps. More trying days at the end of which there was real comfort in spotting a red roof amongst the trees. They gave a sense of homecoming and solidity, those huts. A sense of belonging—not because you happened to be in a place but because you'd earned it.

The buildings themselves were suitably stark, the simplicity of their design outweighed by the grandness of their positioning, the impossibility of their location. Their red roofs seemed to call over the mountains to the men who'd built them—men who carried water tanks and metal pipes through the wildest bush, whose backpacks bristled with axes and nails. Who did it for no reason other than giving their children a place to bunk down in the unruly.

Those men could teach you something, Morris thought. You could learn a lot from those huts if you knew how to read them.

Sometimes when there were no other trampers in a hut he'd want to study every inch of it, to run his hands along the knots in the wood, looking for messages hidden in them by the hut's builders.

Morris remembers the smell of wet boots and wood. Gas burners lined up on a bench. Rachel's poise as she stood at a window, opening a tin. The English tramper who picked up her pack to lift it on to a bunk and commented, teasing, at how such a tiny thing could carry such a humungous load. Then muttered softly (but it was a confined space) that he was only trying to be pleasant, there was no need to get all uppity.

Another father might have leapt up then, told the boy to apologise. Couldn't he see she was just a girl? Sadie would have done that. Or she could just as easily have pulled Rachel aside and said, 'He's a silly boy but honestly, honey, would it be so hard to smile at a person?' Maybe Sadie would have done both and made the boy shake Rachel's hand or invited him to share their meal, overpowering Rachel's awkwardness with bright conversation and funny stories.

Is that what Rachel would have wanted? Morris knows, actually for sure, that she would not. He can picture the lifting of her head, the tightening of her mouth, the turn of the heel as she walked away from the English boy, and he knows he did the right thing. Be quiet and ignore it. They'll be turning to their sleeping bags soon, and tomorrow morning we'll be up and out of the hut before that boy has woken up.

David and Wendy are looking at Morris with one face.

David gestures towards him as if introducing him to a crowd. 'Morris and Rachel, the Goldberg Family trampers.'

'I haven't gone tramping in years.'

'Well, she certainly has. She's been doing it pretty regularly for at least two years now.'

Of course. Morris knows that Rachel returned to tramping some time ago. There'd been that scene at the hospital. Rachel had sent a text to Sadie saying she wouldn't be visiting because was going tramping. Sadie seemed to think it was fine, but David did not. He called Rachel from Sadie's ward, started off all bouncy and light-hearted.

'Thought you'd get away without talking to big brother, did you?'

The bounciness didn't last.

'So when are you planning to come back? D'you think it's a good idea to be away for so long? At a time like this?'

He walked out of the ward and into the passage. Leaving Morris and Sadie.

'I don't mind, you know,' Sadie said. 'Not for me. But David's right. She should be here. She might never forgive herself if I . . . you know.' She lifted her hand slightly so as not to dislodge the drip. 'And I mind for you.'

Why should she mind for Morris? Why should he care if Rachel went tramping? There was no need to mind for Morris.

As it happened, Sadie got better. Went home.

So, after all that fuss it was okay that Rachel went tramping. She could be forgiven for it. Morris wonders if David has forgiven her for it. He looks at his son. And at Wendy. Again the single face.

Then Wendy says, 'Back to business. What do we know about her gear?'

David clicks his pen. 'All right, I'll tell you what I know.

I know that she spends a fortune on sporty-style stuff. She probably spends half her income on that crap.'

'It's not crap.' Morris's voice comes out too loud. 'It's important to have good equipment. You don't want to be caught in the bush with inadequate equipment.'

'Okay, Dad, we get the message. You and Rachel love tramping gear. You're passionate about it.'

And not much else, David wants to add. Morris can almost hear the words, and David's c'mon-Dad-I-was-joking tone as he said them.

'These things are important,' Morris says. He manages to keep his voice down.

'Um, you two,' says Wendy. 'If I can bring you back to the job at hand.'

Now look where you are. You've got yourself so caught up in thinking unjustified thoughts about your own son you've forgotten what you're supposed to be doing. Think about Rachel's tramping gear. Rachel. Tramping gear. That's all.

When Rachel was small she carried a little canvas pack that had once been David's school satchel.

With every tramp the satchel got fuller and fatter until the sight of it, bobbing in front of Morris, embarrassed him. Rachel was nine or ten at the time. The right age for a proper backpack. With a pocket on the top and a pouch on the side for holding the water bottle.

Morris went to a camping shop and found just the right pack. He bought it there and then, even though he hadn't compared prices with other shops. Even though he hadn't consulted with Sadie. He was hungry for the pack. If he paused to consider, the moment might be lost. And they were going tramping that weekend, the gear was ready to be laid out on the lounge floor. It was urgent. Besides, good camping equipment was important. You don't cut corners when it comes to tramping gear.

Morris planned what he'd say if Sadie disapproved of his buying the pack: I saw it in the window and thought, That's what Rachel needs. I know it seems like a lot of money but it's actually quite cheap for something of this quality. It was on special. David got that tape recorder and Rachel didn't complain. Good tramping equipment is important. You don't want to be caught in the bush with inadequate equipment.

Sadie was alone in the kitchen. 'I bought this for Rachel,' Morris said. 'David got that tape recorder . . .'

'It's blue,' Sadie said. 'Her favourite colour. I'll wrap it and we can give it to her when she comes home from ballet. She'll love it.'

Morris remembers Rachel's face, her hair done up in its tight ballet bun, her careful fingers opening the wrapping, her eyes lighting up.

She didn't wait to change out of her ballet clothes. Just slipped the blue backpack over the leotard. And kept it on while Morris laid the gear out on the lounge floor.

Rachel is wearing a pink leotard, pink tights, ballet shoes, a pink slip of a skirt. And a blue backpack. She's standing in the middle of the lounge, surrounded by camping equipment.

'Check,' she says, and she points a toe at the cooker. 'Check and check,' as she jumps over a pile of clothes.

She pauses, one hand on her hip. 'I could make a list of everything that goes into my pack.'

'A list,' says Morris.

'Sorry, Dad, what did you say?'

'A list. She might keep a list to remind her what to take on a trip.'

Wendy says, 'You're right. She might.'

'She's always been a big one for lists,' says David. And then he says, 'Oh bugger.'

'What?' says Wendy. 'What?'

'I forgot to check if she has any ballet classes this afternoon. I should have checked her ballet classes first. Oh bugger.'

'Don't worry about it,' says Wendy. 'We can check now.'

'How can we?'

'We can ask someone. Who would know?'

'No one. No one. I can't think of anyone.'

'D'you think Debbie knows?'

'Why would Debbie know?'

'Someone at the gym?'

'They wouldn't know at the gym. Her ballet is separate.'

On and on like a pair of turkeys until David says, 'That's sorted then.'

And Wendy says, 'Right, Morris, get your coat.'

It's all planned. Wendy and Morris will go to Rachel's flat. They'll use David's spare key to get in. David will wait at home by the telephone. He'll keep trying Rachel's cell phone. Wendy will look for a ballet schedule, and Morris (he feels sick at the thought of it) will search through Rachel's things for camping gear and a list.

He says, 'If she's taken her gear it really doesn't make much sense for me to . . .'

Wendy interrupts. 'It was your idea to look for the list. You're the detective. I can't tell the difference between a tent and a what d'you call it? Ground thingy. For God's sake, Morris, we have to do something. Let's go.'

David waves Morris out.

Sheet, thinks Morris as he follows after Wendy. It's called a ground sheet. And I'm not a detective.

Wendy points her arm in the direction of her car. It beeps in response and the locks pop up to hurry Morris along.

The car's CD player bursts into life. Not loud but full and rich. Inappropriate.

Wendy turns it off.

Later she will turn it on again. Then off, and the radio on. Then off.

They keep their eyes fixed before them.

At a traffic light she turns to him. 'How do you feel . . . feel about . . .'

'Did you hear,' he interrupts, 'about the opening of the Arctic Sea Route?'

The traffic light changes.

'Yes, Steven was telling me about it.'

Steven? Who's Steven? Steven is not Strobelight.

Strobelight is Stewart. Steven is not Wendy's ex-husband. He was called . . . what was his name? David. Sadie used to call him Zowie. Why Zowie? Why was Wendy talking to Zowie about the Arctic Sea Route?

'Steven got quite worked up about it. He finds the whole global warming thing really upsetting.'

'Mmm.' Not Zowie, Steven.

'But you know. I'll tell you something. Don't tell anyone I told you. Especially not Steven.'

Don't tell me. I don't want to know.

'There's a part of me that finds it quite exciting. The whole idea that the earth is changing beneath our feet. It's quite exhilarating really.'

'I know what you mean,' Morris says, and immediately wants to take the words back. He shouldn't admit it. Not openly like that.

She looks away from the wheel to smile at him. 'Don't tell anyone I said it's exciting. I'll deny it if you do.'

Morris smiles. 'I won't.'

'Pinky promise,' says Wendy.

Pinky promise. Sadie used to say that.

Outside Rachel's flat, Morris hesitates before unbuckling his seatbelt. It's as if he doesn't intend leaving the car. As if he expects Wendy to say, 'I'll fetch her and we'll come straight down.' Or Rachel herself to be waiting outside, ready to get in the car.

Wendy notices his hesitation. 'Are you okay?'

'I wonder if—'

'Let's do this thing. What've we got to lose?'

'Do you think she'll mind?'

Wendy rattles her keys. 'Come on, Morris. You of all people shouldn't be squeamish. You spend all day digging about in people's personal files.'

'I don't—'

'Look, I don't like this any more than you do, but if we can get information which might help . . .'

Morris unbuckles his seatbelt.

At Rachel's front door he stops himself from suggesting that they knock before entering.

Wendy takes the key from her bag and then, after the slightest pause, knocks loudly. 'You never know,' she says.

They stand in the narrow entranceway, looking at the door, until Wendy says, 'Well, I guess we know now,' and turns the key.

Rachel's flat is small, clean, uncluttered. Tidy house, untidy mind, thinks Morris, but he doesn't believe it. The tidiness is soothing. He wants to run his hands along the clear surfaces, to feel the smoothness of them.

There's a faint perfume. At first Morris thinks it's coming from the vase on the table but it can't be—the flowers in the vase are clearly dead. He draws back, resisting the temptation to sweep the curling petals into his hand.

Wendy says, 'Why would she buy flowers before going on a trip?'

'Um . . .'

'Unless someone else bought them for her.'

She snaps her cell phone open and calls David. She hardly greets him—just fires a question into the phone about who might have bought the flowers. Could it have been Strobelight? That could mean he told her about the pregnant girlfriend. Thought he'd sweeten the news with a bunch of crappy flowers. Or maybe it means he didn't tell her. Maybe they weren't from him. Anyone could have given them to Rachel. Didn't her ballet students sometimes give her presents? She wouldn't have bought flowers for herself before going tramping, would she? Would she?

Maybe Rachel was seeing someone else and he gave her flowers. But she'd tell David if she was seeing someone else, wouldn't she? Wouldn't she?

Morris looks around the room. There's not much to see. A desk with a telephone and cup of pencils, a sofa, a television and, in the corner, a wooden cabinet with a glass front. The cabinet must be new. Morris doesn't remember having seen it before. He likes it.

Rachel won't mind if he looks more closely. She'd put it there for display.

If Morris had hours to stand before the cabinet he might see the patterns in the items on show. He might understand why she chose to present that particular ballet shoe and why she placed it so close to the green vase. He might know why she wanted the two eggcups to stand on different shelves.

If Morris had hours to stand before the cabinet he'd recognise something. Anything.

Sadie would have known the story behind each item. She would've said, 'I'm so pleased that you kept that sash. I'll never forget how well you danced that night.'

She would've made a joke about the absence of memorials to herself.

Morris kneels down so that he's at the same height as the shelves. The height Rachel would have been at when she filled the cabinet. Did she arrange her belongings on the floor beside her? Did she study each item before deciding if it deserved to be on display? Did she step back once everything was arranged to look at it again from a different angle?

She must have felt optimistic when she was doing it. Like she was expecting visitors.

A shadow falls across the cabinet. Wendy says, 'I wonder where Rachel found that unit. She must've bought it recently. Deco. It reminds me of the furniture your aunt used to have in her house.'

'My aunt. Joan.'

'Your Aunt Joan. Little did we know that her taste in furniture would come back to haunt us. She loved a china cabinet, your Aunt Joan. I don't think I've ever seen one as big as the square one she had in the lounge. Remember?'

Morris remembers no big square cabinet. He is not interested in a big square cabinet. He wants to study the life that Rachel put on display. He wants to look for the gaps left by an item removed. A keepsake from a boyfriend, perhaps.

'Well, we'd better get down to work,' says Wendy. She touches him on the shoulder. 'I'll look for her ballet schedule. You see if you can find a list. Or gear. Whatever.'

Morris touches the glass front of the cabinet. Lightly so his fingers won't leave a mark.

Wendy's task is quickly completed. The ballet schedule is exactly where one would expect to find it, on Rachel's desk next to the telephone. It is clearly labelled: Ballet Students' Times and Contact Details.

There are no classes scheduled for today. Wendy phones David, says, 'So you see, it wouldn't have made a difference if we'd checked earlier. This is good news.'

She puts the book in her handbag and says to Morris, 'People usually keep lists on the fridge. Try the fridge. Oh, and I guess she keeps her gear in the bedroom. You get going in there. I'll check her phone. There may be messages.'

Messages? She can't be intending to listen to Rachel's phone messages.

'But, but, this is the last place she'd call.'

'I wasn't thinking there'd be messages *from* her.' But Wendy withdraws her hand from the phone. 'I'll go outside and have a cigarette. Leave you to it then. Try the fridge. For the list.'

Morris crosses the tiny kitchen to close the balcony door behind Wendy. Rachel wouldn't want to come home to a flat smelling of cigarette smoke. Wendy shouldn't be smoking here at all, making herself at home. She'll be opening Rachel's underwear drawer next, trying to find her hidden diary so she can pop that into her handbag.

The fridge door is a clear white expanse. There are no fridge magnets, no pictures of Rachel with her arms round a group of laughing, tipsy friends. No list of tramping gear. Just a fridge. Just white.

Beside the fridge is a little pinboard. On it is a flier like the one on the gym's website. The classes taken by Rache (aka Goldie) have been highlighted in straight, ruled lines. Morris traces a finger across them.

He wants to call Sadie in from the veranda and show her. He wants to point to the straight lines and say, Look at these lines and you'll understand. Rachel isn't Jekyll Jane. There's no inconsistency between the shy, serious girl you called a cold fish and the exclamation-mark woman who is passionate about exercise. She's good at her job. That's all.

He steps away from the flier, towards the balcony, and sees Wendy's silhouette. She is not the person he wishes to tell.

The last time Sadie came back from the hospital her friends hung about the house like groupies waiting backstage at a rock concert. All dressed up in their thoughtful best, all clutching gifts that they pushed into Morris's hands with words too hushed and meaningless for him to catch.

He thought they'd go away after Sadie died, but for a while they kept on coming. They pressed harder on the doorbell and there was something aggressive in the way they thrust containers of food at him. They wanted to come in and sit down. To talk.

It was okay if David or Wendy was there. They'd take the food, offer tea, explain that it was the Jewish custom for mourners to sit on low stools. They'd tell the visitor how Sadie died in her sleep and how she valued her friends. Then the guest would dab her eyes and David and Wendy would dab theirs. They'd drink tea and the guest would leave.

If Rachel was there she'd offer tea and put some biscuits on a plate, but then she'd disappear into the kitchen, leaving Morris to face the company alone. He could feel them staring into his dry eyes, studying his smooth face, finding him wanting. He felt sure that his lack of tragedy confirmed what Sadie had already told them—he was a man who did not feel very much.

Morris was alone in the house when the surprising woman arrived. On opening the door he'd reached out automatically for the offered Tupperware or still-hot pot, but she was empty handed and he only just managed to turn his raised arm into a clumsy handshake.

Empty handed. That was the first surprise. The next surprise was her voice—rasping and deep, like a man's.

But most surprising of all were her words. She waved off Morris's offer of tea and started speaking before he had lowered himself into his stool. She spoke urgently, vehemently, as if she knew she'd meet opposition and would need to keep her voice strong if she wanted to be heard.

'It doesn't get better. Don't believe them when they tell you that the pain gets better. It gets worse. Time doesn't heal. It scratches at the scar.'

Morris can't remember the name of the surprising woman or how she'd known Sadie, but he remembers the urgent vehemence of her voice and he remembers her words. They are the ones which come back to him most often, which come back to him now, in front of Rachel's pure white fridge. Time doesn't heal. It scratches at the scar. They are the ones which he finds most comforting.

Before comfort, the rasping woman's words gave relief from the judgement that there is something horribly wrong with a man who doesn't suffer agonies at the premature death of his wife—a woman loved and missed by scores of people.

Perhaps today, Morris had thought on the morning of the funeral. Perhaps today I will cry. When we're on our way to the cemetery, or when I see the cemetery gates, or when our clothes are cut.

Maybe when I see the coffin in the ground, he told himself as the rabbi snipped strips off his clothes. Maybe when the soil is thrown over it, or the prayers recited. Maybe when I wash my hands on leaving the cemetery, or when I turn around in the car to see the cemetery receding behind us. Perhaps when I see the house again on returning from the cemetery or when we're in the lounge on our low chairs. Perhaps when I'm alone in my bed. Maybe then I will cry.

Morris awoke the day after the funeral, having slept through the night, and told himself that there is something seriously wrong with a man who cannot shed a tear for his wife of over thirty years.

Before the funeral, a man from the synagogue came to the house and talked to the family about dealing with death—the Jewish rituals. Wendy seemed to know it all already. David asked questions, and Rachel sat straight up in her chair and said nothing.

When the man said, 'Morris, I understand you have lost both of your parents as well as your aunt and uncle,' Morris kept quiet. To speak would be to show his ignorance, to reveal that despite the loss of his mother and father, not to mention his uncle and aunt, he'd never been through the whole period of ritual mourning.

Later, when they were alone together, the man tried to get Morris to talk about those earlier deaths, but what could he say? That he was too young when his father died, that his mother's death came as a relief? That the aunt and uncle were no more than an aunt and uncle, old and far away by the time of their deaths?

It had been David's idea that the synagogue man should come with his explanations. Apparently it was important to him that they did things in the traditional way. So important that he'd started crying when Morris suggested it might be best for them to get back to normal as soon as possible, started shouting that he wanted to do things right, that he needed all the help he could get. Who were they to do things their own way when there were centuries of traditions to help them?

'Who do you think you are to want to do it differently?' he'd shouted at Morris. 'D'you think you're so special that the rituals don't apply to you?'

Morris could have shouted back that he didn't think he was anyone special. He was afraid of getting it wrong. Those rituals were hard and there was so much to remember. He could have hugged David and said, 'I know, I know. I also need all the help I can get.' He could have admitted that he couldn't even cry like a normal person. There was something wrong with him.

'Tell me what you want me to do,' he'd said to David.

'It's not what *I* want you to do,' David had replied, but then he'd relented and said that a man would come from the synagogue to help them.

The man left a booklet, *Death: The Jewish Rituals Explained*. It contained clear instructions.

Morris read the booklet over and over again but either the traditions had different goals or they didn't work on Morris. Maybe he did it wrong. The end of the Shiva period brought nothing but confirmation that his heart was dry.

And all those visitors—was it too much to characterise as torture their comfort and their food and their promises that it would get better? He wanted to scream at them, to yell that he didn't want to feel better, what he really wanted was to feel worse.

He came close to actually shouting at one visitor, a colleague of Sadie's whom Morris knew for the many sentimental gifts and cards he had given her. The man was so overcome with grief that he struggled to communicate, but he did manage, through his soggy handkerchief, to tell Morris that time was a great healer and that even a grief as deep as that which Morris was living with would, with time, recede. 'We will never understand how such a woman could be snatched from us,' he'd sobbed. 'But we must push on through our grief. So we can get to a place of peace. Or if not of peace, at least of closure.'

A place of peace? Morris stood up, felt his hand forming a fist—'I don't want . . .' then, seeing the man's white face looking up at him, sat down again. There was no point in shouting at him. He was just trying to help.

70

They were all just trying to help.

Until the surprising vehement woman with her rasping voice and her knowledge that things get worse. Time doesn't heal. It scratches at the wound.

Before the vehement woman Morris had assumed that the pain comes first and then things get better. After the vehement woman he could tell himself that his assumption was back to front. Bad then better is the wrong order when dealing with feelings. Feelings start at nothing and then get worse. He was still stuck in nothing but that would change. He was just a bit slow in making the transition. The pain will come, he told himself. Don't worry. The pain will come.

Morris could wait. He could be patient.

A year later he decided that the vehement woman must have been wrong. The tombstone was unveiled, and still he didn't cry. Don't those who are most vehement tend also to be most mistaken?

Morris hasn't thought about that vehement woman for weeks but he is reminded of her when he finds himself standing in his daughter's kitchen, looking at her straight ruled highlighter lines, and he is encouraged.

'After my Alex died I kept having conversations with him in my head. I'd imagine him giving me advice,' she'd said, and her voice momentarily lost its rasp. 'Alex always gave bad advice.'

She smiled, and Morris saw a flash of softness before her intensity returned.

'Always coming into my head, his words. His bad advice bothering me all the time. Like counting footsteps. Counting footsteps doesn't make you go any faster.'

Counting footsteps doesn't make you go any faster, Morris repeated to himself, and the phrase had a comforting ring of truth to it.

'What really mattered only came later. What really mattered was not his ghost knocking on my door, reminding me that he was dead. That was nothing. The real thing was when *I* went knocking on *his* door. When I *forgot* that he'd died.'

There was that softness again. 'Sometimes I'd forget that he'd gone.'

She was silent for a long time and Morris looked at her pointy shoes.

Maybe the woman wasn't mistaken after all, thinks Morris. Hadn't he just done what a grieving person's supposed to do? Gone knocking on Sadie's door, forgetting she was gone. Hadn't he turned to say something to her, only to remember she's no longer around?

He wants to rush out onto the balcony, to tell Wendy that he's just found himself wanting to tell Sadie something, that this is a good sign. It means the vehement woman was right and things are finally getting worse.

He catches himself. He's making too much of a stupid mistake.

Morris looks at Rachel's white fridge and wonders what he's doing there.

You are in Rachel's kitchen. Wendy is on the balcony, smoking.

She opens a gap in the door and sticks her head through. 'Try her bedroom.'

Take a breath, collect your thoughts. Slap your forehead. You are looking for a list and camping gear. Wendy says you should try the bedroom.

The bedroom door is open. There's a white bed and a white wardrobe, and Morris is saved from having to enter by the certain knowledge that Rachel wouldn't store tramping gear in all that whiteness. She wouldn't keep it in this clean bedroom at all. There must be a storage space somewhere.

He steps back and looks down the short passage. There's a built-in cupboard near the front door.

Inside the cupboard smells of lavender and something else which Morris recognises but can't place.

It's the smell of ironing and a white tablecloth on Friday nights. The smell of his mother's linen laid out on a paper-lined shelf. The smell of his mother saying, 'You see, Morris, I don't fold these ones neatly along the same place. If I did they'd get stiff lines and permanent creases. These ones we don't fold. It's better to roll them in a wad, carefully but not precisely.'

Rachel has stuck little labels on the shelves: Duvet Covers, Sheets, Towels (Training), Towels (Bath). There are some bags made of a shining satiny fabric which contain, Morris knows this for sure, the lace. And there, behind the tablecloths, are serviettes, stiff from ironing like serviettes ought to be. He reaches out to touch a pile, then pulls back. Wendy would think it weird if she caught him stroking his daughter's linen. It is weird to stroke your daughter's linen.

It's the smell of cloves. Cloves to keep the moths away and lavender to keep the linen fresh. Cloves to invite Morris in and lavender to tell him he can fit under the bottom shelf, close the door behind him and wait for his daughter to come home. Maybe he will cry.

There's a noise from the balcony. He steps back, is about to slam the cupboard door shut, stops himself. There's no need for panic. He's not doing anything wrong. But he does need to focus. Rachel would not keep her camping equipment so close to the linen.

She would keep it—there, in that extra little cupboard above the linen cupboard. The one that you need a chair to get to. She'd use that chair with the hard, scuffed seat which is easy to stand on and balances just right.

The cupboard contains a gas canister, a burnt frying pan and—Oh Rachel, he thinks, my daughter, my clever daughter—sitting right in the front, a yellow notebook. A tidy little thing you could fit in a pocket. She's written on it in her clean straight writing: Camping Lists. And the last page is dated. Five days ago.

Dated and everything. My very clever daughter.

Tent, reads the list.

Check.

Torch.

Check.

Gas cooker.

Good girl, Rachel. Good girl.

Sadie had laughed when Morris bought the little notebook for Rachel. 'First a backpack, now a notebook. Who's playing Santa Claus this week?' She'd kept a straight, artificially firm, I'm-laughing-behind-my-hands-at-you face when Morris explained the importance of keeping a good list in a handy notebook, the convenience of having all your lists in one place so you could refer to past lists when you made out the new one. Then she'd laughed out loud and said, 'Don't worry, Morris. I won't come between you and your little notebooks. All those lovely little notebooks with their lovely little lists.' And she'd teased him about being a man who thinks he can reduce his life to a series of notebooks, a pathway of lists.

Morris had put up with the teasing until she got going on 'that book you write in at the start of the tramp. What do you call it? The Declensions Book? Pretensions Book? Suspension. Suspension. Your Suspension Book. No, no, it's redemption. Your Redemptions Book. Your Books of Redemption.'

'Intentions. The Intentions Book.'

'Yes, yes, that one. I mean honestly, Morris, how restricting is that? Writing out all of your intentions when you're supposed to be free and easy, on holiday, ready to go where the wind takes you?'

Morris looked at Sadie then and thought, She doesn't understand. She will never understand. Thought, She'll tell Rachel the Intentions Book is just daddy's nonsense. She will put our daughter in danger with her silly teasing.

And then he did something. He put his hands on Sadie's shoulders and steered her to a chair. He sat her down and said to her, 'Sadie, please, please be quiet and listen to me.' He explained to her, in as few words as possible, the importance of the Intentions Book. Told her the value of the lists and the notebooks when you're going tramping. He put his case.

Sadie was quiet until he finished. Then she said, 'I shouldn't have teased.' Later Morris heard her telling Rachel that it might be better if she wrote in the Intentions Book ('Let daddy dictate and you write. His handwriting can be messy sometimes but yours is lovely and clear. And you want your tramping intentions to be lovely and clear, don't you?'), and he felt a wave of affection for his wife who did, actually, understand.

Morris looks at the little yellow notebook and wonders if a wave of affection can knock you off a chair. He rests his forehead against the wall for a moment and tries to recall the smell of Rachel's linen cupboard. Then calls out to Wendy that they can go. He has what they need.

She says, 'Let me help you down,' and reaches out a hand.

Wendy's nicotine hand will kill the smell he's trying to hold in his head.

She wriggles her fingers. 'Are you coming or not?'

He takes her hand.

Wendy says, 'Do you know what she took? Is it good

news?' She takes her car keys from her pocket, starts jiggling them. 'Did she take what she needed?'

'I think so,' says Morris. 'She kept a list.'

He clasps his hands together with the notebook between them.

Wendy passes her car keys from hand to hand.

He slips the notebook into his pocket.

She says, 'Morris. We have to get going. It's almost . . .'

Morris looks at his watch.

Wendy's jangling keys lead the way out of the apartment, down the passage and into the grey outdoors.

She walks quickly with her head forwards as if she's dropped something. As if she's at the end of an elastic that's stretched so thin it's cutting her in half at the waist. He trots to catch up to her, and she goes faster. She has her key in the ignition before he's opened his door.

'Jesus Christ, Morris, it's almost four o'clock,' like he's made her late for something, like there's somewhere she's supposed to be. 'Jesus Christ, Morris. Jesus Christ.'

She's hunched over the steering wheel. One tug on her elastic and they'll start speeding across the road, weaving in front of oncoming traffic.

Morris's head tingles, as if the car is actually weaving and spinning and something in the engine's about to give.

A terrible noise breaks into the car. Wendy gives a little yelp and starts flapping her hand towards the floor at Morris's feet.

'My phone. In my bag.'

She bends towards him, hand still flapping. He wants to shout, Keep your eyes on the road, I'll get it. I said, I'll get it.

The car jerks to one side as she tries to lean past him. He has the bag on his lap. Her hand flaps and pecks. 'Unzip it, Morris. Dig around in it. Find the bloody phone.'

Unzip it, Morris. Dig around in it. Find the bloody phone.

Which has gone silent.

Wendy swears and pulls the car over.

She checks the phone, says they've missed a call from David, ignores Morris's apology and stabs at numbers.

She gazes out of the window while she waits for David to answer, says, 'Hi, okay, we'll be there soon,' and shuts the phone.

David's spoken to the police.

A full search is being launched.

The weather's turning.

'Jesus Christ, Morris,' she says.

Search and Rescue have put together an incident team. An incident co-ordinator has been appointed. Her name is Molly. She calls with questions: Does Rachel understand the dangers of flowing water? What do you know about her gear? How about navigation skills? Is she familiar with the terrain?

David and Morris hand the phone back and forth between them, trying to fill each other's gaps.

Molly's tone is firm but calm. It's the sort of tone a doctor would use when talking to family members whose loved one is in surgery. There's really nothing you can do. Go home and have a shower. She's in excellent hands. It will be hours before she's conscious and can see visitors.

She says 'That's good' a lot, and finally she says, 'Okay, that's good. Can I speak to your son again?'

Morris hands the phone over and steps back. He is exhausted.

'What did they want to know?' Wendy asks. She doesn't even bother to whisper.

David turns his back to Morris and Wendy. 'On Wednesday,' he says into the phone.

'Morris, tell me everything. What did they ask?'

Morris is trying to focus on what David is saying, but David's talking really quietly and Wendy is pulling, actually pulling, at Morris's shirt. David walks away, still mumbling into the phone.

Behind all the questions, hiding in Molly's *that's goods*, there's a question that hasn't been asked. A gap in Molly's interrogation. It's in the room with them. Morris can feel the empty space of it. If he could just hear what David is saying.

'Morris,' says Wendy, 'stop torturing me. What did they say?'

When Morris was thirteen and falling behind at school, his mother engaged an English teacher to come to the house and tutor him privately. Miss Robson smelled of laundry soap. Her hands had brown spots and her hair was so thin he thought he could count the strands. When she bent forwards over his book, the desk lamp caught her scalp and displayed little freckles where her hair was supposed to be.

'Now, Morris, this is important. The first thing you do when you open a test. The first and most important thing . . .'

Some other boys had lessons with Miss Robson. One of them said she was nuts. He said she ought to wear a scarf to hide her bald head. He reckoned that his mother was going to buy her one at the end of the year. He said that her head was fuzzy and bumpy, that the freckles weren't freckles but sunspots, probably cancer. You'd be able to feel them if you ran your hand along her head. If you could bear it. I dare you. I dare you to touch it.

Morris didn't need to touch her head. He knew it was neither fuzzy nor bumpy. It was smooth and shiny. Uncomplicated. He hoped that the boy's mother didn't give her a scarf. He didn't see why women wore scarves on their heads. Like they were hiding something dangerous.

At the end of Morris's first lesson Miss Robson said, 'You have a remarkable ability to concentrate. Do you know that?'

Maybe she was a bit nuts.

'But you concentrate on the wrong things. We're going

80

to work on that. I've got a simple technique that will help you.'

Miss Robson's simple technique did help. At the beginning of each lesson, or on starting a test, or on being given an assignment, Morris was to ask himself only one question: what must I focus on? When he had the answer he was to write it, in letters as large as possible, on a piece of paper as large as possible, and he was to put it in front of him where his eyes would see it.

Miss Robson used a huge piece of paper. She wrote *When must I use an apostrophe?* on it with a thick black marker.

'Now Morris, during this class, while I'm talking and you're concentrating on something entirely different, you will find that your eyes wander. You'll gaze at different things—the lamp, that picture. The top of my head. But every now and then your eyes will stray towards this paper. When they do, you will remember—apostrophes. That's what you're to concentrate on. The paper will draw you back.'

Morris used Miss Robson's technique through the rest of his schooling and at university, though he never used a black marker and was ashamed at the thought of a large piece of paper.

If Miss Robson were in David's lounge now, she'd write Rachel on her paper in huge bold letters. Then she'd write the missing question. Then, when she was sure Morris knew what to concentrate on, she'd lean back so her shiny head didn't distract him.

A policeman arrives. He's plump and solicitous. He holds out his hand to everyone in turn and says, 'I'm Tim.' He smiles a lot and says, 'Rest assured,' and, 'You can be confident that.' He has come to offer support. And to give instructions: Search and Rescue prefer it if the family stays away from the incident site. Leave them to get on with their job. Stay near the telephone. They'll keep you informed. You can be confident that we're doing all we can, that the people in the incident team know the area like the backs of their hands, that they'll keep on searching through the night.

There's a lot to be confident about.

He asks to see Rachel's typed notes and her list. When he takes the notebook in his fat fingers, Morris looks away.

'Take your time,' Miss Robson used to say, 'in thinking about your question. Take the time to get your question right and everything else will follow.'

But they won't give him time. They keep interrupting his thoughts with questions and instructions, pulling at his shirt and keep me company while I have a cigarette.

'If smoking helps you get through it, don't let me stand in your way,' Tim says to Morris.

'No, I . . . I don't smoke.'

'Come on, Morris, keep me company.'

'You can rest assured I won't pass judgment. If you need a cigarette, you have it.'

'I don't . . . I don't.'

'Go on, Dad. Keep her company.'

'Rest assured I'll still be here when you get back.'

Wendy looks directly at the policeman. 'I'm going fucking insane here.'

The policeman stops smiling.

'Dad,' says David, 'will you please go outside with Wendy.'

Wendy slams her cigarettes down on outside table. 'Schmuck cop. Fat lot of good he's doing sitting in our living room. Rest assured he's waiting for us to feed him.'

Light your cigarette, thinks Morris. Smoke your cigarette and please, please keep quiet. There's something I need to think about.

Wendy doesn't speak but she's not quiet. She clicks her lighter and rustles the cellophane on her cigarette pack. She sighs and coughs and shuffles about in her seat. Morris wonders whether anyone has ever hit her. Three minutes, he tells himself. That's how long it takes to smoke a cigarette. In three minutes she will be done and then you can escape to a quiet place.

Wendy's cigarette is down to its last thirty seconds when David comes outside.

'Dad, won't you sit with Tim for a few minutes, please. While I phone Debs and make some tea.'

Wendy snorts smoke through her nose.

'I know,' says David, 'I know. But I can hardly shoo him out, can I? Anyway, rather this than if they didn't take it seriously.' He turns to Morris. 'Come on, Dad. Don't want to leave a cop alone in the living room, do we?'

'Even if he is a schmuck,' says Wendy.

Why do policemen always travel in pairs?
What?
Not what. Why. Do policemen always travel in pairs?
Why.
'Cause one can read and one can write.
But if—
For goodness sakes, Morris. It's a joke.

The policeman settles into the sofa. 'The waiting's the worst part. Definitely the worst,' he says, looking at Morris. 'The waiting.'

Wendy's right. The guy's a schmuck. There are surely many worse things. Like if he never works out what his Miss Robson Question is. Or if he does work it out but then can't find the answer. Like if it starts to rain. Or snow. If Rachel is alone in that.

She shouldn't be alone. It shouldn't be allowed.

He should have warned her about tramping alone. And about the Tararuas.

He should have gone somewhere quiet and thought about his Mrs Robson Question.

He should have asked David what he was discussing with Molly, why he walked away when he did.

He should have remembered not to sit on that low sofa.

The policeman starts drumming his fingers on his knees. Morris should have thought to drum. It seems the right thing to do. But now it's too late. The policeman got there first.

Morris's fingers tingle. What will the policeman think if he sits on his hands?

The house is silent, as if Wendy and David have run away, leaving Morris clasping his hands to stop them from tapping in unison with a policeman's.

At last Tim speaks. 'So, what work do you do?'

'I'm retired.'

Morris Goldberg has just lied to a policeman.

Had Morris spent the previous minutes thinking about what might follow rather than focusing on tapping fingers, he would not have had to lie to the policeman. He would have prepared himself for that question.

He should have known it would come. Whenever there was a lull in the conversation or a silence to be filled, that question would float down to fill it. Someone would realise that Morris hadn't spoken much and, in an effort to include him, say something like: 'So, Morris, tell us, what work do you do?'

At David's birthday party it had been the woman in the red dress, the long-suffering wife of the funny man. Her husband had finished his story. The last few laughs had died down, and in the smiling lull that followed she'd turned to Morris and said, 'So, you're David's dad. I seem to remember you had an interesting job. Remind me what you do.'

'Um, I'm in computers.'

The smiling faces looked to Morris.

'What aspect of computers?'

'It's not very interesting. Really.'

'Come on. Don't be shy. Tell us.'

'Um, I'm a metadata analyst.'

The faces around him were serious. Morris looked around for David. Couldn't he wave his baton and restore the smiles? Couldn't he explain? Like Sadie used to do.

Sadie had developed a standard response to the what-in-the-world-is-a-metadata-analyst question. Sadie's response went: 'It's a fancy-sounding term for computer geek. The metadata analyst takes geekdom to new heights. Meet Morris, metadata analyst and ubergeek.' Then she'd give Morris a little pat—on the arm or the back—and no matter where she patted him he always felt it as if it was on his head. And he'd smile and nod and hope that someone would take the conversation elsewhere.

Often someone did take the conversation away. Like that woman at the hospital who'd told a long story about her frustrating battle to get her computer settings right.

'On Day Thirteen I went ballistic,' she'd said. 'I set the

computer repair guy's Asperger's management programme back by about three years.'

That had got Sadie laughing, and then they'd moved on to talking about Asperger's, which Sadie seemed to know a lot about, and Morris was able to sit back in his seat and pick up one of the hospital's women's magazines.

But the topic of Morris's job did not always die such an easy death. Some people were demanding—like that engineer who'd invited Morris and Sadie for dinner and then spent half the evening telling his guests about how he'd put his foot down and said that he was not going back to Nigeria, no matter how many American dollars those oil gluttons throw at me, or the economist who travelled the world advising governments on how to stop spending money.

Some people demanded an explanation of the role served by Morris Goldberg. Or maybe they were not being demanding but were actually trying to be kind, wanting to draw Morris into the group, not wanting him to feel left out.

This would, Morris had noticed, usually be a woman. Someone soft spoken and sweet, or maybe one of those clever women who enjoy collecting information about people. Like the bejewelled wife of the engineer.

'That's really interesting,' the bejewelled wife had said. 'I don't think I've ever met a meta-whatsit before. So tell us more. What do you actually—?'

'I don't get it,' her husband had interjected. 'What *exactly* does a metadata analyst *do* when he's at home?'

The travelling economist had encountered a metadata analyst before. 'We had one of you guys at my work once. He spent three days interfering with all the computers, charged us a fortune and I'm still not sure what in hell's name he was doing there.'

And Morris, poor Morris would try to explain.

'Why don't you read what the encyclopaedia says?' Sadie asked him once. 'Learn their Metadata 101 off by heart and rattle it off every time someone asks you that tiresome question.'

Morris, to his subsequent shame, had done just that. He'd gone to the encyclopaedia and learned that: Metadata is data about data. An item of metadata may describe an individual datum, or content item, or a collection of data including multiple content items.

Morris knew, even as he was learning the words, that it was ridiculous to do so, and he didn't tell Sadie he had followed her advice. He kept his definition close and secret and waiting. For the opportunity when it could spring from his mouth.

Why did Sadie have to be there when it did?

She'd driven him to the garage to fetch his car in for repairs. She could have dropped him and left. There was no need for the two of them to hang about, but Sadie, it seemed, wanted to hang about. She parked the car and went in with him.

'What kind of a mechanic doesn't have a calendar or a page three poster on his wall?' she whispered to him after the mechanic left them in his tiny office while he went in search of his assistant.

'What do you mean?'

But before Sadie could answer, the mechanic was back, squeezing through the space between Morris's chair and the wall.

'My assistant will be here with the keys in a minute. He's giving the car a vacuum.'

That was when Morris should have insisted that Sadie leave. But he missed the opportunity and then it was too late. The mechanic tipped back in his chair and swivelled it to face Morris.

'Nice car you've got there. Tell me what you do to deserve it.'

'To deserve it?'

'What job, I mean.'

It was definitely Sadie's idea that Morris rote-learn the definition. Why then was there such dramatic surprise, such raising of eyebrows and rolling of eyes when he recited, in the mechanic's little office, what metadata was?

Driving home from the garage, blessedly alone in the car, Morris wondered for the first time in his marriage whether he might just keep on driving. Sadie would be home already. She always drove faster than him. She'd be calling Wendy right now. Oh my God, Wends, you won't believe what that husband of mine just did. And when he got home she'd tease him, call him something like her Walking Encyclopaedia and try to hug him as she laughed.

Morris, true to form, did not keep on driving and Sadie (could this possibly be true to her form?) never mentioned the incident in the mechanic's office.

Perhaps she too had done some thinking on the drive home. And perhaps she'd realised that Morris's shame at not being able to explain his own job was something real, not to be trifled with. For if a man can't explain what he does for a living, how can others know that he deserves a place in this world?

They never discussed what happened in the mechanic's office, but from then on Sadie would, if the need arose, explain what Morris did for a living. He was so relieved the first time she did this he didn't even correct her when she got it wrong. Well, not wrong exactly, but not quite right either.

She quickly developed a narrative—What Morris Does: The Palatable Version. And while this version was imprecise and vague, Morris recognised that it was entertaining. And that people understood it. And (this Morris pretended to himself was not important) that people seemed to consider his job, as described by Sadie, exciting. Sexy even. So if Sadie's story exaggerated the thrill, well, it wasn't Morris telling it, and everyone knew that Sadie exaggerated things.

'It's quite interesting actually,' she would begin. 'The best way of explaining it is by example.'

Already the listener would be leaning forward to listen. Morris would stand back a bit.

'Say you're writing a document in, say, MSWord.'

Sadie always said MSWord in full. Not, 'You're working in Word'. Morris liked this touch. It added gravitas to an otherwise slightly frivolous tone.

'You start working on Monday. You work for an hour or two. Then stop. On Tuesday, you come back to it, delete some of what you've done and work for another few hours, and so on. Maybe you send it to someone else in between. They work on it and send it back to you, etcetera etcetera.'

The listener would often be nodding by now. This made sense. This they could understand. Sometimes they'd say something like, 'Et cetera et cetera, story of my life.'

'Tell me about it,' Sadie would respond. 'Okay, so the document you have produced with all this to-ing and fro-ing is your information. The data. But, there's something more there, something—' She always paused at this point, lowered her voice. 'Something hidden.'

Even after Morris had heard Sadie's story repeatedly and he knew that word was coming, he found it surprising. Something hidden. And he, Morris Goldberg, was the man to find it.

The listener might look over at Morris now, respectfully even. And he'd immediately feel like a fraud. Once or twice he'd started to explain himself. 'It's no big deal really. It's just computer—'

Sadie wouldn't allow him to spoil her story. 'Something hiding there, wondering whether it will be discovered.'

Hiding and wondering. Sadie could take things too far. Morris was relieved when she brought things back down to earth.

'The computer keeps information about the file too. When it was opened, and by whom, when it was closed, what actions were performed, et cetera. This is information about information or, to be la-di-da, metadata. So, for example, the metadata might say that the file was opened at 3 p.m. on David's computer, that it was kept open for two hours, during which time words were deleted, that it was then opened on Sam's computer, that words were then added, et cetera.'

At this point Sadie might cross her arms or hold them akimbo as if to say ha and the listener would nod, pleased with himself for having learned something new. Morris could almost hear them thinking, I must remember that. That's something worth knowing. That's a term I can use sometime. But they wouldn't get to use the word. It is not the sort of word you get to throw into conversation. Morris could tell them that.

You'd think that would be the end of it but no, there was always someone—the engineer's brother or the long-suffering wife—who'd say something like, 'That's really interesting, but tell me, what does *Morris* do,' or, if it was the travelling economist, he'd point a finger towards Morris's chest and say, 'That's all very well, but I'm still not sure, *exactly*, what *you* do.'

'I . . . I analyse the metadata.'

'Yes, but for whom? And why? For what *purpose*?'

Sadie was quick to step in. 'Let's say someone is stealing information from a company. Say he opens confidential documents, saves them under a different name, emails them to a friend, then deletes the saved document and the emails. A metadata analyst would be able to tell the company what files were opened by him, when he opened them, and so on. The actual files may be deleted but the metadata about them would remain. Or say someone downloaded porn, printed it, then deleted it. The porn might be deleted but the information that he'd downloaded and printed it would be the metadata.'

Morris hated those examples. They made his work sound sordid, like he spent all his time digging about in people's personal files. This didn't seem to bother Sadie at all. She seemed to revel in the examples, embellishing and expanding them. She said the examples helped people to understand and were, anyway, a true reflection of what he did. 'Whether you like it or not,' she'd fired at him once, 'that is where your work goes. It does have practical implications, you know. It's not just you in a room with a box.'

The examples gave people the wrong idea. Morris was sure of it. They encouraged responses like, 'Ooh, industrial espionage. Sounds very 007 to me.' Or, 'Does that mean Morris is the one I should speak to if I want some tips on how to download porn without leaving a trail?' Or Morris's very worst: 'Tell me. I promise not to tell anyone. Have you been involved in any juicy cases lately?'

Then Morris would mumble that he was just the guy who worked on the computers and all he saw was numbers and formulae and strings of letters. The listener would lose interest then, and the conversation might finally shift.

When Sadie was in hospital there'd been a doctor. A young man who seemed to spend a lot of time at Sadie's bedside, chatting. Just chatting. Morris did not mean to disapprove of this doctor. After all, having a doctor close by was something to be pleased about, and you could hardly complain that the man was paying too much attention. But did he not have places to go? Other patients to visit? On one occasion Morris found himself standing outside Sadie's ward, waiting for the doctor to leave. He'd stood there for maybe five minutes when a slow nurse on shuffling feet came past and, opening the door, said, 'Go right in. Family can visit any time.'

The doctor stood up when Morris came in. He stepped towards the door, but Sadie detained him with small talk and soon he was asking Morris what he did.

Sadie seemed quite lucid, though she must have had morphine because she seemed to have forgotten her shtick. There was no Palatable Version.

'My husband,' she said, 'sees the spaces left by absence. Where others see only emptiness, my husband sees, if not exactly a presence, then the gap left behind.'

Morris never heard the Palatable Version from Sadie again.

At David's party, when the long-suffering lovely wife asked the question, Morris had to clear his throat before answering. 'Me? I'm just a metadata analyst.' When the second question came, when it was time to explain what a metadata analyst did, he had, like the man in the funny story he'd just heard, found himself wondering where he was and what he was doing there.

'Um . . .'

Then David was there to say, 'Did I hear someone ask what my father does? Well, let me tell you, 'cause it's really interesting.'

He'd stood there, half-full bottle in his hand, and given Sadie's Palatable Version.

He's learned it off by heart, Morris thought. He must have. But no, David's version was slightly different and ended with, 'He's supposed to be retired, but you know, some men!' Then he'd clinked the wine bottle against Morris's glass in a movement which caught Morris completely unawares, though it was, he later recognised, the equivalent of Sadie's pat on the head.

'Let's face it, there are some people who can never really retire. My father's one of them. He's doing a job for the Competition Commission at the moment.'

David had taken it too far with that last bit about the Competition Commission. Sadie wouldn't have said that. She would have realised it was opening the door to questions which Morris would have to answer.

'Tell me about the Competition Commission,' asked a small woman whose glass David had just replenished. 'Do they sort out competitions like Lotto?'

'I, um.'

'Oh my God,' the long-suffering wife interrupted. 'Lotto. Has Simon told you what an ass he made of himself at the Lotto counter?'

And so Morris had been saved, first by David with his Almost Palatable Version, then by Simon and his still funny folly. But he should have known better than to relax into his seat and sip at his wine. Next time might not be so easy. Next time David might be out of the room and Morris might be alone with a policeman.

The policeman doesn't realise that Morris has lied to him. Either that or he doesn't care. All he says is, 'Retired huh. Lucky you,' and goes back to his drumming. He keeps at it until David comes back.

David has tea on a tray, home-made biscuits and a copy of the flier which Rachel had up on her pinboard.

Morris says, 'Where did you get that?'

'From Debbie's gym bag. It's got all her class times.'

David smooths the flier against his chest. It must have

got crumpled in the gym bag. People don't look after those fliers. They throw them in amongst their sweaty sports clothes and forget about them. They let them get damp and crumpled. They don't care about the person whose photo is being kicked by their dirty shoes.

David hands the flier to the policeman. 'I thought you might want to see this. It has some information about the training she does. Confirms that she's as fit as I said she is.'

'That's good to know. You wouldn't believe how many people go rushing off on tramps that are way beyond their fitness level. And without any bush skills. Only the other day I heard about this Japanese tourist . . .'

For a moment Morris thinks—this is absurd, he knows it's absurd—that they should make copies of the flier and post them up in the area where Rachel is missing. They could put them at bus stops, on poles, on trees.

Like Sadie and David did that time Rachel's cat went missing.

When Rachel's cat went missing, Sadie and David made fliers and headed out to post them up like they were going on an adventure, Sadie chanting, 'The sooner we're ready the sooner we'll leave, the sooner we'll find Miss Genevieve.'

The cat was not called Genevieve.

Morris and Rachel stayed home.

David and Sadie did a thorough job. Pictures of Rachel's cat were everywhere. It greeted Morris at the bus stop and was there waiting for him all along the route home. From trees, fences, lamp posts, the lost cat peered down at him, charting his course. And wherever the cat went was the word *Lost* in thick red ink. The cat was more present than before it went missing.

And then it was gone—really gone. Run over.

They'd held a funeral. Sadie must have insisted on it. She'd stood beside Rachel, holding her hand. She'd given Rachel a poem to read, but Rachel had refused so Sadie had read it herself.

Morris remembers looking across at them over a great deep hole, but that can't be right. It would have been a small hole—the size of a shoebox. They would have been standing quite close to each other. He would have kept his eyes on Sadie, waiting for her to signal that he could cover the box, pat down the earth and be done with it.

Morris was secretly relieved to be burying that cat. Rachel didn't seem too perturbed either. The spurt of affection she'd once shown for it had died down some time earlier, as quickly and unexpectedly as it had sprung up in the first place.

Morris blamed the short-lived infatuation on a girl from ballet who'd come to the house to play with Rachel and spent the whole visit fussing over the cat. For the next few weeks Rachel had fussed over the cat too. She used the same words as that overbearing little ballet girl, bubbling and crooning, 'Oh this fur is so soft. Oh it is. Oh it is. Oh it is.'

It was, Morris thought, all a bit much. The cat must have thought so too. For weeks Rachel's hands and arms were littered with tiny scratches—the gentle wounds from an unassuming cat that wanted simply to get to his food, slink in the night, mind his own business. How many times had the cat dashed for the flap only to be swept off the ground? 'Oh, the naughty torty. Trying to run away, were you? Come to mama.'

It made Morris uneasy to watch.

Then one day Sadie picked the cat up and tried to hand it to Rachel. 'Naughty Torty wants a cuddle,' she crooned.

Rachel turned away.

Sadie kept thrusting the cat at Rachel, though it was clear to Morris that Rachel was no longer interested.

Maybe she was also relieved when they finally buried it.

There had always been at least one cat. Sadie had seen to that. 'A child must have a pet,' she'd said, emphatic when Morris reminded her that she'd once promised there'd be no pets. Every child must have a pet. A promise to the contrary was simply not binding.

Always at least one cat. Still to this day. And if Morris doesn't exactly love the current cat, he has got used to having one around and sometimes, perhaps, feels pleased it is there when he comes home in the evenings.

But if the cat goes missing no fliers will be put up. That Morris will not do. Not for a cat.

The policeman has drunk his tea and left.

'You should never have offered him tea,' Wendy says. 'Cops can't resist a cup of tea. Rest assured.'

David collects the tea cups.

'I'll help,' says Morris.

'Dad, just sit. I can manage,' says David, but he leaves without the milk jug and sugar bowl.

'He needs some time alone,' Wendy whispers and then, as if Morris hadn't heard her the first time, 'Give him some space to breathe.'

When David comes back he looks blankly at the jug and bowl, then flops into a chair. A moment later gets up and leaves the room empty handed, then comes back empty handed. He stands in the doorway, runs his hands through his hair and turns to leave again, muttering that this time he'll bloody remember what he went for.

He's gone before Morris can tell him that sometimes a person forgets what they're doing in a room. It happens to everyone. It happened to David's friend Simon.

'It's because he blames himself,' Wendy whispers when David is out of earshot. 'He's all shaken up blaming himself.'

'Blaming himself?'

'Be careful what you say to him, okay?'

'But what has he got—'

'Morris, we've already discussed this. A bit of sensitivity is in order here.'

'But he hasn't done anything.'

'And don't say that to him, whatever you do. He's cut up enough already about not doing something earlier.'

'But he couldn't—'

'Oh for God's sake, Morris. How would you feel if your younger sister had gone off? All alone? And got herself lost?'

Wendy is right. David must be blaming himself. Morris must be more sensitive. He must watch what he says. Or say nothing at all, to be safe.

'All alone,' says Wendy.

'—'

'Couldn't she have asked someone to go with her?'

'—'

'Anyone. I mean, honestly, if she couldn't find someone to go with her maybe she shouldn't have gone at all.'

Keep quiet, Morris. There's no point in challenging her. She sighs loudly and theatrically.

He says nothing. There's a feeling building in his throat. His face feels flushed with it. Morris feels . . . burned. That's the word—burned. One of Sadie's words. She used to use it all the time, to cover all manner of irritations.

Newsreaders burned Sadie. So did the plastic clasps on top of bread bags. She was burned by the woman who lived across the road, the babysitter whom the children loved though she was, Sadie told Morris repeatedly, even thicker than two bricks. Half the children's schoolteachers burned Sadie, as did ballet mothers, shop assistants, bus drivers. Morris's resistance to having guests at the house burned Sadie. As if to confuse him, so did people who wanted to stay longer than one night.

When David was a teenager he burned Sadie. Rachel did not. This burned her too. 'She's a teenager, for crying out. She's supposed to burn me. That's what teenagers do. Remember how David used to burn me? My God, he could piss me off. But Rachel's so well behaved. What kind of a teenager doesn't burn her mother? Damn it, Jim, it burns me.'

Sadie got burned so often, so readily, you could hardly take it seriously. And the word was imprecise. It suggested that Sadie was the victim, the burnee, the passive bystander who just happened to be in the firing range of 'that sanctimonious little prick who calls himself a school principal'.

The principal business had been too much for Morris. 'You burn him as well,' he'd finally told her. 'You give as good as you get.'

She seemed to like that. 'I know. But the difference is, I'm right.' Then she'd laughed, whether to undercut the smugness of her words or because she was proud of her own rightness he wasn't sure.

Morris left it to Sadie to feel the indignation. He never burned along with her. But faced with Wendy's shooting eyes and disapproving sighs, he understands precisely how Sadie felt. Wendy is burning him. She's the one doing the burning. He, on the receiving end, feels strangely empowered.

He knows what he could say: I've had enough of the implication that David has to be protected from me. And as for Rachel—I get it. She doesn't have friends. So what? Maybe she likes to be alone. Did you ever consider that she might prefer her own company to being with a bunch of silly girls?

David interrupts Morris's thoughts. He's standing in the doorway. 'Are you two okay to phone the ballet mothers? I'll just . . .' He turns and walks away.

See, Morris thinks, I'm right. Wendy is wrong. There are people who will miss her. But he can't sustain the burn for as long as Sadie could. He just feels tired.

And there's something nipping at the edge of his mind—a question which needs to be asked.

Then come the phone calls. The endless phone calls. And the waiting in between, and the checking whether Search and Rescue has called. The wondering whether they should call Molly in case she tried to get through while Wendy was on the phone speaking to ballet mothers. Rachel has hours and hours of students.

Wendy does the talking ('Don't worry, Morris, I won't force you to'). Morris runs a finger down the list, ticking off names, grateful to Rachel for her neat lines, her straight margins, her organised columns: student's name, parent's name, time slot, phone number.

Wendy takes a deep breath before each phone call. 'Jesus Christ, Morris, this is hard.' Then: 'Hello, Mrs Burdon, my name is Wendy. I am the aunt of Rachel, your daughter's ballet teacher. I'm afraid that there won't be a lesson tomorrow . . . no, she's not ill . . . she's missing . . . tramping in the bush . . . We're sure she'll be back tomorrow, but just in case . . . She's been doing it for years actually, yes, I know, not many people knew she did it. In the Tararuas . . . yes, yes, I know. Classes as usual next week. Unless you hear from us. Classes as usual.'

There is no theatrical sighing when the calls are over. Just a soft, 'Jesus Christ, Morris, I had no idea Rachel has so many students. No idea at all. I don't think Sadie knew. Rachel should have told her. She would have been so proud. Jesus Christ, Morris.'

The phone rings. Morris snatches it up, sees David come rushing into the room, and hands it over to him. David grabs the phone, 'Hello . . . yes . . . yes.'

Wendy shrugs and mouths the word, 'Molly?'

David says, 'Thank you for calling. Thank you. Thank you. Goodbye.' He stares at the phone. 'That was Search and . . . Molly. They've checked all the huts. Rachel didn't sleep in any of them, but she passed by four and signed in. Last time she signed in was yesterday afternoon. She wrote that she was going to sleep in her tent.'

Wendy says, 'So they know where she was yesterday afternoon. That's good news.'

David says, 'Confirmation that she had her tent with her.'

As if a ticked-off list wasn't confirmation enough.

Wendy says, 'This is definitely good news. Good news, David.'

'Yesterday afternoon,' says Morris.

'Actually,' Wendy says, 'not yesterday afternoon—more like this morning. If she slept in her tent last night then she would've woken up in it this morning, so actually, actually, she wasn't even missing this morning. This is really good news, David.'

They're rattling on about tents and knowing where she was, but there's something they don't mention: as long as Rachel was signing in, she was sticking to the rules. For a moment Morris feels comforted by this knowledge and considers raising it with the others. But the comfort passes and he says nothing. They'll only ask whether he ever doubted that she'd stick to the rules. Then they'll ask why, if she's so good at sticking to rules, no one has heard from her. And he won't know what to say.

Wendy picks up her handbag. 'Come on, you two. Keep me company while I have a cigarette.'

'You go out,' says David. 'I'll come and join you. I'll just call Debs.'

Wendy is hunched over in her chair with her hands tucked into her armpits. She's rocking slightly.

'Can I get your shawl?'

She shakes her head and sits up straighter, but her hands are still tucked into her armpits and there's still that rocking.

'Thanks, but I'm not cold. It's just my hands. They won't stop shaking.'

Morris keeps his hands in his pockets, ashamed of their calm solidity.

Wendy's hands shake so badly that she struggles to light her cigarette.

If Morris wasn't so ashamed of his steady hands he could take the lighter from her, lean in and light her cigarette. Or he could light a cigarette for her and take a drag himself before passing it on. If he wasn't so ashamed he could hold the cigarette between her lips, let her drag on it and take it away until she was ready for the next drag. Like the good cop does for the handcuffed prisoner.

Like Wendy did for Sadie when she was so sick from the chemo.

Morris was walking down the path when he saw it. It was night. The light was on in the lounge, illuminating the sofa which Sadie was lying on. It was like watching a stage show or a silent movie. Sadie, playing the sick patient, lifting one languid arm. Wendy, the attentive sister perched on the side of the sofa, holding a cigarette up to the patient's mouth. The patient draws on the cigarette. Her arm falls. She lies back. Her sister strokes her arm, brings the cigarette to her own mouth.

Morris clutched his briefcase and stood dead still. He could have watched their performance all night.

He should have watched how Wendy helped Sadie. He could have learned something. He could have taken up a little lesson and saved it for an occasion such as this. How to help someone smoke a cigarette when their wrists are handcuffed or their hands are shaking so badly they can't light their own. Or they've just come home from the hospital and can only raise one languid arm.

He tries to draw the memory out but there's something wrong with it. She wouldn't have smoked for years, and definitely not after chemo. Morris must have his memories mixed up. Wendy must have been feeding Sadie—soup, probably. Chicken soup. Sadie always made chicken soup when someone was sick.

'I make it because it's good comfort food,' she said once.

'You make it because you like playing the caricature Jew,' Wendy said.

'Caricature Jew. Is there any other kind? I mean, honestly, look at us. Look at Morris!'

They both turned to consider him. He shrugged and did up a button on his cardigan—an action that clearly amused them.

Chicken soup can't be the right memory. There was smoke. Morris clearly remembers the smoke rising from Sadie's face, and the smell that lingered in the lounge.

'Marijuana,' he blurts out. 'You gave Sadie marijuana.'

Wendy looks up sharply. 'Sure, Sadie had weed after her chemo, but what makes you think of that now?'

Your shaking hands, he can't say. 'I don't know.'

She gives a half-smile. 'Sadie and the weed. There was a thing. Sadie and her weed.'

After a while she says, 'You know how sometimes you can be reading a book or watching a movie, and you see someone doing something that seems believable when you're watching it. But afterwards, when the movie's over or you've finished the book, you think about it and you realise that you can't actually think of anyone doing it in real life? It's not so strange as to be unbelievable in the story but it's unusual enough that you think, Not in my world. In someone else's maybe, but not mine. D'you know that feeling?'

When Morris was ten years old, his mother made him accompany her to her boss's house. The doctor was going on a long holiday and Pearl had to drop off papers from the surgery. Morris wanted to stay in the car, but his mother insisted that he come in and play with the doctor's children while she and the doctor discussed what they needed to discuss. He stood behind her in the doctor's entrance hall. There were suitcases everywhere, and children's running feet.

The doctor's wife threw her hands in the air and said, 'Did you ever see such chaos?'

Morris's mother said, 'It must be a big job, the packing.'

'Lord knows it's hard enough to pack for our family, but to think of catering for four families whose only access to the mainland will be a boat that comes every few days. Think of feeding all those children for three weeks. Think of it!'

The doctor's family was going on holiday. With other families. There would be fourteen children in all. They were taking over a whole campsite. Morris looked around at the washing baskets and piles of toys, and thought, It looks like something from a film.

That evening he wondered whether his life looked like a film to other children, whether the doctor's sons might look at Morris and his mother as they sat listening to the wireless and think, Not in my world. In somebody else's life that might happen. Not in mine.

He imagined the doctor's sons lying in their bunk beds. The oldest one leans down from the top bunk. 'It must be funny to be that boy Morris, eh.'

'Yeah,' replies his younger brother. 'It's only him and his mother. Just the two of them. Must be funny to be just you and your mother.'

'His mother's a widow. Father's dead.'

The younger boy bangs his feet on the bottom of the bunk above him. The older one leans down again. 'Yeah?'

'Morris and his mother are Jewish. What do you think it's like being Jewish?'

'I dunno. I guess it's kind of funny.' The head retreats

back to the top bunk.

A few moments later the younger one gives three sharp bangs on the bunk. 'What's being Jewish?' he asks the head which is hanging down towards him again.

Wendy is wrong to think you only get that feeling after watching a movie or reading a book. It happens in life. All the time.

He says, 'Mm. I know that feeling.'

'Well, it was like that with the weed. I'd read about people who smoked weed to help them through chemo. I'd seen it in a movie but I never thought I'd know someone who actually did it. When you see it in a movie, you think it's only done by movie people—bigger, braver, story people.'

'Mm.'

'Well, Sadie was that person—the bigger, braver, larger-than-life story person who actually did things. She really, truly smoked the weed. It helped her get over the nausea and gave her a bit of an appetite. Just like in the stories. Bloody hell, it even got her laughing.' Wendy gives a strange half sob. 'How many people can say that some of their funniest memories of their deceased sister are from just before she died, when she was riddled with chemo, bald and skinny? Jesus Christ, Morris, she could still laugh. She couldn't eat but she could laugh.'

It takes Wendy a few moments before she can speak again. Morris busies himself with a cigarette, waits for her to collect herself enough to say, 'Christ, that woman could laugh.'

David comes outside. He's holding a box of cigarettes. 'Come on, Dad, you can't smoke that menthol crap. Have one of these.'

'I didn't know you still smoke,' says Morris.

'I don't,' David replies. He holds a hand out to Wendy and she passes him her cigarette so that he can light his off the end of hers.

Morris excuses himself to go inside. There's something he needs to think about.

Morris lays the flier on the table.

Rachel smiles up at him. He tries to smooth the flier down, but no amount of stroking will remove the cracks over her face where the shiny paper is crumpled and bent. She's smiling at him through chicken wire. He feels unexpectedly, desperately sad for her. His daughter whose fridge is white, who is passionate about spreading the word on fitness training, considers herself lucky to be paid for doing what she loves best and must, for her exclamation-mark job, provide for herself a new name.

His Rachel whose linen smells of lavender and who left him a notebook in her cupboard.

They eat store-made soup which Wendy brought.

David has the phone on the table next to his soup bowl. He picks it up immediately it rings, swallows hard before saying hello.

It's Molly. She has good news and bad news. David uses these words when he puts the phone down. 'Search and Rescue has good news and bad news.'

The good news is they've spoken to a tramper who saw Rachel's tent this morning at about nine o'clock. The tent was erected exactly where Search and Rescue would have expected it to be, given Rachel's plans—five or six hours walk from the car park. The tramper didn't speak to Rachel or see her. He assumed she was sleeping.

Wendy says, 'That *is* good news. She probably decided to sleep in 'cause it was the last day and all. I bet she got going late.'

They start doing sums.

'So if she slept in, say until ten—'

'Then it could be almost eleven before she'd packed up her tent and started walking.'

'And she'd still have five or six hours' walking to go.'

'That means she's hardly even late.'

'Hardly. And for all we know she could have slept later, say until 10.30 or eleven.'

'Any minute now she'll walk out of the park right as rain and ignorant of all the fuss.'

You don't sleep in on a tramp, thinks Morris. On a tramp you get going with the sun. And Rachel is an early riser. Always was. As a baby she'd start crying at precisely five o'clock. Morris would hear her cries in his dreams before he heard them in the house. She'd cry only for a minute or two—just long enough for him to get out of bed. She knows I'm coming, Morris would think. She doesn't need to make a fuss to get my attention.

David used to giggle and coo when he had his nappy changed. Not Rachel. She gazed up at Morris, solemn and serious, as if recognising that the start of a new day is a matter of some weight. She'd wait patiently while he warmed her milk, and when he was ready she'd settle softly, softly into his arms.

Rachel and Morris alone in a world that hasn't yet woken.

Then David would come crashing in and tickle Rachel's toes to make her giggle. Sadie would follow. 'I want my baby girl and I want a cup of tea. Come on, David, I want a cuddle before we get you ready for kindy. I want a kiss from my husband.'

One swoop accomplished both the kiss and the removal of Rachel from her father's arms and on to her mother's shoulder. Rachel kept her eyes on Morris, gazing at him from over Sadie's shoulder as she receded from the room.

When Rachel got older Sadie started leaving a bowl of cereal out for her at night, with a little jug of milk so she could help herself to breakfast while everyone else slept. Sadie even bought a special milk jug with pictures of cows jumping over moons. They made Morris sad, those endlessly jumping cows.

One morning he found Rachel sitting at the window with her cereal bowl in her lap. She glanced over her shoulder at him, then turned back to the window, saying, 'When I get up early I feel like I'm the only person in the world. That's nice.'

The only person in the world, thinks Morris. That's nice.

Wendy says, 'I suppose I'd better ask about the bad news.'

The weather's turned. It's raining hard. Has been for

some time. Rivers are rising. There may be landslides.

Morris is holding a spoon. Above a soup bowl. There's red tomato soup in the spoon. He must have been intending to bring it to his mouth but he can't do that now. He looks down at the spoon, at the bowl. You don't, on hearing such news, calmly go on with your soup.

The spoon clatters against the side of the bowl. There are red spatters on the table.

'Rising rivers,' says Wendy. 'Landslides. Jesus Christ.'

The soup spatters look like ink stains on an old man's pocket.

'Jesus Christ.' Wendy looks to Morris, as if expecting him to provide an explanation for the rising rivers.

'She knows how to deal with rivers,' he says.

'Are you sure?' Wendy asks.

'I taught her.'

Sometimes on a tramp Morris and Rachel would find themselves among other walkers doing the same route. This could lead to greetings, small talk and, if they were unlucky, invitations to combine pasta dinners or for Morris to have a sip of the whisky which Peter here lugs around with him on every single tramp. Like that time when he . . . If they stopped too long for lunch there were always other trampers, looking for conversation, whispering about a father and daughter tramping together. It's quite sweet really. Maybe the parents are divorced.

Always feeling sorry for Rachel and wanting to include her in their activities.

It was like that on the tramp of the washed-away bridge. For two days they were shadowed by a party of three families. Two days of boys tearing through the bush behind them or bursting into the quiet spot where they'd stopped for lunch.

Two nights in the same huts. The more the merrier, come and join us for dinner, we've got instant chocolate pudding for dessert.

On the first night Morris and Rachel allowed themselves to be chivvied into socialising, but on the second Morris managed to stay firm. 'We'll be turning in early tonight. We have an early start tomorrow.'

'Very early,' added Rachel.

It was still dark when they crept out of the hut next morning. They had their breakfast outside. Morris wondered whether the sleepers would consider them rude for sneaking away and found that he really didn't care if they did. It was those families who were rude, violating his bush and scaring Rachel with their whooping. Sadie would say he shouldn't care what they think. She'd say that he shouldn't worry about people he'd never see again.

They made good progress that morning. The sun rose to a clear mild day. They were alone in the world. They need never see those families again.

At mid-morning they reached the stream. A bit later, the spot where the bridge was supposed to be. Had clearly once been. Morris pointed to some rocks on the other side. 'It must have been there. It's been swept away.'

Rachel thought it might be a bit upstream. Became increasingly insistent that it was definitely upstream. Or downstream. Morris trotted after her. He knew she wouldn't get far either upstream or down. The bush was dense. The path overgrown. The bridge had definitely been washed away. Finally she stopped and said, 'Well then, we'll have to cross here.'

'Rachel, we can't—'

'Let's go, Dad.'

'Rachel, the bridge has been washed away. We need to think this through. We need to take it slowly.'

'Those others—they're only an hour or so away. I don't see why we can't cross,' Rachel said.

'It's flowing water.'

'It's just a little stream. It's hardly even moving. So what if we get a bit wet?' Her tone was derisive.

Morris knew where Rachel had learned that tone. She was mimicking her brother who over the past few months had become increasingly scornful of his parents. Sadie said David's behaviour burned her but they shouldn't take it personally. David was just being a teenager. He had to scorn his parents to establish himself as his own person. She said Morris must have done it, and nagged him to tell her about his teenage rebellion. She wouldn't accept there was nothing to tell, said, 'Come on, Morris. You know you can't hold out on me.' She said, 'If you don't tell me what you did, how can I be expected to know what David will do?' So Morris snapped at her. 'David is nothing like me. If you want to know how he'll behave, ask yourself what you did at that age.'

'Me?' said Sadie. 'Me? I didn't have to rebel. My parents were too busy doing it themselves.' She looked sad then, and Morris felt sorry for snapping at her. He said, 'Well, I suppose I was a bit irritable with my mother,' and she said, 'But you wouldn't have been really bad, would you? You're not like that.' She still looked sad, so he said, 'You know, you're right about David establishing himself as his own person. It's good that he's doing it,' and she said, 'You and me, we didn't need to do it. We were already our own person . . . people . . . person.' And she smiled. But then she looked sad again and said, 'Rachel had better get a move on if she's going to do it. We don't want her doing it when she's twenty-five. There's nothing uglier than an old rebel. Nothing uglier. Trust me.'

Sadie would have been happy to hear Rachel's irritable

tone. She would have liked the derisive note when Rachel said, 'Come on, Dad. Will you just get a move on. We're not made of sugar.'

Sadie would not have snapped.

'Rachel, for God's sake, shut up. This is important. Important.'

She looked away.

'Rachel, it's just—'

Morris was okay with Rachel becoming her own person. He understood that she would one day draw away. But not that day. Not when they were faced with flowing water. Not when there was an important lesson to be learned.

Morris himself had learned that lesson about twenty years earlier.

About twenty years earlier, Morris had sat at a river bank with a group of people and listened to a giant of a man explain the dangers of flowing water. Craig looked tall even when he was sitting down. When he spoke everyone listened—even the boys who'd been drinking beer and trying to put their empty cans in other people's packs. Even the girl who'd kept up a steady stream of chatting since they set out that morning.

When Craig spoke they kept quiet. Craig wouldn't let them go any further until they'd listened.

Morris would explain to Rachel as Craig had explained to him. Even if she didn't want to listen, he would explain. He took off his pack and sat against a tree.

She glowered down at him.

He had to explain. He was her father.

'The thing is, Rachel, water is dangerous. Even if it's

just a shallow stream. Even if it looks calm. There's often a hidden current.'

She wouldn't meet his eye, but he knew she was listening. 'Promise me you won't try to cross flowing water on your own,' he said, and she gave a small nod, then went to sit at a bit of a distance from him.

When they heard the other family approaching, he picked up their packs and went to sit beside her.

One of the boys said, 'Who have we here?' and another one said, 'You thought you'd slip out on us, didn't you?' before their mother shushed them and bent down to ask Rachel how she was.

The men stood on the side of the river with their legs planted wide. Stones were thrown in and the water speed measured with sticks before it was decided (I've been trying to tell you this since you arrived, thought Morris) that it would be safe to cross if they held each other across their backs, in a chain. 'Like we were taught in Scouts,' said one of the boys. 'Strongest on the outside, weakest in the middle.'

They put Rachel in the middle. A young boy on either side of her, then the mothers, then the larger boys, Morris (making one side longer than the other and so destroying the symmetry) and then, on either end, the fathers.

There was no doubting that Craig would go on the outside. Morris was next to one of the beer drinkers. The boy was breathing fast. He gripped Morris's waist hard and, when they were about halfway across, whimpered. Morris's feet lost the ground and flapped useless in the current. Someone gave a grunting sound. A stone hit against Morris's calf. His foot found a rock, then lost it, and both his feet were sweeping away, down the river and away from him.

It must have taken about thirty seconds to reach the other side. Someone said they could have died. Someone said, 'Man, I'm pleased we decided to cross. That was the right decision.'

Craig didn't say anything. His beard was red against his face.

One of the fathers kept shouting instructions. 'Arms around backs. Arms under packs. Hold on tight to those on either side of you. Hold tight now.' Morris looked down the line to Rachel. If she turned, the others would turn with her. If she moved, the whole line would move.

'Ready, steady,' called the shouting father.

Rachel was the first to step forward, toes pointed.

'Hold your horses,' said one of the boys.

'One foot in front of the other,' called the shouting father as they went.

The water wasn't very deep and they kept their footing, but still there was a fuss on the other side. One of the mothers said that Rachel had done really well for such a slip of a girl.

They walked as a group for the rest of the day.

'Smallest on the inside,' one of the boys joked. Rachel went and walked near the back. They'd made a mistake to put her in the middle. A mistake to think her the weakest.

David sits down heavily and reaches across the table towards Wendy's hand. 'The good news is better than the bad news is bad.'

'The bad news isn't even that bad, 'cause your dad says she knows what to do around water.'

'And she'd know how to deal with landslides. She's always been sure footed.'

'A broken leg is probably the worst we're looking at. A broken leg at worst.'

'A broken leg isn't the end of the world.'

'Don't come running to me if you break your leg.'

The soup stains look like the ten plagues, spelled out in wine on the Passover saucer. Blood, Locusts, Pestilence, Killing of the First Born.

Then there are the hours of waiting. The dark hours when the rivers are rising, the land is slipping. The world is sleeping and the family is not.

They have the drugged-out look of people who have just stepped off a midnight aeroplane—glassy eyed, fiddling with their watches, testing the ground with each step as if unsure it will hold them, telling themselves to be alert, there is still passport control to get through, and Customs. There are still questions to be asked and answered.

Wendy takes Panadol. She offers one to Morris and he refuses it. Later, when it feels as if the throbbing in his head must be visible, he reconsiders but doesn't ask.

David will make up beds for Wendy and Morris. Morris isn't thinking of going home is he?

Morris is thinking of going home. He wants to be alone with a desk, a pen and paper, a computer. A door he can shut behind him. He wants a large sheet of paper and a thick black pen.

He has a reason for needing to go home—the cat must be fed.

David tries to make a joke. 'Oh all right then, but come back. Don't try to make a run for it.'

Neither Wendy nor David offers to accompany him, and Morris realises that David hasn't been to the house in some time. It's not that he and David haven't seen each other. They've seen plenty of each other—dinners at David's house and trips accompanying David to garden centres, hardware stores, Benjy's clinic visits. If Morris's phone has rung in recent months it's probably been David with an invitation. 'On Sunday Emma's playing soccer. Come on, come and see a bunch of four-year-olds kick a ball around. It's good for a laugh. And a hot chocolate afterwards.'

The invitations are well meant and generous but behind their warmth Morris hears whispers of shame, as though David is embarrassed that his father has not planned on seeing another human being for the whole weekend. 'You can't pass an opportunity for hot chocolate,' David would say. 'The whole weekend,' his scandalised shame would whisper down the phone line.

'If you're not back in half an hour,' David is still trying to joke, 'I'll send Wendy to come looking for you.'

At the front door Morris lifts his jacket from its hook and finds, hiding behind it, a row of little hooks at child's height like in a kindergarten or an orphanage. The red hook holds a red raincoat, bright and shiny. Red is a good colour for a little girl's jacket. Clearly visible. Morris bends down to the hook, reaches out to the jacket, feels the earth sliding beneath his feet.

'Back already?' says David. 'Couldn't keep away? Dad, you're pale. Sit down. I'll get you some water.'

David is all activity, calling Morris's neighbour who has a key.

'Sorry, Dad, I should have thought to call her in the first place'

A neighbour has a key?

'Yeah, yeah, you know, Mrs Mac. She used to come in sometimes if Mum was going to be alone . . . when you . . . were at work or something. Mrs Mac. She's had a key for ever.'

Mrs Mac still has her key. Mrs Mac will be happy to feed the cat and no, David assures her, no, there's nothing more she can do.

You can give me back my key, thinks Morris.

David conducts phone calls, glasses of water, tea. He

provides toiletries, shakes sleeping bags into duvet covers.

Morris gets the spare room, Wendy Emma's room.

Morris wonders how David made the decision. Did he consciously avoid putting his father in little Emma's room, worried that Morris might fall over the plastic ballet bar or get tangled in the plastic chandelier? Bump his head on the top bunk. Leave a trace of what? Farce?

Morris stands in the doorway of the spare room, turns on the light and finds himself gazing into a room which is at once completely strange and wholly familiar. It seems to be furnished entirely with things that Morris and Sadie once owned. He recognises the chair, the desk, even the curtains and bedspread. Things he has forgotten he ever possessed or ever lost. Things that left no gap when they were removed.

There was a time when a lot of construction work was being done in Wellington—buildings being demolished, rebuilt, demolished again. Sadie would point out building sites as they drove. 'Look at that, children—not you, Morris. Eyes on the road, hands upon the wheel—see that crane.'

She'd wonder aloud what was going to go in all those new buildings, who would be living there. And what of the shops? What would they sell? She'd make up stories and Morris, eyes on the road, hands on the wheel, would try to remember what had stood there. Before the To Let signs and the building site there had been something. It worried him that he struggled to remember what it was.

He never mentioned this worry to Sadie.

I would have told you that no one remembers what used to stand anywhere. We forget. We adapt. That's the beauty of human beings.

It worried Morris that the world could shift around him. Whole buildings could be created to fill a gap he hadn't even noticed. Chairs and desks, curtains and bedspreads can move from house to house without your noticing their absence. Linen can take its smell of lavender and cloves and you'd never even notice they were missing. The earth can slide beneath your feet.

He switches off the light and turns from David's spare room without stepping over its threshold.

David says they have to sleep. There's no point in being exhausted. But for now they sit at the kitchen table. There's a bottle of wine. Wendy turns it round and round.

'It's not like I'm going to be driving anywhere,' she responds to Morris's glance when she refills her glass.

He pours himself a glass to show that he didn't mean, that he wasn't suggesting . . .

His head aches and no amount of brushing with the tiny airline toothbrush David supplied will get rid of the dry, dull mouth of too many cigarettes for a man unaccustomed.

He wants to ask David about the furniture in the spare room. He'd like David to remind him where each item used to stand.

David would know but Morris can't ask him. If he did, David's face would crease and Wendy would burn. She'd point her finger at him and ask him who he thinks he is, making the boy feel bad about a few chairs, things that he never missed anyway. At a time like this. She'd drag hard on her cigarette and demand to know what kind of a man gets upset about the gaps left by a chair but finds himself thrilled—yes, thrilled, he told me—by the gaps left by the melting Arctic ice. She'll say something biting about priorities and working out which gaps are important. Morris will be at a loss.

There's a bowl of nuts which David eats, replenishes,

eats again. Morris has brushed his teeth and hadn't intended eating anything more. But now he's drinking wine and he's going to have to brush his teeth again anyway.

They talk about Sadie. David's face gets its creased look. He covers his mouth with a handful of nuts and says that he really misses her jokes.

'The only jokes I get now are those awful ones that are mass emailed. Even if they're funny they're not as funny as Mum's. It was something in the telling.'

Wendy picks up her glass. 'She was telling jokes right until the end. You have to wonder where she got them. I mean, could the nurses have been sticking their heads in to say, "Mrs Goldberg, have I got a joke for you"?'

'What was that joke about the definition of a schlemiel?' Morris asks.

'Oh God, I remember that one,' says David.

Wendy shushes him and raises her glass. 'What,' she asks the wine, 'is the difference between a schlemiel and a schlimazel?'

'No,' says Morris, 'not that one.'

'The schlemiel,' David says, 'spills his soup on the schlimazel!'

'The schlimazel spills his soup on the schlemiel,' says Wendy.

David makes a sound which is part laugh, part sigh.

Wendy takes a large gulp of wine. Her eyes are shining.

Morris's head throbs.

'The schlimazel spills his soup on the schlemiel,' says Wendy. She brings her shawl to her face.

'Not that one,' Morris says again. 'A different one. About a man who lives in a vacuum.'

Wendy lowers the shawl to look at him blankly.

'I mean, a man who sucks the air from the room.'

'Are you sure it's one of Mum's? I don't remember it.'

'It's about a schlemiel or a schmuck or something.'

'A schmuck,' says Wendy. 'Now there's a different variety altogether.'

'When he walks into a room it's like the air leaves,' Morris says.

'I know that one,' Wendy and David say together.

'But it's not about a schlemiel.'

'Or even a schmuck.'

'It's definitely not about a schlimazel.'

It's like watching a comedy routine where they're the jokers and he's the fall guy. Any minute now one of them will punch his nose while the other pours water over his head.

'It's about a nebbish,' says Wendy. 'When a nebbish walks into the room you feel like someone's left. When he leaves you think someone's arrived.'

'A nebbish,' says David, 'Not a schmuck. Or a schlemiel. Definitely not a schlimazel. A nebbish.' He smiles. 'Try to keep up, Dad.'

Wendy gives a wild laugh.

It's a laugh that Morris has heard before.

Sadie and Wendy were eating cake and laughing. They laughed so wildly, so hard, that crumbs flew from their mouths. Their eyes watered. Their noses dripped. Sadie put down her cake, wiped her hands on her pants, made a show of trying to stop laughing when Morris entered the room.

'You know how some people say that depression makes them want to stop eating?'

'I know, I know,' said Wendy. 'God, I hate those people. They're the same ones who say, "When I'm busy at work I completely forget to eat."'

Sadie spluttered and picked up her cake. 'Well, when I'm

grieving, I can't stomach a mouthful.'

'Tell me about it.' Wendy ran a finger through the icing. 'I'm afraid I might waste away altogether.'

Their father in faraway England had died. Neither of them was going to the funeral. They said they couldn't afford it.

They thought it was a joke.

Now David's doing it too—laughing and joking like he's at a carnival. He and Wendy are carrying on like circus clowns.

Wendy abruptly stops laughing and says, 'God, I wish she was here now.'

'Me too,' says David.

They must mean Rachel.

David is going to sleep. There's some discussion as to what to do with the phone. It's finally agreed that Morris will keep it close to him. He's a light sleeper and he'll wake the others if there's any news.

Wendy stands up to hug David at the door, to tell him he mustn't worry and she's sure that when they wake up it will be to good news.

Morris expects Wendy to go too, but she sits down opposite him.

Morris is alone with his sister-in-law who seems to have used up all her softness in hugging David and is facing him now with a hard, tight face. His sister-in-law who is (he can almost see the smoke coming out of the top of her head) burning. He can smell her cigarettes. He can taste the ash in his mouth.

If Wendy is burning, then Morris must be the burnee.

'You never were a great one for hugging, were you?'

'I . . .'

'Or touching.' She pours them both some wine, as if he's going to need it. 'Sadie used to complain about it.'

Sadie complained? She discussed this?

'Oh come on, you must have known she would complain to me. I know she complained about the touching to you, and if she complained to you, chances are I knew all about it.'

Sadie *had* complained to him—repeatedly.

When David left home: 'There goes the only person in this family who's not tactile defensive.'

When she was worried about Rachel: 'Have you noticed

how she stiffens when I try to hug her? She's like you in that way.'

When he pulled away in a movie, surprised by her hand on his thigh: 'For God's sake, Morris, I wasn't going for your popcorn. I was trying to touch you. Mind you, you probably find that way bloody worse.'

'I did touch her. We . . .'

'Don't even think of mentioning sex. I'm not talking about sex. Sex doesn't count.'

'Sex doesn't count.' Sadie's exact words. 'This is not about sex. I'm talking about a hand on the knee in the movies, holding my hand even for three small seconds. Hugging me maybe. Once or twice a year. Every six months. Turn back the clocks. Check the fire alarm. Hug your wife. How hard can it be? Humour me.'

And even—Morris blushes at the memory—'I'm not having sex with you if you haven't touched me at least three times since we last had sex.'

She should have known that would cause a stand-off. She should have realised that he couldn't, even if he wanted to, touch her after that. It would have been forced and dishonest, done just so he could get her to have sex with him.

Wendy takes a large gulp of wine. It does nothing to soften her face. 'What good was sex to her when she lay in that horrible hospital bed? That awful metal bed. And when she came home you still slept in your bedroom even though she was downstairs in the spare room.'

'She couldn't make it up the stairs. The spare room was best for her.'

'Of course she had to be downstairs. But so, Mr Morris, should you have been. You should have slept downstairs with her. Not up those fucking stairs and so far away.'

'It was a small bed. I thought it was best. I . . .'

'Well, it wasn't best. She needed someone close. Even if

124

you couldn't bring yourself to sleep in the same bed as your dying wife you could at least have sat beside her, held her hand. Something. Anything. Jesus Christ, Morris, I know this sounds corny, but couldn't you see that she needed to be touched?'

'I . . . she didn't mind. She understood that I needed to sleep, that I had to go to work.'

'Don't even get me started on the fact that you were still working.' Wendy points a burning finger at him. 'Right until the bitter end you went to work. What is the matter with you?'

'There were always people with her.'

If Wendy wasn't there, the nurse was. And that neighbour —Mrs Mac, in and out all the time. In and out with her key.

'Why do you think they were always there? Because you weren't. We couldn't leave her alone, could we?'

'Always people there.'

'Not good enough, Morris. You didn't change your routine one iota. "My wife is dying. Well, that's no reason to miss that very important deadline so I can sit with her and watch crappy videos. Some neighbour will pop her head in every now and again. My wife is dying—no reason to move to the spare room with her or break the habit of a lifetime and maybe hold her hand." Come on, Morris, how hard would it have been for you to break your routine enough to buy her a bunch of flowers? Jesus Christ, Morris, what the fuck was the matter with you?'

'I—'

'You know what, forget it. Forget it. I'm going to have a cigarette.'

She is burned out. Maybe she won't come back.

Morris leans on the kitchen table, holds his head with his hands. The air is heavy with all the things he could so easily have done and what, what the fuck is the matter with you, Morris?

Wendy's right. There is something the matter with him. He knows it, has always known it, was reminded of it with every visitor who came to sit by his stool after Sadie died. Morris Goldberg, as husband, son, nephew, father, has always had something the matter with him. Sadie knew it too. She complained about it but she understood. He thought she understood. Not all the time, but sometimes—usually even. She seemed to understand that he didn't mean it. That he couldn't help it. There was something the matter with him.

D'you remember that programme we used to watch, Frasier, *the one about the shrink?*

Shrink? Don't talk to me about shrinks. You told her—you told her everything.

Of course I told her. She's my sister, for crying out. So, in that programme—

I don't want to think about TV programmes. I thought you understood, sometimes. Most of the time you understood—

Frasier, the radio shrink.

Frasier.

And his brother. What was his name again?

Niles.

Yes, Niles. So, do you remember that one where Frasier and Niles were pretending to be Jewish? Something to do with a woman, and they had to pretend to be Jewish.

They put sugar in the wine. To sweeten it.

Sugar in the wine. Yes, and then they got in a big fight. They were shouting and screaming at each other and they couldn't stop.

I don't want to think about Niles and Frasier fighting. I don't even remember a fight.

You do. You do. They couldn't stop fighting, and then one of them said, 'We can't do this. We're not really Jewish. We can't start screaming at each other 'cause we don't know how to stop.' And then their father hobbled next door, or that Daphne, and fetched their Jewish neighbour to help them make up.

To help them make up.

That's it. The neighbour came and told them to pull themselves together. If they wanted to fight like Jews they had to learn to make up like Jews, and next thing they were hugging and crying and the neighbour was hugging and crying and that Daphne was hugging and crying. Then the neighbour left and they got all withdrawn with each other again. But the fight was over.

You liked that programme.

Well, you and Wendy. You are Jewish. You don't need the neighbour. Dammit, Jim, you don't even need to cry and hug each other. You two can get over this. You have to. Ask her something about herself. Ask about Steve.

What if she doesn't come back?

She'll come back. Ask her about her Steve.

Wendy comes back. She's pulled her hair back from her face, so that she looks both stern and child-like, like a school girl who's playing at being teacher. She hands Morris the telephone, says, 'You probably want to keep this close.'

Morris says, 'About Sadie—I would have got in the way. She had you and her friends. She didn't need me hanging about.'

'Of course she needed you. You were her husband.'

Wendy's smile is so slight that Morris almost misses it. 'That and she carried a torch for you. Yup, Sadie always carried a torch for you.'

Ask her about Steve.

Morris wants to know more about the torch but he says, 'Tell me about Steve. I haven't met him, have I?'

Wendy rests her hand on his shoulder, and he knows that she's ready to take the conversation in this new direction. She says, 'Sure you have. You remember.' And then she says, 'Just joking. I only met him a few months ago, eight months ago to be exact.'

'Eight months ago.'

'I know it was soon after Sadie's death but I guess I was lonely. He helped me through it.'

Morris says the right thing: 'Sadie would have wanted you to get on with your life. She would have been happy for you.'

She smiles. 'I wish she could have met him. They would have liked each other. Steve and David really get on.'

So David has met Steve.

'Debbie also likes him. Emma calls him Steve Irwin.'

And Emma has met Steve.

'Steve Irwin?'

'The crocodile man.'

'Oh, that one. But why should Emma . . .'

'She started it the first time they met. He pretended to be a crocodile. Chased her round, snapping his hands like a giant mouth. You know what I mean. Emma Kabemma laughed like a drain.'

Morris wants to ask more about how he got Emma to laugh, and how did it sound, her laughing like a drain? He wants to put his hands in front of his body and try snapping them like a giant mouth. He wants to ask how the crocodile man managed to get so close to Emma and David and where was he, Morris, when all that snapping of hands was going on? Where was Rachel?

'That crocodile man died, didn't he? Eaten by an alligator or something.'

'I think it was an eel, but that's not the point. Aren't you interested in where I met him?'

'Can't have been an eel. Eels don't eat people, do they?'

'What do I know? Maybe there's some kind of giant killer eel. In Australia. Not in New Zealand. Who knows? Who cares? We're talking about *my* Steve. The one who wasn't eaten by an animal unknown.'

He actually laughs. 'Tell me about your Steve, the one who wasn't eaten by an animal unknown.'

'My God, man,' says Wendy, 'I thought you'd never ask.'

Later Morris will look back on the next half hour and wonder whether it could really have been as pleasurable as he remembers. It seems contrary to imagine that it could have been. And yet there's something so companionable, so familiar and familial, in putting your arms behind your head, leaning back in your chair, maybe even closing your eyes—to rest them, not to sleep—while Wendy tells him how she has finally, 'at the ripe old age of fifty-something, and completely out of character, I'll grant you that,' found herself a 'jolly decent chap'.

Maybe it isn't the lulling chatter which is the source of that pleasant feeling, but rather the words which bring it drifting to an end: 'A jolly decent chap. Someone I can count on. Like my sister Sadie found for herself.'

Wendy stretches, open and wide, as if she would embrace the room. Or Morris.

Wendy is dozing on the sofa. It's like she's naked, with her drooping head, open mouth, her socks sagging round her ankles.

They're getting old, those left behind. Old and undignified. And left behind.

Soon they'll be gaps and no one will remember who used to fill them.

Morris closes his eyes and tries to picture Sadie. She's carrying a torch. A flaming one, like the Olympic torch. A giant joint. She's holding it out in front of her so that he must run if he's to stay within her light. But she's running too fast and he can't keep up. Her running feet are making cracks in the ice. If Rachel steps on the ice she'll fall down, down, into the icy water and the waiting crocodiles with their snapping jaws. He wants to call out. Stop. You're melting the ice. Stop. You're making gaps.

Morris jerks his head upright. Did he fall asleep in front of Wendy? Was he dreaming about Sadie?

The vehement woman spoke about dreams.

'You know how people tell you that you'll think you see your loved one in a crowd?' she'd asked.

'Uh huh.'

'Well, it's nonsense. That sort of thing only happens in movies. In life you don't see them at all—well, not in your waking hours. But in your dreams—now that's a different story. In your dreams you see them all the time.'

Her voice seemed to be losing its vehemence, and Morris

found himself leaning forwards, almost tipping off his stool to hear what she was saying.

'When I first moved to New Zealand I used to have dreams about my old home. I'd be standing in my kitchen and there'd be lots of sunlight. They felt so real, those dreams. It felt like I was really there. Not dreaming I was there but actually, really there.'

Other visitors would bend down towards Morris. Some sat on the floor next to his stool. But not the vehement woman. She sat straight and distant so that he had either to focus on her pointy shoes or strain his neck to see her face.

'I told Sadie about my dreams once. She lent me a book about the dreams of holocaust survivors. Sadie always lent me books. There was a piece in that book where a young man told how he used to dream of walking up the stairs to his front door, how he'd stand at the door, lift up his hand to open it.' The woman looked around the room, as if expecting to see the book or the front door described in it. 'It had, I think, a red cover . . .'

'Red. I don't know.'

'Well, in that book the man described how his dream was so real that it wasn't like a dream at all. He thought he was actually at his front door. That was what made the disappointment so sad, when he realised he couldn't open it. So tragic when he couldn't open it . . . So tragic.'

Morris wanted to tell her to stop digressing, to switch off her low musing voice, go back to her vehemence and tell him more about how things will get worse. Before other visitors arrived and interrupted them.

'I don't dream much.'

'Yes, yes, the dreams. When you lose someone you love, the dreams are so real you forget you're dreaming. You think you're really with them. And when you wake up you hate yourself for forgetting. And you hate yourself for waking up. You hate those dreams but you long for them also.'

Things will get worse and you'll dream of the person who died. Two promises the vehement woman made to Morris. Two promises that might finally be coming true.

But the dream, like the urge to tell Sadie about Rachel's flier, does not stand up to Morris's scrutiny. The vehement woman's dreams were so real she forgot she was dreaming. His dream was bizarre. It wasn't even a real dream—more like the ramblings of a half-awake man who's supposed to be listening out for the telephone.

Wendy snores, opens her eyes and says she's going to sleep in a bed like a human being. She stands up. 'Don't you want to go to bed? You can still keep the phone close. You'll wake up if it rings.'

'I'll go soon. I'll just sit here a bit longer.'

She bends down to pull at her sock, and he finds himself hoping that she won't leave just yet. 'Um, Wendy—'

'Hmm?'

'There was a vehement woman who came to the house after Sadie died.'

'Vehement woman? What vehement woman? Morris, I'm exhausted. You'll have to give me more information.'

He describes the rasping voice and pointy shoes.

'Of course, it must have been The Tsarina. That's what Sadie used to call her. The Tsarina. She came from Russia. She had a whole lot of funny little sayings that Sadie thought were Russian proverbs full of great wisdom but were probably nonsense.'

Tsarina. It fitted perfectly. What Morris took for vehemence was a Russian accent. Tsarina captured her pointy shoes, her straight back, the Eastern European knowledge that she knew a thing or two about tragedy.

Wendy says, 'She worked with Sadie. Could she have taught maths maybe? Economics? I met her once at some do at the school. Sadie said the kids mocked her accent, and there was something else . . . some other reason to feel sad for her . . . she'd lost a son, I think.'

Wendy stands up. 'Enough of The Tsarina, and enough of this sofa. Go to bed. Get some rest. You can put the phone on your pillow if you're worried about hearing it.'

She releases her hair from its band, says, 'It's hard not being able to do anything to help. Just waiting.'

'The policeman said the waiting is the worst.'

'Who'd've thought that schmuck cop could be right about anything?'

At the door she turns around. 'It's okay for you to doze, you know. You don't have to sit here wide eyed and bushy tailed all night. As long as you hear the phone.'

When she has gone, he picks the phone up, listens to the dial tone.

Enough of The Tsarina. You're obsessing about her. What about the other stuff Wendy said to you? What about the touching? And how you were working when I needed you to be around? What about that, Morris. What about that?

You shouldn't have complained to Wendy about the touching. It was private. Our private stuff.

Nothing is so private that a woman can't complain about it. Especially when it comes to husbands and children. Every woman complains about her husband and her children. I did it. My friends do it. Your mother did it.

My mother never complained. Or spoke about private things.

Of course she did. You can bet your bottom dollar she did.

She never did.

136

Nonsense. She must have complained to someone. What about Joan of Arc?

Joan of Arc?

You know, Joan. Your Aunt Joan. Wife of The Norman Conquest. Owner of the biggest china cabinet in the southern hemisphere.

Morris's mother, Pearl, had one much younger brother, Norman. He lived with his wife Joan and their dogs in Levin.

You know I often wondered why they lived in Levin. It must have been—what, a three-hour drive from Wellington in those days?

Two hours at most. So what?

Well, I mean, three hours. That's quite far. I would have thought they'd want to be closer to their beloved nephew. And your mother.

They liked Levin. Norman's work was there. Joan liked walking her dogs on the beach. My mother liked Wellington. It's no big deal. It was only two hours away.

Two, three hours. I'm surprised Joan didn't insist on staying close enough to do the pop-in. Can't you picture her, yoo-hooing and carrying a cake?

Yoo-hooing?

Levin—I mean, you'd need a reason to schlep out to Levin. Jewish holiday, birthday, that sort of thing. You wouldn't go to Levin just for the hell of it. And the pop-in was definitely out. You wouldn't go there much in the evening, would you? Unless you slept over.

They never slept over.

What about in school holidays? You must have gone and stayed with them for a few nights during the holidays to give your mother a bit of a break. Like we used to leave David with them before they moved.

I never slept over.

What about on Passover? Didn't you do Passover at Norman's house? You couldn't have driven home on Passover. It would have been too late when you left. Unless you didn't do the full Seder. You did the full Seder, didn't you?

Yes, yes, we did the Seder. The full Seder. At Norman's. And we didn't bicker about which bits to leave out like your family did.

If you're referring to the Seders Wendy and that husband of hers used to have—well, I can tell you the bickering there was nothing. Nothing. Anyway, of course we bickered. That's what the Seder is for. How do you think the Jews spent their time when they were wandering about in the desert? I'll tell you how—eating manna and bickering. Probably about which bits they'd tell their children and grandchildren. Picture it: the plagues are over, the waters have parted, they're crossing the Dead Sea. Bobba turns to her grandson. 'Remember this, Hymie, something to tell your children and grandchildren, something to put in your diary so you can remember exactly how it happened. People will study that diary one day, when you're a great scholar.' If Rivka Levy would let me into her toga that would be something to put in the diary, thinks Hymie. To Bobba he says, 'Enough with the grandchildren already, and I already told you, I'm going to be a singer, not a scholar.' 'This is how you speak to your grandmother?' says Bobba.

Okay, Sadie, all right. I get the picture.

Well, I'm just saying. Your family must have bickered about the Seder. Only you don't remember it.

Morris does remember. There is no bickering in his memory. There is food and ritual, and Uncle Norman at the head of the table, for this is his house, his Seder. Norman is wearing a kaftan. No, no, it wasn't a kaftan. It couldn't have been. It was a woven open-necked top. Cream coloured, with some sort of embroidery around the collar.

Uncle Norman—your sweet Uncle Norman wore an embroidered collar? He of the pen stains on the top pocket of his shirt? Norman, the bald accountant with pen stains? Talk about the caricature Jew. Almost too good to be true, those pen stains.

Morris is six years old. He's standing in the middle of a carpet in the middle of a room. His new Aunty Joan is standing at the door. She's holding a blanket. Norman is on the carpet with Morris. He's crouching down on his haunches so that his face looks directly at Morris's. Morris wants to step back, but Norman has his hands on Morris's shoulders, holding him fast. He speaks softly. Coaxing.

'Morris, big boy, take off the shorts.'

There are ink stains like spots of blood along the bottom of Norman's pockets. Blue blood like the Queen's. Morris wants to take a finger and trace them. Poke at them. But that would mean taking his hands out of his pockets. If he takes his hands out of his pockets they'll make him take his shorts off. And he's not doing that. Ever.

He of the pen stains and polyester tie—he wore an open-necked woven top for Passover? What was it? Some kind of costume party Passover re-enactment?

No, no, Morris is tired and confused. There was no kaftan, no open-necked shirt. Just Norman wearing a white shirt and tie. And yet there was, on those Seder nights, something of a Pharaoh about him. He lifted the matzo high above his head and broke it into two clean, sharp pieces.

He determined which portions would be read and which omitted. There was no bickering at his Seder. He was the man of the house.

I guess you would have been the one to ask the four questions.
I was the one who asked the questions.

Year after year the only child at the table. Year after year the one who the adults turned to, depended on. The one who God depended on. To get it right.

When the other children from cheder had long since moved off the four questions, the task having been taken over by younger siblings or cousins, or some kid visiting from overseas who hadn't learned the questions properly, there was Morris, still asking. Still standing. Still forgetting.

Come on, they couldn't have made you stand.
I'm remembering this. I stood.

Stood and faltered and mangled his way through the four questions. His mother kept her head bent over the book, following the words with him. Norman smiled up at him, encouraging. When it was over, Norman would praise and Pearl would look up from her book.

Joan would give an extravagant gift when he found the hidden matzo, and Morris, his throat drier than the bread of affliction which his ancestors ate, would know that he was undeserving.

The problem was that Norman and Joan never had children. They never wanted them, the younger Morris supposed, and why would they? They had each other and their dogs and Morris to ask the four questions. Morris to look for the matzo. Morris to hug and sometimes, where Joan was concerned, to hold too close so that he'd try to wriggle away and his mother would have to apologise and say that he didn't like to be held much.

When Morris got older he began to wonder whether Norman and Joan had sex. Or did Norman wear a condom? And still later, when he got old enough to understand, he felt sorry for them both and tried to bring himself to withstand Joan's hugs. It was easier to do when done out of pity.

One Passover they were joined by a cousin on holiday from Australia. She wasn't a real cousin but Joan's niece, come to visit with her parents. How proudly Joan had presented the girl to Morris, how bravely she presented Morris to the girl. 'Becky, Morris, you're cousins and I love you both, so go on, be friends.'

Morris watched Joan patting the girl's red cheeks, smoothing her blond hair, and he thought of Moses coming down from the mountain to the sight of his people bowing before false idols. That red-faced Becky was just like the golden calf. She wasn't his cousin. Not even nearly.

I always felt sorry for Moses. Can you imagine what it was like for him, to go through all that he did, leading a bunch of ungrateful slobs through the desert, only to be denied, at the last minute, entry into the Promised Land? And for what? Some silly infraction. I don't even know what he did wrong. Do you remember what he did? See, you can't remember. And for that completely forgettable infraction he gets to die in the desert. Unfair, I say. You always reminded me of Moses.

Me remind you of Moses? I'm not a bit like Moses. He was a hero.

When Morris was at university he once went on a long tramp with a group. The hikers found themselves hemmed in by thick bush and impassable terrain. Morris suggested a way through. His route started by taking them away from where they were heading, and it was rejected out of hand by most of the group. But the tramp leader said, 'Hear him out,' and Morris's friend Murray said that no one had come up with anything better. So Morris explained, and was surprised (and concerned) to find that he had convinced them.

When they burst through the bush into the open and saw the lake before them, Murray gave a loud whoop. The tramp leader said, 'Behold, the Promised Land.' And someone said, 'Morris, our hero, our Moses.'

Morris could have been a hero to the not-cousin. He could have found, then pretended not to have found, the hidden matzo so that Becky could lift it up and lisp, 'Thee what I got, Morrith.' The adults would have seen that he'd let Becky find it, and been proud of him. But he'd sat on the cushion that was hiding the afikomen, and crushed it.

Becky gave a loud wail and punched him in the stomach.

Joan told Norman he was silly to have hidden the matzo where the boy could sit on it. Becky's mother said she didn't care what the tall boy had done, Becky shouldn't have hit him, and Morris, with matzo crumbs all over his corduroy pants, wondered how Goliath had felt at finding his forehead suddenly struck by some little pipsqueak with a catapult.

First Moses, then Goliath. You were having a biblical evening of it. Goliath is another one to feel sorry for. He couldn't help himself. He wasn't bad, Goliath. Just himself. Like Moses. Moses was a stutterer, you know.

What?

He stammered. He couldn't speak for himself. A bit like your mother.

My mother didn't stutter.

I know that. His brother spoke for him.

Norman?

No, no, not your mother's brother. Moses' brother. But since you've brought up the topic of Pearl—

The topic of Pearl?

The topic of your mother. Where was your mother in all this?

Pearl was agreeable with her family. She was pleasant to her sister-in-law, helped in the kitchen and was an easy, undemanding guest. She remembered birthdays, bought exactly the right gifts—tidbits for the dogs.

Pearl did everything right, but she moved through the gatherings with the air of a woman who has learned the names off by heart, who, on being presented with a relative, runs through a list in her head before settling on . . . Joan, Norman's wife. Your friend. What would you do without her?

Once she found Morris sitting alone in Norman's study, flipping through a magazine. She looked at him from such a distance that he wondered whether she was running through names in her head before coming to . . . Morris. My son. Who should be in the kitchen keeping Joan company, not hiding himself in Norman's study.

'Come and join the family, Morris. Dinner will be starting soon.'

She set a slow pace down Norman's passage. When they reached the dining room where the noise was coming from, she breathed in sharply through her nose and seemed to pull herself erect before glancing down at him and opening the door.

Later, when the evening was over and the car doors closed behind them, she let out a sigh so loud that Morris wondered whether she'd been holding her breath all evening.

Morris should have been in the kitchen keeping Joan company. He should have learned the four questions better, should have phoned Norman and Joan more often, let them know how things were going at school, at university. He should have gone with Sadie to visit them after they moved to Australia. He should not have stiffened when Joan came to hug him. Would it have been so hard really, Morris, to pat those dogs once in a while?

It was different for Sadie. She liked having family nearby. She liked maintaining contact with them. She wanted to phone Joan when the babies smiled, walked, said mama. She chose to discuss school reports, Morris's job, what they'd be doing for Norman's birthday. 'His sixtieth, can you believe it? No, I don't think Morris will make a speech but I'd be happy to tell the world how much I adore that husband of yours. I'll shout it from the rooftops. Joan's Norman is the sweetest man in the world.'

She was sorry when Joan and Norman moved to Australia. She kept telling them how much she'd miss them. She told them so often that it was all told up. She'd used up all the words, all the ways of saying I'll miss you, before he even knew they were going.

Joan phoned Morris with the news. 'We wanted you to know first. You're like a son to us. So we wanted to tell you first. That we're going trans-Tasman. Can you believe it? We're crossing the ditch. To live. At our age we decide to up and move. To Australia, no less. Melbourne. I'm going back to my roots. Where my brother is.'

I bet she told Sadie ages ago, Morris thought. She'll have discussed with Sadie when and how to tell me. Now she's waiting for me to say something. What does she want me to say? She already knows we'll miss them.

Joan said, 'You know my brother's in Melbourne and your cousin Becky's got three children. I'd like to get to know those children.'

Say something, Morris. Anything.

'Three children.'

'Two girls and a boy and I hardly know them. Oh, I tell you, Morris, they're as cute as can be.'

'What about Norman's work?'

'Oh, Morris, you know Norman pretends to work but really he's retired. There's nothing keeping us here any more and—' she lowered her voice, as if letting him in on a big secret—'to tell you the truth, I never loved Levin much. I'll be happy to see the back of it.'

Now that your mother has died, Joan might have said. There's nothing keeping us here now that your mother has finally stopped lingering and finally died. We've been wanting to move to Australia for ages, Joan might have said, but we couldn't leave, could we? Not with your mother lingering. We could hardly leave her, could we? Or Levin.

She might have said that, and she might have also said, It's not like you made the effort to visit us very often. Instead she said, 'We'll miss you. And Sadie. And the children. The children will have to come over for holidays and you'll come and visit us, won't you? We'll have lots of lovely holidays together. You're like a son to us.'

Of course I knew they were going before you did. I knew everything before you did. Joan and I discussed how to break it to you. Joan was worried that you'd feel let down by them leaving so soon after your mother died. She didn't want you to feel forsaken.

Had Morris felt forsaken? He remembers feeling only guilty. It was his fault they'd stayed in Levin all that time. His fault and his mother's.

Forsaken. Guilty. It doesn't matter. You should have made more effort to see them. You definitely should have come with me and the children when we made that trip to Australia.

I had work. I couldn't go running off to Australia. I spoke to Joan on the phone every week. You spoke to her all the time. They didn't expect us to go there. It wasn't necessary.

Not necessary! Never expected it! For crying out loud, Morris, sometimes you can be so infuriating.

What? They didn't.

You were like a son to them.

Well, they weren't—

You know what were pretty much the first words you said to me when we first met?

The first words?

Pretty much. The first words you said to me were, 'Joan and Norman. Not my parents.'

Not my parents. Why would I say that to someone I hardly knew?

Why indeed? Anyway, the point is, you should have—

I had my own parents.

Joan and Norman loved you like a son.

I had my own parents.

Okay, okay, I'm not asking you to deny your parents. You had your own parents. I admit it. A mother. And a father. Pearl and Joe Goldberg. Mother and father of Morris Goldberg.

Pearl and Joe.

Pearl who brought you up and Joe who taught you the importance of good tramping gear. Equipment and lists. Check and check. You don't cut corners on tramping gear. From your tent to your shorts. And for you, my boy, we start with the shorts.

'Good gear. You don't cut corners with tramping gear. From your tent to your shorts. And for you, my boy, for you we start with the shorts.'

Morris's father is taking his six-year-old son shopping for shorts. Next week they're going tramping together. Man and man. Father and son. Next week tramping. This week shopping.

Joe waves away with a laugh and a kiss his wife's suggestion that they take the tram. 'But this is an outing, an adventure for Morris and me. We'll go in the car and we'll eat in a tearoom and we'll buy shorts. Who knows, we might even bring back a little something for you.'

Did you? Did you bring something back for her?
I don't know. I can't remember. What does it matter?

Pearl stands in the bay window, watching them walk down the path to the garage where the car is full of petrol, waiting, ready for adventure.

Joe holds Morris's hand. He turns suddenly, too quickly, to face the house, and does not let go. Morris trips and is pulled around in a circle about his father to face his mother, who is still at the bay window.

Joe shouts, 'Cheerio,' and stretches Morris's hand into the air.

Pearl doesn't wave back. The light must be shining in her eyes.

Did they bring something back for her? Morris can't remember, can't imagine that it would have made much difference to her, and anyway, it's not part of this story. This story is about him and his father who made the shop girl laugh and got a discount from the shopkeeper, who twirled his hat when they walked down the road. His father who sped up to overtake the tram, who sang love songs as he drove and made the car dance across the road in time to his singing. 'Something's gotta give. Something's gotta give. Something's gotta give.'

So this is after the first time you were supposed to go tramping together.

The first time?

Yes, yes. The first time your father blew you off.

Blew me off?

Oh for crying out loud, Morris. The first time your father cancelled on you. He went without you. But now we're on the second time. About a week before you were supposed to go a second time. That's where we are now. Are you sure you remember correctly? Just a week?

I don't know, Sadie. You tell me. You seem to know so much. I was only about six.

Six. You were six at the time.

This is a story about Morris's father, who laid their provisions on the lounge floor and stood looking down at them before reading aloud from a list: 'Tent. Billy. Hip flask for your father. Backpack big enough to take provisions for two.'

Joe had a new backpack. It had come on a ship from America. Months before the backpack there was a catalogue laid out on the kitchen table. Joe called Morris and his mother to come and look.

He said, 'Trapper Nelson,' and ran Morris's finger along the letters. 'The best backpack money can buy.'

Pearl shifted the washing basket on her hip and leaned over her husband's shoulder.

'It could take months to get here. It's not cheap.'

'That may be, but if there's one thing I've learned in my long and varied life, it's the importance of good gear.'

A long and varied life, Morris thought. Will I have one of those?

'Long and varied,' said Pearl. 'You're thirty-five years old—'

'Exactly, precisely right, and you wouldn't want it ending prematurely with me getting washed away down a river, a flooding river—'

Morris shifted closer to his mother. He wanted to grab her skirt.

'—for the want of a decent backpack! Now would you?'

Morris shook his head.

His mother shifted her basket to the other hip. 'No,' she said at last. 'No, I wouldn't.'

Joe lifted Morris on to his knee and pointed to the picture. A man stood beside a tent. A dog lay panting in the open entrance flap.

'You see, big boy, your mother and I agree. We are at one. *Ad idem*. There are few things as important as good camping gear.'

Pearl said, 'It's not cheap and we need—'

'Few things as important, as important.' Joe's leg shook. Was he playing Phar Lap and the jockey? Morris giggled. Phar Lap got faster. Morris clung to the table. Phar Lap kept jiggling. Morris was scooped into his mother's arms.

'Come with me, Morris, you can try out the new puzzle from Uncle Norman.'

'But I want . . .'

'Few things as important as . . .'

'I said, come. Now.'

The pack arrived two months later. Joe stuffed it full of blankets and walked around the garden 'breaking it in'. He wanted to put Morris in it, but Pearl wouldn't allow it. She and Morris watched him through the window. Morris wouldn't have minded climbing into the pack. He knew he'd be safe in it. His father said it was the best quality money could buy. You don't cut corners when it comes to tramping gear.

This is a story about Morris who stood next to his father

as he studied the provisions laid out on the lounge floor. Morris who jumped from item to item as Joe read from his list.

'Tent. Billy. Hip flask for your father.'

'Yes. Yes. Yes,' and, for the Trapper Nelson, a double yes because it can take provisions for two.

And a yes for the shorts which didn't go into the backpack.
Because I would wear them.
Because you would wear them on the tramp. Which you were doing with your father.
In the morning.
Early.

Morris has worn his new shorts to bed, along with the rest of his tramping clothes. Right down to his socks.

His mother can't understand this silly behaviour. He is six years old and should know better. She asks him over and over why, in heaven's name, he wants to do such a ridiculous thing as to sleep in his tramping clothes.

Morris won't relent and he won't tell her why, but he has a good reason. If he sleeps in his clothes he'll be ready to leave as soon as he wakes up. And if he's ready to leave there's less danger of his father going without him. He can be at his father's side in a second. He'll be waiting in the car while his father's still packing it.

'Pyjamas are for night time. Clothes for day time. Come on, Morris, don't be silly.'

Morris holds his arms stiffly on either side, pinning the blanket down over his body. His mother will have to wrestle the blanket off him if she wants to get to his shorts.

'Morris, please, Morris. This is silly. You'll disturb your father.'

'But I want to wear them,' he whispers.

'Morris,' his mother whispers back. Then she suddenly relents and with a shrugged, 'Well, if you must you must,' gets up to leave the room. Before she closes the door, Morris hears his father approaching.

His mother comes back later to kiss him on the forehead and tell him to get a good night's sleep, but by then any triumph he felt at getting his own way has given way to a strange feeling of homesickness, as though he's missing his mother before he's even left her. As if it would be better if his father did go without him.

It's not that he doesn't want to go. And he doesn't want his mother to come with. This is to be a boys' weekend. Father and son. Man and man. Morris has boasted at school about this weekend, couldn't sleep for the wanting of it. But when his mother bends down to kiss his forehead he wants to throw his arms around her and cry, 'Keep me here. With you.'

It doesn't help that she looks sad, or maybe she's cross about his nagging. 'I'll lie still,' he promises her, 'so that I don't crumple them.'

At the door she turns back to look at him. She stands there so long it feels as if she's not expecting to see him again for the longest time, as if she won't be there when they get back from their trip.

'Go to sleep now,' she says at last. 'You've got an early start in the morning.'

Morris closes his eyes and tries to sleep, but his mother looked sad and the shorts are uncomfortable. He's thinking about the story his father told him earlier and there's a song going round in his head. Something's gotta give. Something's gotta give.

That song—it's from the movie Daddy Long Legs. *Wendy and I watched it on DVD. When we were doing our Oldie Mouldie movie marathon. Not so very long ago.*

Not so very long ago Morris paused at his front door. Put his bag down. Unbuttoned his jacket to get the key from his inside pocket. Buttoned it up again. Put his key to the front door and found that it was off the latch, that a simple push with his shoulder would open it.

There was a part of Morris that would have liked, at the end of the working day, to have the front door opened for him by his wife. That was how he'd imagined married life when he was younger—a wife who would take his hat at the front door, hand his briefcase to their son and give him maybe a small peck on the cheek.

Sadie might have met him at the door if Morris had asked her to, but she would have made a song and dance of it. There would have been hands smelling of garlic all over his suit, music jangling in the background, and something mocking in her tone as she said, 'Hi honey, you're home.'

Maybe Morris never really wanted it anyway. Putting his key in the latch made him feel like the man of the house, a provider, an owner. If Sadie and the children opened the door for him he'd feel like a guest. Also, he'd have to give up the moment of pause that he allowed himself every evening when he reached his front door, pulled out his key and drew himself erect.

Anyway, the children were long gone by then, and it wasn't as if Sadie was suddenly going to start waiting for him at the front door in an apron. Even if she owned an apron.

Even if she could still stand.

Not so long ago, Morris pushed the front door open, put his briefcase down and closed the door behind him. From the spare room came the sound of music and talking. He hung his jacket on the hook, called out, 'Hi, it's me,' and wondered whether he should leave his laptop in his study or in the kitchen. Kitchen, he thought, it's warm in there. But first he'd better go to the spare room and see who was with Sadie. He should probably offer to make them tea.

Wendy was in the bed next to Sadie, lying close. Sadie's eyes were closed. She was wearing a garish red scarf that seemed to mock her sunken face. Morris wished she wouldn't wear it. He wouldn't mind her bald head.

Wendy lifted the remote to pause the DVD.

'We're watching golden oldies. We've had a marathon of them. This is number three—*Daddy Long Legs*.'

She pointed to the screen where a man was frozen, mid-leap, his edges out of focus, his face a blur.

'That's Fred Astaire,' Wendy said. 'Sadie's developed a mid-life crush on him.'

They both looked at Sadie. She stirred, murmured, opened her eyes. 'We're watching oldie mouldies.'

'Golden oldies,' said Wendy, 'like us.'

'Moulden oldies,' said Sadie, 'like me.'

'Can I get you anything?' said Morris.

Wendy replied, 'Nah. I've got my wine and Sadie's got her meds.'

Morris closed the door behind him.

Something's gotta give. Something's gotta give. Something's gotta give.

Morris must get a good night's sleep because tomorrow he's going tramping with his father. Only the two of them.

But he's got a song going round and round in his head and what if he oversleeps? If he oversleeps his father might go without him. He must go to sleep but how can you sleep when your shorts are digging into your waist and what if he's forgotten something?

Something important, like the torch. What if his father really needs the torch, keeps on looking for it—Where's that blasted torch. Pearl? I've looked everywhere. The boy must have lost the blasted torch.

If he doesn't sleep he'll be too tired and he won't be able to keep up with his father. Then he'll fall behind and his father won't hear him calling because he'll be marching forwards, further, looking for the torch, looking for some peace and quiet. Something's gotta give.

Something's gotta give—busting into the kitchen where Morris was pouring himself a glass of juice. Wendy must have turned the volume up on the DVD. They were probably singing along—Sadie's mouth just moving, Wendy loud enough for the both of them.

He would have liked to ask them to turn the volume down. He would have liked to tell them that he didn't like that song. But then they'd ask him what he had against it. It was a classic. What was not to like about it?

He didn't have a reason not to like it. It bothered him. That was all. They'd never accept that for an answer.

Sadie would say something like, 'Don't deny me this pleasure. I have so few pleasures left.' Then they'd both laugh and cry and he'd stand in the doorway.

He turned his computer on.

Later Wendy came in and said the DVD was over and Sadie was dozing. She said there was some soup in the fridge. Debbie had brought it. She'd warm it up for them.

Morris turned from his computer. 'I'll do it. You stay with Sadie.'

He carried the soup through on a tray. Wendy sat on the bed next to Sadie, and tried to get her to eat a few spoonfuls. 'Debbie made it. Imagine the farible if she finds out you wouldn't eat it.'

She removed the scarf from Sadie's head so that the edges didn't fall in the soup.

Sadie tipped towards the spoon, and her head, as it came into the light, was smooth and shiny and almost perfect. It reminded Morris of someone else. Maybe a character from a forgotten film.

He pulled a chair out from the dressing table and turned it to face into the room so that he could see Sadie. But it was difficult balancing the bowl on his knee and he almost spilled his soup. 'I'll just . . . eat at the table.' He turned the chair back and sat facing the mirror to eat.

Did you notice how Wendy and I were together on the bed? How you were sitting at a distance?

What did you want? I wasn't going to get on to the bed with Wendy on it. That would have been too . . .

Okay, I know. All three of us would have been a bit weird. But did you see how she touched me? Wendy was right, you know, you aren't much of a toucher. What do you have against touching? Was it your mother? Intimacy issues maybe.

Intimacy issues. What are you talking about? My mother and I were fine. Just fine.

So sue me for a bit of pop psychology. Did you hear the one about the Jewish woman whose son's in therapy?

In therapy?

It's a joke. There's this Jewish woman and she says to her friend, 'My son's seeing the best shrink in town. It's costing him two hundred dollars an hour.' 'Two hundred dollars an hour!' says the friend. 'That's a lot of money.' 'I know it is. And you know what he talks about for that whole hour? Me!' It's a joke. You can laugh.

My mother and I were fine. We never had, what did you call them?

Intimacy issues.

Intimacy issues.

Fine, then give me an example of intimacy. You and your mother. One example. Only one. Give me one and I'll leave you alone.

Leave me alone?

One example. That's all I ask.

One example? I can give you plenty. Well, the same example.

The same example?

Every day. Sadie. The same example. Repetition and consistency. That's intimacy.

Listen to him—the intimacy expert.

It's late in the afternoon. Morris is nine years old. He's hunched over his desk, bent into homework which is never ending. He's supposed to be checking his work for spelling errors, but how can he? If he knew they were errors he wouldn't have made them in the first place. It's been hours and hours since he pulled out his English book. His room is getting cold.

Pearl opens the door. 'It's nearly 5.15.'

Morris is simultaneously relieved and frustrated at this news. Relieved because it means release from the work before him. Frustrated because he has achieved so little since he sat down. There's still so much to do. He hasn't even started on the volcano project. It's not fair. Others got to do the project at school, when they'd finished correcting their writing, and here he sits, writing still uncorrected. Project still waiting.

'Fetch the ironing board,' says his mother.

The ironing board stands between the wall and the sink. It's wedged into a tight space and is liable, when pulled out, to fold in on itself, catch his fingers, bang his nails against its wood. Morris must be careful.

He staggers, rests the board on the floor, changes his grip, and carries it proud and straight into the kitchen.

The kitchen is warm. The dinner's in the oven. He sets up the ironing board at exactly the right height.

'Thank you,' says his mother. She's carrying the laundry basket. 'Turn on the wireless. It's just about 5.15.'

'It is 5.15,' says the radio announcer. 'Is everyone sitting ready?'

Morris nods.

'In today's episode of Children's Session . . .'

Morris sinks into the settee, rests his feet on his mother's foot stool. Homework project be damned. His mother is doing the ironing.

Pearl is ironing a serviette which she will roll in a serviette ring and put in a drawer. When they are sitting at the dinner table, she will pull the serviette from its ring, place it on her lap and smooth it out. After dinner she will lay her serviette on the table, flat against the tablecloth. She will fold it, flatten it, fold it again before rolling it back into its ring.

She will run her hand along the tablecloth, collecting crumbs into a small pile, smoothing the cloth as she goes.

She will shake the tablecloth outside, then bring it back, spread it over the table, and bend past the chairs to make sure it is flat, crisp, smooth.

Later, when the dishes have been washed and Morris has cleaned his face and brushed his teeth, they will turn the wireless back on. At 7.30 there's a serial. Pearl will do her sewing and she will rest her feet on the foot stool. Morris might, if the evening is cool, take the soft blue blanket from the linen cupboard and wrap it round himself. The blanket will smell of the lavender and cloves which his mother uses to keep the moths away.

Sometimes, at school, Morris would overhear kids talking about the programmes. Once, on the tram, he'd found himself joining in their discussion, expressing an opinion, surprising them with his memory of tiny details. 'The woman who won a scrubbing brush turned down seven pounds ten to get it.'

'Ha,' a boy said. 'You just won me a bet.' He grinned at Morris, then turned to his friend. 'Seven pounds and ten shillings to be exact.'

'So what?' said his friend. 'It doesn't matter how much she turned down. The point is she shouldn't have kept going for the bag. She should've taken the money.'

He turned to Morris. 'She should've taken the money, shouldn't she?'

'I, um—'

Of all the wireless shows that Morris and his mother listened to he liked 'It's in the Bag' least of all. His mother didn't love it either. She complained that the questions were too easy, but for Morris it was the terrible stress of making the correct choice of prize, the horrible loss at getting it wrong. All those voices from the audience shouting, 'Take the money. The bag. The bag.' The too-friendly host saying, 'Make up your mind now, Mrs Deans. You have to choose one.' Just last week a man had lost out on a washing machine by choosing ten pounds. How would he explain that to his wife?

'I prefer John Maybury,' said Morris, but the boys didn't hear him. They were talking about rugby, which Morris did not play.

It's because you're Jewish.

Jewish?

Jews don't get rugby. Or sports more generally. We're genetically predisposed against sports.

I like rugby.

No you don't.

And cricket.

You're genetically disposed against that too. Anyway, I don't want to speak about rugby or cricket. I'm genetically predisposed against them. I want to talk to you about your mother and intimacy.

I've told you about my mother and intimacy.

Intimacy? You call that intimacy?

Oh Sadie, let it go.

Listening to the radio. Ironing and smoothing. Being allowed to wrap yourself up in a blanket if you're lucky? A bit anal, don't you think, your mother. All that smoothing and ironing. Ironing and smoothing. A bit uptight maybe?

She liked things to be smooth. Even. That's all. Rachel too. She likes things smooth. You saw her bed. And her linen.

Cloves and lavender. Morris can almost smell them.

Sure I saw Rachel's bed. And the linen. Not sure that I liked what I saw though. Where does it end, all that smoothing?'

It ended, in the case of Morris's mother, in an old persons' home in Levin.

Joan chose Pearl's new home. It had to be done quickly. It couldn't wait for Morris to finish his exams and return to Wellington. And they certainly wouldn't want him doing anything foolish like missing classes. Not in his final year.

Pearl had a stroke. Two neighbours coming home from work saw the milk and paper still at the gate. They banged on the door but got no reply. Eventually they opened the front door and walked in. She was clutching the iron when they found her. She'd fallen over and the ironing board had somehow landed on top of her. They had to pry her fingers off the iron.

They could thank God that the neighbours cared, said Joan. Cared enough to go and investigate when they saw the milk left uncollected. And they could thank God that the iron pulled out of its socket when she fell. And they could thank God that the neighbours had the good sense to go in. Who knows what would have happened if they hadn't been so quick thinking? Joan made biscuits for the neighbours. Morris might want to go over and thank them himself when he was back in Wellington.

Norman and Joan made a special trip to Christchurch to discuss the matter with Morris. They took him to a hotel restaurant.

Norman waited until their orders were placed and the waiter gone, then he laid his hands on the table before him. 'We think it would be best if we moved your mother to a home in Levin, close to us.'

Joan said, 'I can help to look after her. We can go on outings together. It will be a pleasure. You'll be starting work soon. Honestly, a pleasure.'

They looked at Morris. Did they fear an outburst? Is that why they chose a public place for their announcement?

Norman said, 'A decision has to be made soon, and you still have six months of university ahead of you.'

Joan said, 'It will be nice for Pearl to be close to us.'

'Very nice,' said Norman.

Joan said, 'You'll be moving back to Wellington soon and the drive will be a doddle for you. You're such a good driver.'

'And don't worry about the cost of petrol. Or any costs. We'll have to sell the house, of course, unless you . . .'

Morris excused himself to go to the toilet.

'Oh my God, Norman, follow him.'

'No, no, Joanie, let the boy be for now.'

Morris washed his hands, looked at his face in the mirror and asked himself what sort of reaction they were expecting from him.

Think, Morris, think.

Maybe you're supposed to feel insulted. Enraged that they should imagine you can't look after your own mother. Maybe they want you to refuse point blank, to say that you are your mother's son and she is your responsibility. Maybe they want to be able to explain to you slowly, as if to a child, why this really is a good idea.

You're being ridiculous, Morris told his reflection. Why would they want that? They want you to be grateful. Grateful to them for assuming the burden.

Guilt—you're supposed to feel guilty. For being such a bad son that you can't even look after your own mother. After all she did for you.

Grief, that's it. This is a sad day for you. The day you have to admit that your mother can't look after herself.

No, not grief. If you feel grief then they're going to want to comfort you. Joan is going to want to hug you. Not grief.

Any minute Norman will come in. Joan will have sent him. What will you tell him? That you feel nothing at all? Except maybe a little bit relieved? You can't tell him that.

The food was on the table, but they hadn't started eating. They looked up when Morris came in. Norman clapped him on his back when he sat down.

'It's for the best,' he said and, as if this was the blessing they'd been waiting for, they picked up their cutlery.

So who packed up the house?

The house?

Your mother's house. Your house. The one you were brought up in. The one your father bought when they got married. She'd been there for more than twenty years. She must have accumulated a lot of stuff in all that time. Who packed it up?

Was there a lot of stuff? Could some of it have ended up in David's spare bedroom? Maybe later, when Morris goes to bed, he'll look around the spare room and see if any of the things he recognises could have been his mother's. For now he'll sit in David's lounge and try to picture her house. He'll start at the entrance hall with its umbrella stand. Coat hooks behind the door. The bathroom off to one side. Not much stuff in there. Or in the tiny lounge. Or the kitchen.

After so many years it's still easy to run through the house in his mind. Morris knew where he was in that house.

Things stayed where they stood. Things did not jump from room to room or out of the house completely, only to be missed, only to be told that a friend of Sadie's had left her husband (finally, he was such a pig) and really needed a chair.

Things did not suddenly appear, picked up at a junk shop or found in someone's basement (they were going to throw it away, can you believe it?).

Morris knew where he belonged in that house. Things stayed where they stood.

There was only one real change in the furniture in that house, and that marked a life-changing event—Morris's bar mitzvah.

For a bar mitzvah furniture can arrive.

Well, not every bar mitzvah, but if your bar mitzvah happens to coincide with the introduction of television into Wellington and your uncle and aunt happen to love you very, very much and be so very proud of how well you did, so proud that they buy you an Admiral Television with a wooden finish and special table for it to stand on. If that happens, furniture arrives.

'Your surprise present is arriving on Friday,' said Norman on the telephone.

'Tell him he can invite some friends over to watch with him,' called Joan into the silence.

Morris's mother knew the television was coming. Norman and Joan would not have bought such a huge, imposing thing into the house without consulting her. That would have been like arriving with a kitten in a box and saying it was a gift. They wouldn't do that. They'd discuss and warn and remind her that it was arriving on Friday, and had she thought about where she'd like to put it? The corner furthest from the door might be nice.

She knew it was coming but she hadn't thought about where it would go. Or she'd thought too much and got confused. She looked at the delivery men blankly and didn't answer when they asked where she wanted it. Morris stood in the passage, waiting for her to direct them, but she seemed puzzled and reluctant to let them in. They made a great show of labouring under a heavy load. The younger man looked at his watch and muttered about the number of televisions they still had to deliver. Finally the men left the television on its trolley at the front door, and Pearl stood to one side so they could come in and survey the lounge.

The older man decided that the middle of the living room would be best. 'It doesn't have to stay there for ever. You two can easily slide it to the correct position when you've decided where you want it.'

'If you ever decide,' muttered the younger one. Morris glanced at his mother. She must not have heard the man, because she just ran her hands over the box and said something about possibly covering it with a nice piece of lace.

She never put lace on the television and they never decided on a better place for it. It stayed where the movers had put it. Morris liked it there. He thought it was good for the reception if the television had free space around it.

A neighbourhood child from Morris's class came over, all sudden friendship and trailing younger sister and let's see that new television you got.

Morris, puffed with the pride of possession, the power of owning something first, waved his neighbours into the living room. 'It's best to put televisions in the middle of the room so they have air to breathe.'

'Is that so?' said the neighbour, still smiling, still friendly. 'Tell me about it.'

He wanted to come back that evening to watch, but Morris told him they were going out. 'I mean, getting visitors. And tomorrow night as well.'

Maybe that was why the boy turned on him, told others that Morris Goldberg thought a television's reception was improved by standing it in the middle of the room. Ha, ha, in the middle of the room, because televisions, get this, need air around them so they can . . . wait for it . . . breathe!

Another child in Morris's position would have scoffed at the boy. Another child would have smirked and asked how he got to be so knowledgeable about televisions. Had he seen the packaging they came in? Did he have one in his living room? Morris did. He owned one. He would invite others to come and watch it but not you, you . . . teaser. Not you. Another child would have said that.

Morris said nothing.

That afternoon he got a book from the library about how televisions work. The librarian encouraged him to take other books as well. 'If you're interested in how things work you might like this one about wirelesses, and this one has toasters and ovens. Cameras. It shows you how to make your own.'

Morris took the offered books, though he had no interest in wirelesses, toasters or cameras. The boy hadn't mocked his knowledge of those.

He spent a week studying the book and poring over the manual which came with the television. He wrote up tests for himself, and spent the weekend checking and rechecking his understanding. Just let that boy say something on Monday. Let him say something about Morris and televisions. Morris was prepared. He'd explain to him, slowly and methodically, like he was talking to a stupid child, like some teachers spoke to him, about the waves and the particles and, actually, you need to own a television to really understand what I'm telling you. You don't actually own a television, do you?

On Monday the boy had a new catapult. It was all he was interested in, all he spoke about. He wasn't interested in Morris.

When Morris returned the book, the librarian asked if he'd liked it. He thought about it and realised that he had found it interesting. He'd actually enjoyed spending a weekend reading.

'Isn't it amazing,' she'd said, 'to think that we are surrounded by particles and waves, electrons and things? All moving. We don't even know they're there, but some clever men have managed to . . . to harness them. All we have to do is turn a switch on a big box. Isn't it amazing?'

It works because the particles and waves move in patterns, Morris wanted to say. They follow their route like they're supposed to. There are rules for their behaviour. That's why it works.

The television stayed in the middle of the carpet and it reminded Morris that he had done something important. Norman said the important thing was becoming bar mitzvah, becoming a man. Morris didn't feel like a man, but still he'd done something significant: he'd learned that he was surrounded by pre-determined patterns and waves. Morris found this knowledge both comforting and empowering. It raised the possibility that the world was not always erratic and random. For some things there were rules. Nature had laws. These laws could be studied. Maybe he could do that. Once he'd learned the rules he could—what was the word the librarian had used?—harness. He could harness the energy. All he had to do was learn the rules.

It was like that teacher with the black beard had said. Things don't go bumping into each other, colliding at random, wasting energy. There is order, even if we can't see it. That's why things work. Because they are predictable.

They know their place.

The television's place was in the middle of the room. Things stayed in their place in that house.

Except for your mother's room.
My mother's room? What about my mother's room?
It moved.
Moved?
When you were six. Your mother moved out of the bedroom and into the lounge. She swapped the two rooms.
She didn't. The lounge was always the lounge. With the television in it.

You knew where you stood in that house.

Until they kicked you out of it.
Kicked me out? I left to go to university.
Kicked out to go to university.

Morris was eighteen when he left home to go to university. He went to Canterbury and stayed in a hall of residence.

Morris knew that he wouldn't be sleeping in a hall, that he'd be sharing with only one person, but he couldn't help thinking of it as being like a school hall, only packed with beds. Row upon row of them and, in the one closest to the middle, pinned in on all sides, Morris Goldberg and his locker which didn't close properly.

Hall of residence—it made Morris think of that school trip when they'd slept in a school hall. Sixty boys in sixty sleeping bags in one room.

In the bus on the way to the host school, Morris had felt sick, not from the windy roads which caused some boys to make a great fuss of falling over, banging bags and Miss, Miss, I think I'm going to throw up. Windy roads didn't bother Morris. He knew that if you kept your eyes focused on a point in the vehicle you'd be fine. He chose the back of the driver's chair. The driver kept his head quite still. Boys rattled around him and he kept on driving, his hands firmly planted on the steering wheel. As long as Morris kept staring at the back of his chair he'd be fine.

One of the boys said that the driver had learned to drive in the war, driving tanks.

That's why he's so steady, thought Morris.

'That's why he doesn't look back,' said another boy. 'Soldiers never look back.'

Morris had picked a good point to focus on. The driver was steady. He wouldn't move. He'd never look back. Soldiers don't.

But still he felt sick.

It was the thought of sleeping in the hall. One room. Sixty boys. Sixty sleeping bags.

The boys scrambled to lay their sleeping bags in the best positions. Morris found a space next to the wall, close to the door. You can handle this, he told himself. Face towards the wall. Don't even think about the others. Block your ears. Read your comic. You'll be fine.

He was fine—until the teachers left and the lights went off and the torches went on and his classmates turned into warriors, stamping their feet and banging on their thighs and pulling savage faces. Morris sat up wide eyed in his sleeping bag, pressed his back against the wall. You will not cry. You will not cry. You are fourteen years old and you will not cry.

He pulled his comic close to his face. Someone tapped him on the shoulder and a voice said, 'What a bunch of morons, hey?'

It was James, the boy who was good at English. He was inviting Morris to join him and some other boys who were above this sort of bullshit in a cigarette outside.

Outside. Morris hadn't thought of going outside. He nodded and followed James.

There were four others outside, sitting on their haunches close to the wall.

One of them said, 'You look pale. Have a cigarette.'

Another said, 'Of course he's pale. It's a stomach-turning scene in there. What would those idiots do if a real Maori soldier came along? They'd shit their pants, that's what.'

'There was an old Maori guy sitting round the back,' said the boy with the cigarettes. 'I bet he was a soldier. He asked for a fag and I gave him one.' He paused, fiddled with his lighter. 'I wonder how he knew I smoke.'

'They can tell these things,' said James, ''cause they're more spiritual.'

The boys considered this in silence, then the one with the cigarettes said, 'So did you want a fag, Goldberg?' And before Morris could answer said, 'I'm not surprised you were put off by it, Goldberg, you being Jewish and all.'

'Yeah,' said James, 'Jews are really sensitive about racism and stuff.'

'They make damn good soldiers. It's in their blood,' said another. 'The Maoris, I mean.'

'Um yes please,' said Morris, 'I would like a cigarette. Please.'

He didn't cough. No one laughed at him.

Later, when boys were being disciplined, 'Not only for the mess, not only for the noise, the nuisance, the wild behaviour. What are you? Savages? But for the dis-re-spect,' Morris felt himself blushing with pride. He had not taken part in what he now knew to be racist mocking. He was Jewish, sensitive about such things. He had stayed outside, mature and superior. He had smoked a cigarette.

James started greeting Morris after that, and the boy with the cigarettes asked him a few times if he'd be joining them for a fag at lunch, behind the changing sheds. Morris never went. They were clever boys. It wouldn't take them long to see through him, to realise that he wasn't being sensitive at all. He was scared.

The hall of residence would be nothing like that. He'd pretty much have his own room. Morris knew that. But there would be the communal bathroom and communal dining room and, God help him, dances. Morris had heard stories of new boys being pulled out of bed in the middle of the night, being made to dress up in girls' clothes, made to drink huge amounts of beer, being soaked in water, in flour, in feathers. The boys may be older but they would, underneath their beards and their pipes, still be waiting for the lights to go out and the torches to come on.

It made much more sense for Morris to live at home. The local university offered all the courses he wanted.

'It's not the money, I hope,' said Norman when Morris told him that he intended applying to the university in Wellington. 'Canterbury offers engineering. There's enough money for you to go there, or anywhere else.'

Joan said, 'I understand you don't want to leave your mother. It's good of you to think of her, but she understands, honestly she does.'

Joan came forward as if to grab his cheeks. Don't pull back, Morris, don't pull back. But he did and she saw it and her hands looked like she was squeezing an invisible balloon, like she wanted it to pop.

'We're all so proud of you,' she said, dropping the balloon. 'Your mother is so proud of you. Going to university and all.'

Norman phoned two days later. 'Your mother and I have discussed it, and she's decided . . . we've decided. She thinks you should go to Canterbury.'

Norman didn't ramble like Joan did when faced with Morris's silence. He waited, quiet himself. Sometimes, behind the silence of the telephone, Morris could hear Joan instructing Norman in urgent tones. Tell him we'll bring him a present next time we come. Ask him if he wants to bring a friend to Levin for the day on Saturday. Tell him we only want what's best for him.

Norman waited, and when Morris finally said, 'I don't want to. I want to stay here,' Norman's voice was sad. 'I know you do.'

Just that week, on television, Morris had seen a boy of about his age slam the phone down on his sister. A vase had fallen off the table, such was the violence of the boy's anger.

The phone was left dangling and Morris imagined that he could hear the sister calling through it to her brother.

He could do that. He could walk away. He could leave Norman gulping into the silence, Joan's 'Tell him the Smith boy, Brian, is going to Christchurch' trapped in the cords that wound between their house and his own.

But his mother was standing at the door looking at him, listening in. Later she said to him, 'You're going to Canterbury. I'm putting my foot down.'

The next day at the bus stop Morris met an old man from the synagogue. The man said, 'I hear you're going to study at Canterbury. Mazel Tov.'

His accent was so heavy that Morris had to lean forwards to hear what he said.

'Mazel Tov,' the man said again, louder this time.

Morris gripped the slats on the bus-stop bench, and didn't let go when the bus came.

The old man looked back at him from the step and Morris shook his head. He'd sit there and shake his head at anyone who came near. He wouldn't fight with them or slam telephones. He'd shake his head until they went away. They couldn't make him go anywhere.

He boarded the next bus. His mother would worry and phone Joan if he wasn't home in time for dinner. He'd go home to save her embarrassment, but he wouldn't be gracious about it.

At dinner he told Pearl she shouldn't go around telling everyone their business.

She smoothed the serviette in her lap. 'There's no point in hiding from it. You are going. Don't be petulant.'

Morris slammed his bedroom door and turned the volume on his wireless way up loud. He didn't come out of his room to say goodnight to his mother. In the morning he lay in his bed and listened to her getting ready for work. His blankets flattened him into the bed.

Joan phoned. 'I know you're worrying about leaving your mother but you shouldn't. She'll be just fine. She's an independent woman, Pearl. Independent and strong. She doesn't want you worrying about her. She wants what's best for you. We all do.'

Norman phoned with the suggestion that they go out for lunch. 'A celebration that my brilliant nephew has chosen to study engineering at Canterbury. A new French place has opened in Wellington. We'll have something exotic and European.'

Morris said, 'I can't go out. I'm not well. And my mother doesn't like foreign food.'

But it seemed that Pearl was only too pleased to go. Norman had already discussed the matter with her.

In the silence while Morris tried to understand this, Norman said, 'She's happy for you. She wants the naches.'

'I'm sick. '

'It will do you good to get out.'

'I'm not well.'

'Twelve o'clock tomorrow. We'll come and fetch you. And Morris, Morris, wear something smart. We're going fancy.'

Pearl wore a dress which Morris didn't recognise. And red lipstick. When they got in the car, Joan said, 'Isn't that the lipstick we chose together? I knew it would look good on you.' Pearl said, 'Thanks,' and she took a little mirror out of her bag and touched up her lips.

Norman said, 'Who's ready for a little French?'

'French,' said Pearl, 'but that means we must be going to—'

Norman interrupted her. 'I know. I know. My treat.'

'Oh but Norman, it's expensive. It's not necessary.'

'For my nephew,' said Norman.

'For Morris,' chipped in Joan.

'Nothing is too much,' they said together.

'My goodness,' said Pearl, and she nudged Morris.

Morris edged away from her.

'A little French,' said Norman. 'Who's ready for a little French?'

Pearl nudged Morris again. He kept quiet and she said, 'I am.'

Norman said, 'Well, that's good because I hear that French waiters are very short.'

Pearl gave a little sigh which could have been laughing or maybe breathing out. Joan said, 'Oh, Norman and his silly jokes. He's just pulling our legs.'

'Legs,' said Norman. 'Frogs' legs. D'you think they'll serve frogs' legs? What do you think, Morris?'

Morris saw Norman trying to catch his eye in the rear-view mirror, and looked away.

Norman ordered wine. He joked with the manager, with the waiter. He waved the folded serviette in front of his face as if it were a fan. Joan laughed and said, 'How I put up with him I'll never know.'

Pearl said, 'I never thought I'd see the day when I would eat in a place like this. Thank you, Norman.'

'Don't thank me. Thank Morris. He's the one who's given us something to celebrate.'

'It's nice to have something to celebrate,' said Pearl.

Norman poured wine for Pearl and Joan, said to Morris, 'When the waiter's not looking I'll sneak you a sip.'

Joan gave Norman a pat on the shoulder. 'Don't be naughty now. The law's the law. And teenage boys like Coca-Cola. Don't they, Morris? Don't they?'

Morris looked at the French flag, the picture of the girl on a bicycle, the menu. When he glanced up, he saw that his mother was staring at him. She'd probably been studying him for some time. Her mouth was set in a tight smirk of distaste.

Joan was laughing and Norman was laughing. Pearl was studying her son and her red lips seemed to say, 'I don't think I like you.'

She caught his eye, then looked away. She twirled her glass and said, 'Isn't this nice? It is so kind of you, Norman, to take us out.'

Then Norman said, 'A toast. To my nephew.'

Pearl looked down at her glass and Morris was able to consider her expression. There was no distaste in it. He had misread her face. The red lipstick had confused him. He said, 'Thank you, Norman. This is very nice.'

Pearl smiled at him. She sipped at her wine. Morris laughed at Norman's next joke.

During dessert, Joan said that she was jealous of Morris, going off to study. She would have loved to have gone to university. She would have liked to study law. Norman said she'd be good at that. She could certainly argue circles around him.

'Why didn't you go?' Morris asked, and Joan said that women didn't do it in her day and someone had to help her parents in the shop.

Pearl said, 'I also would have liked to go to university.'

'You too,' said Joan.

Norman said, 'What would you have studied?'

Pearl ran her spoon along the outside of her bowl as though she was scraping the edge of a baking bowl with a spatula. 'I don't know. I would have made myself someone new.'

Norman said that she'd never escape being his sister, and Joan said that wasn't the point. The point was that men got to go out and make something of themselves. 'Doctor. Lawyer, architect. Women of our generation never had those choices. That's what Pearl means. Isn't it, Pearl?'

Pearl nodded, but Morris knew that Joan had it wrong. Pearl really did mean making herself someone new. She would have gone to university and re-created herself. She would have come back a different person. One who wore red lipstick every day.

Over the years Morris had made innumerable resolutions to be a better person. With every new school term: I will keep up in class. I will not forget my books at home. I will keep a focus in every single lesson. I won't be scared to read aloud in class.

With every school holiday: I will go to the public swimming baths. If I see boys from my school there I will talk to them.

With every Yom Kippur: I will help my mother more. I will let Joan hug me. I will attend social events at the synagogue.

In primary school Morris spent the last week of the summer holidays designing the title pages of his exercise books. They were always neat, always painstakingly illustrated, always optimistic. In primary school these neat title pages gave Morris hope. By secondary school all hope was pushed out by the certainty of unravelling, the inevitability of ink splotches and unfinished sentences.

In his sixteenth year he decided not to fast on Yom Kippur. Having thus denied God, he didn't see that he could also pray for a better year ahead.

The next year he returned to fasting, the guilt of not doing so being greater than the spike of liberation which eating on the High Holy Day offered. But still he didn't make any resolutions for the year ahead. He didn't even pray for a sweet new year. He wrote 'I resolve never to make another resolution' on a piece of paper and threw it in the bin.

That resolution lasted until Pearl's red lips said, 'If I went to university I would have made myself someone new.'

And so Morris came to be at the first meeting of the Canterbury University Tramping Club, listening to an extremely hairy man introduce himself as Craig, the club president.

'You can all congratulate yourselves,' Craig told the meeting, 'for having the good sense to join the only club on campus worth belonging to.'

A few days earlier Morris had gone to a friend of Norman's for Friday night dinner. (Norman had arranged it so that Morris could have an introduction to the Jewish community in Christchurch.) Norman's friend asked what Morris's first impressions of university were, and Morris blurted out that the men there were very hairy. The children at the table giggled. Their father said it was refreshing to hear such a sensible young man. He himself was increasingly disturbed by the facial hair and messy locks which were sprouting all over campus. There was something, something—Norman's friend paused, choosing his words—wanton. That's it, wanton. All that hair on campus was wanton.

Morris was ashamed of himself for agreeing with Norman's friend. Ashamed of being a sensible young man. But the hair on campus *was* wanton and Morris thought slightly scary.

The president of the Canterbury University Tramping Club was not wanton. Craig was no lazy layabout, too drunk or too lazy to have a proper shave. His hairiness spoke of strength and purpose. He was too busy to shave. He had mountains to climb.

He was also, according to the boy sitting next to Morris,

the guy who led that party that got stuck in the snow in that national park.

Morris said, 'Oh,' and the boy said, 'They built an igloo.'

Morris said, 'Oh,' again, and then, remembering his resolution, put out his hand. 'I'm Morris.'

The boy took it. 'Murray. I suppose I'd better shut up so we hear what he has to say.' He smiled and Morris, without even thinking of his resolution, smiled back.

Everyone had to say their name and what made them join the club. Craig pointed to Morris. 'We'll start with you right at the back. Name and reason for joining.'

Morris thought, I want to be someone new. He said, 'I'm Morris. My father was a tramper.' And immediately wondered where those words had come from.

Craig said, 'Brilliant. So was mine. Actually, he helped build some of the huts that we stay in.'

It was as if someone had lifted a corner of the failure that flattened Morris to his bed in the mornings.

Morris is four years old, in his pyjamas and dressing gown. He's waiting with his father on the front steps of their house. Pearl brings him hot milk with honey mixed in. It's just getting light.

Joe says, 'We're going to build a new hut on Mount Ruapehu. One day, when you're older, we'll go there together and you'll sleep in the hut your father built.'

Joe's friends come in a big truck. Two men in the front and two at the back.

Joe picks Morris up to show him the water tank in the back of the truck. He says, 'If Huey is kind to us I'll be back on Sunday afternoon and there'll be a new hut on Ruapehu.'

Pearl says, 'Be careful.'

She takes Morris from his father and puts him on the

ground. Joe throws his pack on to the back of the truck. Then his axe. Then himself. Morris waves and waves.

Morris's father carried an axe into the wilderness.

Joe's axe and Pearl's red lips. They said 'Go' when the first annual meeting of the Canterbury University Tramping Club moved to a bar for a drink.

Joe's axe and Pearl's red lips and Murray, who pushed Morris into a seat next to Craig's and said, 'You make sure no one takes these seats. I'll get us some drinks.'

Murray returned with a jug and three glasses. He handed one to Morris.

Morris sipped on his first beer and realised he was breaking the law. He looked up at Murray, who winked and said, 'The barman knows my brother,' then turned to Craig and said, 'Speaking of friends of my brother's—one of them was with you that time you did Milford in the snow. He reckons he'd do it again any day. D'you think you would?'

Morris listened.

Joe's axe. Pearl's red lips. Craig's stories when the first tramp turned out to be little more than an outdoor drinking session. When the second tramp was rained out and Morris had to spend a night huddling under a tarpaulin with five other people. When naked swims were suggested and crude jokes made about double bunking and pit swapping.

Joe's axe. Pearl's red lips. Craig's stories. And Murray.

Morris could go weeks without seeing Murray. Then one day there'd be a knock on his door or a note with his mail: 'Weekend tramp leaving Friday. I didn't see your name on the list.' 'Mount Oakden. Snow snow snow!' The first time he received such a note ('Have you put your name down for Walker Pass yet?') Morris wrote to Norman and Joan that he would not be having Friday night dinner with their friends because he had been invited to go tramping with other members of his club. He pictured Joan reading the letter out loud to Norman, underlining the words 'invited' and 'other members of his club' with her voice.

As the year progressed Murray's notes changed from 'I've booked you a place on Bush Skills for Beginners' to 'Glad to see you've already signed up for the weekend of 15th.'

Around October there was a note reading: 'Some guys are putting together a group of four to try Nelson Lakes. Are you keen?'

They met in Murray's room. Murray introduced him to the other two as 'Morris Goldberg. He's level headed, always punctual and a damn good tramper.' They discussed routes. They discussed supplies. Morris took notes. He left with a shopping list and an excuse not to attend the spring ball.

After Nelson Lakes there was Richmond Forest. After Richmond, Arthur's Pass. During the evening of one tramp they planned the next. They spoke of doing Mount Aspiring one day.

Morris bought a new pair of pants. The shop assistant recommended a modern style, saying that Morris's old style was cut for a completely different body shape. He bought two new shirts with short sleeves. Sometimes in a lecture he'd sit with his elbows on the desk, gripping his upper arms. He started lingering over getting dressed, allowing his body to be caught in the mirror. His muscles were getting harder. His legs were getting stronger. He was improving.

Once, on returning from a three-day tramp, Morris found a group of guys playing cards in the lounge. They groaned about hangovers and disinterested girls and the month's money gone in a single weekend. Morris found himself overtaken by an unfamiliar feeling: he felt better than them. His legs throbbed with it. He was not Morris Goldberg, too scared to ask a girl to an informal social. Not Morris Goldberg, too terrified to take part in a night raid on the other hall of residence. He was Morris Goldberg, tramper, club member, buddy of Murray.

Morris wrote to Joan and Norman about Murray and how they'd shown their slides at a club meeting. He referred to the weather as 'Huey' and his sleeping bag as his 'pit'. He described how Murray had exaggerated their exploits to get the attention of a female club member.

To Pearl he wrote of the lakes and the silence.

When Morris went back north for the long summer break, Joan quizzed him on student life. Morris spoke about tramping. When pressed for details he told her about the club's rules—the express ones like filling in the proper forms before you headed out, and the silent ones which Morris was slowly learning: you don't eat on a rest day. You listen to everyone's suggestions about which routes are best.

She asked about Murray, and Morris said, 'We're tramping buddies. It's good to have a buddy like that when you're tramping.'

He almost but didn't tell her that sometimes it felt as if Murray could read his mind. Like when they were choosing a path through the bush or when a decision had to be made about stopping for the night. He didn't tell her that he and Murray could go for hours without speaking to each other, that sometimes a gesture towards the river bank was enough to say, How about this as a spot to stop for lunch?

Morris had found a way to be amongst people and to be silent. When he did have to talk, it was about concrete things like what time they'd make a start in the morning and who would be responsible for putting the billy on. Even when they spent a whole day stuck in a hut or when they were sitting around the fire and someone had a bottle of whisky, the conversation was desultory and marked by long silences. No one noticed that Morris didn't speak much. No one spoke much.

To Joan he said, 'I'm thinking of getting more involved in the planning side of group tramps.'

She lifted one ear of the little dog that was sleeping on her lap. 'Did you hear that, Sammy? He's thinking of getting more involved.'

In Morris's second year of university he was asked to help plan the three-week Christmas hike. Joan and Norman glowed down the telephone lines.

'How many of you did you say are doing it?' Norman asked, then, 'Fifteen, Joanie. He says there are going to be fifteen of them.'

Back to Morris: 'Is that boys and girls?' and to Joan, 'Yes, Joanie, girls too.'

The next week a parcel arrived for Morris. An early congratulations on finishing your second year present—a new backpack. Joan had filled it with food.

Morris already had a backpack. He'd got it when he came home for his first Easter break. The Easter backpack was waiting for him on the floor in his bedroom. His mother had laid an old towel down on the floor and put the backpack on top of that. Morris circled it a few times before kneeling down to study it. It was khaki canvas. It smelt damp and had discoloured patches on it like it had been dragged through dirty water. A Trapper Nelson. It looked familiar to Morris, as though he'd seen it in a picture.

When he thanked his mother for it, she said it had been in the basement gathering dust. When he asked where it came from, she said it needed to be washed. Morris wanted to say, There's nothing dusty about this backpack. He wanted to say that it shouldn't be washed. That its stains were something to be proud of. Something that told you it had been places.

But it did smell mouldy so he spent an afternoon scrubbing away at it, and when he was done it looked good. Clean but still old, still experienced.

Craig had a Trapper Nelson. People teased him about how heavy and uncomfortable it was. Craig laughed the teasing off. He said the backpack was based on a Red Indian design. The Indians carried theirs long distances. If it was good enough for them, it was good enough for him.

The Trapper Nelson gave Morris unexpected cachet with the club. Someone drew a cartoon for the newsletter of Morris and Craig lying flat on the floor, pinned down by their packs. Two Trapped Half Nelsons. Murray stuck the cartoon on his bedroom wall. Morris considered sending a copy of it to his mother but decided against it. Instead he sent a photo of him in a group of trampers, their arms around each other.

In Pearl's next letter she said, 'If you can get another copy of that photo for Joan that would be nice.'

Morris got an extra copy. Joan had it framed.

Morris didn't mind the jokes about his pack, and he laughed along when Murray put it on and pretended to stagger about under its weight. The discomfort of the Trapper was somehow appropriate. Tramping was not meant to be a walk in the park.

Even so, Morris recognised that the Trapper would not be suitable for longer tramps. He should have been grateful when the new pack arrived, and he should have been happy that it was filled with food. But the sight of Joan's card made him feel ashamed. Her handwriting reminded him of the old man at the bus stop.

For weeks he couldn't look at the backpack without feeling that he was letting someone down.

At the end of Morris's fifth year of study, Murray moved to England. He sent one or two letters and Morris sent one or two back. Craig took a job in Australia. Someone said he'd given up tramping in favour of surfing.

Morris went back to Wellington after university. He rented a flat, which Joan helped him furnish. 'Most of your mum's furniture was pretty old,' she said, 'and you'll want to start afresh, with nice modern things.'

He bought a new television.

Joan had got rid of the bar mitzvah television when Pearl moved to the home. She'd got the Salvation Army in.

So Joan packed up your mother. Bim bam boom. And she packed up your childhood house, bim bam boom. And by the time you came back from university your home was gone. That would've been upsetting.

Upsetting? I hadn't lived there for years.

That may be so, but this is your childhood home we're talking about. The house that was frozen in time. The house that never changed. Except for your mother's room.

My mother's room?

The room that moved.

My mother's room never moved, I tell you. I can picture it.

All right then—tell me what she had in there.

In my mother's room? A bed, bedside table. The usual.

What else? Describe it for me.

It was a room. A bed. Bedside table. Just a room. A lamp.

Describe it for me.

Enough, Sadie. Enough. I hardly ever went in there.

Hardly ever.

That's how it was in those days. Children kept out of their parents' room in those days.

How you preferred it.

Yes, actually.

David, four weeks old, in their bed. 'Of course I won't squash him, Morris. Stop worrying. Go to sleep.'

David, four months old, in their bed. 'Just until summer, Morris. It's too cold to get up and go to him in the night.'

David four years old, in their bed. 'He had a bad dream, poor baby.'

Rachel, three weeks, three months, three years. 'She was sitting all alone in the lounge, gazing at the television, which was switched off, weren't you darling, weren't you sweetheart? Move over, Morris. Make room for Miss Gorgeousness. Close your eyes, honey bun, I'll tell you a story.'

Sometimes both of the children would be in there, Sadie singing songs and making funny noises, and all three of them kicking their legs and waving their arms and laughing like monkeys.

Snuggling. We were snuggling. Bonding. I was supergluing our family together.

Morris, at seven o'clock on a Sunday morning, in his study with the heater pulled close to his chair. Because there wasn't space for him in the bed.

Don't give me that no space nonsense. You didn't want to be there. It made you feel uncomfortable.
Well, it was cramped.
It was supposed to be cramped. Snuggling always is. And it's good for children. Especially Rachel.

Morris, seven o'clock on a Sunday morning, listening to Sadie singing off key and David trying to whistle, wondering how Rachel feels about all that racket first thing in the morning when she's still sleepy, wondering whether she wouldn't rather be in a quiet room where there's space to think.

She had more than enough quiet and space, more than enough alone time to think. She needed cuddling and tickling. That's why I did it.

Why you did it?

You know how Stormin' Norman insisted that you leave home and stay at the university residence, even though you didn't want to?

Yes but—

He knew what you needed, even though you didn't. That's what parents are for.

What parents are for?

Well, maybe there was a bit of that with me and Rachel. I knew what she needed, even if she didn't. She needed to be cuddled. I couldn't let her go through life afraid of the snuggle, could I? Couldn't let her be a snuggle-phobic person, could I? What kind of mother does that to her child?

Snuggle-phobic?

Look here, Morris, she was my little girl. We cuddled. Mothers and children do that, you know. Parents cuddle their children. You do know that, don't you?

Morris is four years old. Outside is howling wind and blustering storm and dark, though it's past waking-up time on Sunday morning. Morris listens to the rain. He wonders how much wind it would take to blow their house down.

From down the passage comes the sound of singing, whistling, clapping hands and marching feet. His bedroom door is flung open, his blankets pulled off and he's on his father's shoulders, in his parents' room, on his parents' bed, at risk of slipping through the gap between the two single beds that have been pushed together.

His father lies back on the pillow, knees up. He pulls Morris up on to his knees, calls, 'Hold on tight, the horse is going to gallop,' starts jiggling his knees up and down, faster and faster. Morris holds on, shrieks, laughs, falls in a heap on his mother's side of the bed.

Luckily she isn't there. She's standing near the door, pulling her dressing-gown belt tight, tying it in a knot.

'Again,' cries Morris. 'Again.'

His father's knees pop up, Morris takes his hands.

'It's six o'clock, a beautiful evening in Melbourne. The horses are in their stalls. At number seven, the favourite, Phar Lap, ridden by that famous jockey, that wonder of wonders, Morris Goldberg . . .' Joe whistles through his teeth, jiggles his knees. 'And they're off, ladies and gentlemen.'

The horse is galloping, the wind is blowing. From behind the roars of the crowd comes the sound of Morris's mother vacuuming.

Stop jiggling for a second and look around. That's not your mother's room. It's the lounge. Before she moved rooms.

She never moved rooms.

Okay, if you're so sure, describe it for me.

It's too long ago. I can't remember.

Look, Morris, look. You're seeing the storm through a flat window. But the flat window was in the lounge. Your mother's room had a bay window.

Enough, Sadie. You can't expect me to remember every little detail. I wasn't even five then. And I was only six when she swapped the lounge and the bedroom.

Aha. Got you. Freud would have been proud of me.

Freud?

Would've been proud of me for getting you to admit to the swap.

Okay, so she swapped. Can I rest now?

So the house wasn't always frozen. Furniture moved there. When you got a television and when—

When I was six.

And the last move. When your mother went to the home.

Joan kept phoning Morris in Christchurch. Do you mind if I get rid of Pearl's bed? Do you want your mother's recipes? Don't say no without thinking. You might want them one day. Your wife might want them.

At last he said, 'Please, Joan, I don't want anything. Take what you like and get rid of the rest.' He heard her sharp intake of breath and said, 'Sorry, it's just that I'm studying and . . .'

'I understand. I understand. And don't you worry. Your things will be neatly packed up for you.'

'Joan, I'm sorry, I . . .'

'Morris, sweetheart, you get back to your studying and don't worry about a thing. It's a small job. Your mother lived . . . carefully. She lives carefully. And as for you, my goodness, Morris, your things could fit in a few boxes. But then I guess you took most of your things to Christchurch with you. Didn't you? How will you manage to get it all back now? Should I get Norman to arrange for you to rail it up?'

Oh Morris, she was needing support. Don't you see she needed you to help her through it?

I didn't want to . . . to interfere.

She needed you to interfere. It wasn't fair to leave her to make all the decisions on her own.

But she said it was a small job. She said my mother lived simply.

She said. She said. Of course she said. Joan always said. She'd say anything to protect you from distressing things.

Distressing things?

Like packing up your mother's personal things, having your fingers in her tshatshkes.

My mother never had, what do you call them?

Tshatshkes. Except for her linen.

Linen's not a tshatshke.
My God, all that linen.

Joan said the linen would be easy to pack, just a matter of moving from shelf to box, box to shelf.

Shelf to box, box to shelf and, later, when Morris and Sadie announced their engagement, on to Joan's dining-room table.

A bottle of champagne on Joan's dining-room table. Four of Joan's special glasses and a cake with M & S! piped in white icing. Norman all gruff and proud and pats on the back. Joan strangely shy, as if she'd been hiding something or caught stealing. Flustered and uncertain, making three trips to her linen cupboard to bring out all the linen, refusing offers of help.

'I told your mother you were engaged. I popped over as soon as I heard the news. That's what's so good about being close to her. I can pop over any time. She . . . she's thrilled for you. You know how sometimes she really seems to understand . . . She . . .'

Norman put his arm around his wife. 'Pearl wants you to have her linen. Joanie's been keeping it for you.'

Still starched. Still ironed. Some pieces still in the soft bags Pearl had sewed for them. Joan said she knew some of the pieces weren't folded nicely and that they looked kind of wadded, but that's the way you store them so they don't get fold marks in the same place.

'Your mother taught me that. It's the way she used to do it. It's the way she would have wanted it.'

Sadie said there were too many pieces. They couldn't possibly take them all. They didn't have the storage space in Morris's tiny flat. Joan must keep some. She'd have more use for it.

'Especially the tablecloths. Please, Joan, you must choose

189

the pieces you like best. Keep them for yourself. Give some to the synagogue. They'll be nice on the brocha table for Friday night, won't they?'

She took a tablecloth from the pile, laid it across the table. 'This is a nice one for the synagogue. Give them this one. Keep the lace for yourself.'

Joan protested. 'No, you keep them. They're yours. Put them away for when you have children. Your daughter will like them one day. She'll give them to her daughters.'

Sadie said, 'Isn't it a big job to look after them? Not shy with the starch, was she?' And Morris wanted to shout at them both to shut up, wanted to push Sadie aside, roughly even, to refold the cloth carefully, gently, you can't leave it hanging over the edge of the table like that and actually there's exactly the right amount of starch. Then, when it was laid just so, to run his hands along it, to feel its flatness. Its crispness. Its starch.

Did Morris think about the linen when presented, in a hotel restaurant in Christchurch, with the decision that his mother who had recently had a stroke would be moved to an old persons' home in Levin? Did he worry about practical things, wonder who would pack up the house, who go through her things, who put some clothes (not too much, the room is small) into a big old suitcase? Who place a few framed photos on the top of the clothes before closing the suitcase? Who call the Salvation Army to fetch the television which actually still works?

Did he consider who would put the suitcase in the boot, strap his mother into the back seat like a child? Did he think these things through or was he too busy wondering, aged twenty-three and holed up in a hotel restaurant bathroom, what emotion to present to his uncle and aunt on returning to the table?

Had Morris thought through the implications of the move he might have had an emotion to present to the table, but it came to him only later, and by then the decision was made and he was trapped. Had the emotion come to him at the restaurant, he couldn't have taken it to the table anyway. It was too shameful. What son, on being told that his helpless mother is to be moved to a town two hours away, feels a great dose of fear?

But fear is what Morris felt when, some weeks later, newly returned to Wellington, he set out on his first trip to visit his mother in her new home. For then he understood what the journey meant, and he knew it would not be the doddle that Joan had promised.

It wasn't the driving—Morris liked driving. And it wasn't

the thought of seeing his mother in that place. That was sad, yes, but not scary.

It was the thought that he would be expected to stop, either on the way in or out of Levin, to visit his aunt and uncle.

Joan would expect him to stay for a meal, to answer questions, to describe friends and what he was doing on the weekend. She'd want to know how he was settling into his new flat. Did he need cutlery? Crockery? Food? Was he eating enough? How was the job? What were his colleagues like? Her dogs would try to jump on to his lap and lick his face while she ran to the kitchen to pack a parcel of food for him to take home because she knew that young people never take the time to eat properly.

It wasn't the visits to his mother that frightened Morris. It was the visits to his aunt.

He pulled the car on to a verge so as to think the matter over. He could slip in, visit his mother and leave again. No one would be any the wiser. But if he did that, they wouldn't know he'd been there and Joan would be on the phone, saying, 'Morris, Morris, I don't mean to pry, but when last did you visit your mother?'

He'd have to make his presence known. And that meant visiting them. Or going at a time when they wouldn't be home. Maybe he could leave a note. When were they least likely to be home?

Morris started his car, did an illegal U-turn and headed back towards Wellington. It was all too damn scary.

He got halfway home before he did another illegal U-turn to face his car back towards Levin. He was an adult. He had responsibilities. His mother was one of them. Joan and Norman another. He would visit his mother every single week. He would phone Joan first to confirm the time. He would have a cup of tea with Joan and Norman unless he had a good excuse. Like today. Today he had to rush back to Wellington before the shops closed. He was already running late. But next week . . . next Saturday he'd have more time.

So Morris's visits to his mother became visits to Joan and Norman too. On his third visit, Norman pulled him aside and thanked him for including them. It made Joanie happy to see him. He was a good nephew.

'Maybe some good has come of your mother's illness,' said Norman.

Every week with his bag of fruit, because that's what you take.

Every week wondering what he would say to his mother. Once, even making a list of things to talk about but then being too ashamed to pull out his notebook—Pearl might have had a stroke, but she wasn't blind.

Every week looking at his watch before he went into her room, telling himself that he had to talk for at least fifteen minutes. Fifteen minutes and not a minute less before he could open the cupboard, take out the radio, sit with his mother and be quiet.

The radio stayed on a high shelf where Pearl couldn't reach it. The management had insisted. A stern woman with hair that looked like a helmet had called Morris into her office and told him that she was terribly sorry but Mrs Pearl simply could not have access to the radio. The problem was that Mrs Pearl kept fiddling with the dials, turning the radio too loud, blasting interference.

'Electric noise,' the stern woman said, 'disturbs the other residents. Electric noise disturbs the nurses. I have had complaints from visitors about electric noise.'

When Morris was in primary school, the class had made marbled paper. The teacher dropped little circles of oil paint into water and told the children to draw a toothpick through the paint. She laid paper on the water and used tweezers to pull it off. Then she hung the paper on pegs and invited the children to walk around, hands behind backs, and look at them.

Someone said, 'That one's the best,' and pointed to Morris's. 'Hands behind backs,' said the teacher, and then she said, 'It is nice, isn't it?'

Morris knew why his marble paper looked good. It was because he hadn't stirred and stirred at his paint. He'd run the toothpick through it lightly and gently like his teacher said, then he'd stepped back while the others continued to poke and mix and get everything jumbled together. When he looked at his paper, he could see traces of the perfect pools the paint had once been.

It was like that with Pearl after the stroke. Someone had run a stick over her, but they'd done it with a light hand. There were still traces of her smooth round circle.

The helmet-haired woman stirred at Pearl's circles like a child with a stick.

'No doubt Mrs Pearl doesn't mean to do it,' she said, 'but we can't have one resident disturbing everyone else with their racket, now can we? And it's not just the volume but the nature of the noise.' She put her hands on either side of her helmet head and frowned. 'So electric.'

Morris said nothing, and she said she was glad they'd sorted that out. She wouldn't confiscate the radio but the nurses would ensure it was kept high, where Mrs Pearl couldn't reach it. It was only to be used under supervision.

So, fifteen, no, ten minutes of talking before he could open the high cupboard. Then they could sit together, Morris and his mother, and listen to the wireless.

Every Saturday, setting out with his bag of fruit and, later, with Sadie. Sadie who said it was unnecessary to take fruit from Wellington. They'd stop and buy some from one of the cute little fruit stalls on the way. It would be cheaper, fresher. It would be fun! Sadie who chatted all the way there, Morris thinking I must remember that, that's something I could tell my mother. Sadie, who stayed at Joan's house and presumably kept on chatting for the hour (exactly) that Morris spent with his mother.

Dun dun dun dun . . . Surprising English girlfriend to the rescue. Go, Sadie.

Dun dun dun dun?

Sadie to the rescue. I came with you. I visited Joan and Norman. I let the dogs lick my face. You visited your mother. We both got the hell out of there. You could at least have thanked me. I mean, how many girlfriends do that for a bloke?

You liked visiting them. You told me so. You said that it was nice to have family to visit, since your own family was so far away. You said—

I said a lot of things. Okay, so I'll grant you I liked going there well enough. It was quite nice to be spoiled by them. But every weekend? Give me a break. And we weren't even engaged when I started going with you. Come to think of it, you probably asked me to marry you for fear that I'd stop accompanying you. Leave poor little Morris to visit his family alone.

You think that's why I asked you to marry me?

No, I don't think that, but you could have thanked me for going with you.

At first Morris didn't want Sadie to go with him to Levin.

He didn't want her seeing Joan's house with its walls of photos and its huge furniture. He didn't want her stepping over dogs' toys to get to Joan's open arms. He didn't want Joan squeezing her or Norman being kind to her. And he certainly didn't want her going to the retirement home and seeing his mother. Sadie did not belong in Levin and she did

195

not belong to his family. She was *his* Sadie and she belonged in Wellington.

She had other ideas.

They were walking to town when he told her where his mother lived. It was after their first night together, and Morris would have preferred to stay on at Sadie's flat, having sweet tea and biscuits for breakfast. If he couldn't be at her flat, he would have chosen to be alone at his. He could have sat at his desk and thought about the night before. He could have let his mind run through all the things she'd let him do. He could have planned what he'd say to her next time.

Sadie wanted to go to town. She wanted to have tea in a tearoom—the new one with the nice cream cakes—and she wanted to 'show my new boyfriend off to the world. Well, at least to Wellington.'

You don't refuse to be shown off to the world. Not when you had sex the night before. Not when she's calling you her boyfriend. You smile and say you'd like that, and when she takes your hand in public you don't pull away. Not even when she swings your arm and asks you how come you had your graduation dinner with your aunt and uncle? Where were your parents?

Sadie's arms stopped swinging when Morris told her that his father died when he was a child and that his mother was in an old persons' home.

When he told her that he visited his mother on Saturdays she stopped walking altogether, turned to look him full in the face and said, 'You know you can judge a man by the way he treats his mother, don't you? You are a good man, Morris Goldberg. I think it's the sweetest thing on earth that you drive all that way to visit your mother every week.' She stood on tiptoe to kiss him. Full on the mouth on a public footpath.

The sweetest thing. 'My mother's not . . . we're not . . .'

196

he tried to say, but she silenced him with her mouth.

Three weeks later, on a Saturday morning, she arrived at his flat unexpectedly. 'Wendlet and I were supposed to go out and about today but she's cancelled on me. How about I come with you to Levin?' Morris must have hesitated, because she said, 'Or are you getting bored with me already? Need some time on your own already?'

So he agreed that she should accompany him. Sadie confirmed that he was the sweetest thing on earth, and went home to change and pack food for the road.

'My aunt will want to feed you,' he called to her retreating back, but she was already out the door.

Morris spent the next hour worrying about what Sadie expected to find in Levin.

Would she want to go to Pearl's home and also to have tea at Joan's?

She might change her mind about him being the sweetest thing on earth if she saw where his mother lived.

Was it even a good thing for a girl to think you the sweetest thing on earth?

Was it normal for a girl whose been dating a man for less than a month to want to visit his mother in an old persons' home? In Levin?

No, Morris decided, it was probably not normal. Not something you see people do in movies when they're in love. And it was not something he wanted.

He would insist that Sadie stay with Joan while he visited the home. Bad as his aunt's furniture, photos and dogs were, they were preferable to the old persons' home. Overpowering as Joan was, she was at least responsible for herself.

The decision to leave Sadie with Joan brought new doubts. Would Joan attach special significance to his bringing his new girlfriend to visit? Would Sadie? Should he? Was Sadie actually his girlfriend? They'd had sex a few times and she kept referring to him as her boyfriend, but her tone seemed mocking when she did so and he'd seen enough at university to know that having sex with someone didn't necessarily mean you were in a relationship.

Morris could, literally, tear his hair out. He could grab a clump near the front and pull it really hard. He gave an exploratory tug and, like a bell on the end of a rope, the phone rang.

'Are you one of those people who can't bear the thought of cheese and jam?'

'Cheese and jam? I don't know. I've never—'

'Well, do you have a treat in store for you! A new taste sensation. I'll be ready in ten minutes. I'll wait outside.'

Before leaving to fetch her, he wet and combed his hair.

She was standing on the footpath in her good dress, bought for a job interview. When he pulled up, she opened the back door first, to place her basket carefully on the seat.

'You'll have to wait until Raumati before you enjoy the new taste sensation. It's the rule.'

'The rule.'

'That you can't eat your sandwiches until you're a decent distance from home.'

When Raumati was safely behind them, she poured tea into a plastic cup and held it out for him. 'Your reward for having stuck to the distance rule without complaining.'

He found the combination of cheese and jam strange but not unpleasant.

As they drew up at Joan and Norman's house he said, 'I'd prefer it if you stayed . . .' The rest of his words were drowned out by dogs yapping and Joan calling for them to be quiet. It was just Morris. Just Morris and . . . 'My, it's the English girl from the restaurant. Sadie, that's your name, isn't it?'

Joan was full of praise for Morris's parking, for Sadie's dress, full of apologies for not looking better herself but her forgetful nephew neglected to tell her he was bringing a friend. Not that she didn't want Sadie there. Of course she wanted Sadie there. 'When this silly nephew of mine told me that he'd gone to a party with you, I thought wow. Wow is all I thought. I've been wondering and wondering when he'd bring you to visit us. Now here you are and here's me in my Saturday schmutters and all the time I've been wondering when Morris would bring you to visit us.'

'Oh my goodness,' said Sadie. 'Did Morris not tell you I was coming? I am sorry.'

She pulled a funny face which Joan couldn't see.

'We've actually come to visit my mother,' Morris found himself saying. 'Sadie's coming with me to—'

Sadie got herself between him and Joan. 'But I'd really like to get to know *you*,' she said. 'Morris won't mind visiting his mother on his own. You and I can have some time together.' She opened her eyes wide at Morris. 'You don't mind if I stay here with Joan, do you?'

'Of course I don't mind. It's just that I forgot to tell—'

'Oh, I knew you'd understand, Morris. You really are the sweetest thing.'

Joan clapped her hands like a little girl. 'I love the way you say "mother". It's so English.' She brought her hands to her lips as if to kiss them, and clapped again before saying, 'Morris *is* the sweetest thing, but he's also the naughtiest.'

'I couldn't agree more.' Sadie wagged a finger at Morris.

Joan put her arm around Sadie. 'Come and see Norman. He'll be so happy to see that Morris has finally brought you to visit us. You won't mind if Norman pulls your leg, will you? He's a bit of a joker, you see. Then we'll have some tea and you can tell me all about yourself.' They turned together towards the house.

'I always wanted to go alone,' Morris, following, told the slowest, oldest dog.

If they'd given him time to formulate his words, he might have managed to make up a story about wanting to surprise Joan. But it's hard to think of the right words when the woman you've had sex with is pulling funny faces and raising her eyebrows like someone in a silent movie who's trying to scare the villain off just by looking at him.

In the lounge Sadie picked up a dog, faced it eye to eye and said, 'Who's a pretty boy then?'

Joan's eyes shone. 'Oh, oh, I am overjoyed. Simply overjoyed to have found you hiding away in that restaurant. Had silly shy Morris taken any longer to ask you out, I would have done it myself.'

'And I would have gone,' replied Sadie. She had a dog on her lap and another on the cushion beside her. She scratched their ears and tickled their tummies, and when one of them jumped up to lick her face she made a joke about the prettiest boys being the most forward.

She was a dog person. She'd be wanting a pet. Morris could see it.

Joan and Norman smiled. At Morris. At Sadie. At each other.

When they left the room to fetch the tea things, Sadie pushed the dog off her lap, stood up to brush the hairs off her skirt and whispered something about that being the grossest thing she'd ever experienced. Morris wondered whether it was possible to be relieved and insulted simultaneously.

Driving back to Wellington, Sadie apologised for not going with Morris to see his mother. She said that her preference was to be with him but there was something so sad about Joan. 'Did you see how disappointed she looked when you told her we'd come only to see your mum? I couldn't leave her. I just couldn't. You didn't really need me to come with you, but she . . . she needed me to stay, don't you think?'

Morris didn't answer. He was relaxing into the possibility that Sadie both recognised his aunt's needs and was able to separate them from his own.

As if to confirm his thoughts, she said, 'You didn't really want me to go with you to the home, did you? Even though you told Joan that I was coming with you. Tell me the truth now, Morris.'

This time her wagging finger made him smile.

'You're right. The truth is I didn't really want you to come.'

'I knew it. But then why did you say I was coming with you to your mother?'

'I don't know. I don't know. Sometimes words run away with me.'

'I think you mean *without* you. Words run away *without* you.'

They were silent for a while, then she said, 'Can't you picture it?'

'Picture what?'

'Your words running away without you.'

'My words—'

'Bear with me. Don't laugh. Picture it. You're standing in front of Joan and Norman's house. The dogs are approaching. So are your aunt and uncle. All around you are your words—everything you could possibly say to them gathered in their front garden. Your words are jumping up and down around your feet. They're waving their little arms in the air, beckoning to you, shouting in their tiny little voices, "Quickly, Morris. Quickly. There's no time to be lost. Run away with us. Run away."'

Morris grinned. 'There are red words and green words—'

'Even a few grubby little blue ones, and they're all shouting—'

'My words are all shouting—'

'Run away with us, Morris. Quickly.'

'The problem is they do run away and I can't keep up.'

'Of course you can't. They've got fast little legs, those words of yours.'

Sadie stopped grinning. 'You know what?' she said at last.

'What?'

'I think I've got the opposite problem.'

'The opposite?'

'My words hang about. They won't leave me. Even the ugly ones that should never be spoken just won't go away. They're always following me about, trying to trip me up, clamouring over each other, hanging on my skirt, waving their little arms and saying, "Speak me. Speak me."'

'Speak me. Speak me.'

'So I do. I speak them and then I regret it.'

She turned to look out of the window and was quiet for a long time. He thought she might be dozing, but then she said, 'I've been thinking about your mother and I think it might be kind of, you know, confusing for her to be suddenly introduced to me. Also Joan seems so—well, she seems to like me. Maybe I should stay with her next time. If you don't mind, that is.'

She put her hand on his thigh. 'Damn it, Jim, but aren't those dogs something?'

'D'you think you'll ever want to have a pet?'

'Oh God no. I most certainly do not want a pet. It's bad enough that I'm going to have to be nice to the royal corgis every time we go to Levin.'

She was talking of a next time and she didn't want a pet. Morris chose relief over insult.

She rested her head against the window pane and was silent. When he looked again, she was sleeping.

Her hand felt warm and heavy on his thigh. He fell into the rhythm of the drive.

Years later Sadie arrived home with a kitten in a box. 'It's for you, Morris, a gift.'

He tried to remind her of her car-drive declaration.

She said she didn't care what he thought he distinctly remembered, she'd never said she didn't want pets and, even if she had, she could change her mind. It was a woman's prerogative. Besides, David loved animals and everyone knows that a child needs a pet. Morris had gone and spoiled her surprise with some ancient conversation which didn't matter anyway.

After that first visit to Levin, Sadie seemed to assume that she would always accompany him. Joan did too and, once, when he arrived alone, Morris saw Joan's smile drop and something that looked like fear flit across her face.

Every Saturday Sadie went with him. So did her thermos flask and sandwiches. 'I know it's a case of coals to Newcastle but I eat sandwiches on a journey. That's what I do.'

Every Saturday she brushed her hair when they pulled up outside Joan's house, joking about the need to be both mentally and physically prepared when you're about to face a pack of killer lap dogs. Every Saturday she threw herself at the car door, at Joan and Norman, at the killer lap dogs.

A quick hello was all Morris had to give before turning the car towards his mother's home. Sometimes Norman would drive with him to see Pearl and sometimes not.

It was a good arrangement. Everyone seemed satisfied with it. It lasted until they got engaged, when Sadie suggested that it might now be appropriate for her to meet his mother.

Morris's first inclination was to make up some excuse. They weren't married yet. She could still leave him. She could return to England on the pretext that her own mother needed her. There was probably an ex-boyfriend who'd be happy to have her back. She could tell him how Morris was a liar who'd misled her into believing he looked after his mother when actually, actually, he'd left his mother to get sicker and sicker in an old persons' home. In Levin of all places. They'd laugh about what a backwater Levin was, how the closest it got to culture was a Jewish-sounding name. She'd run her hands through his long hair and thank God she'd escaped all that.

'Sadie, I don't know if—'

'So you know Jen?'

'Jen?'

'Jen, my friend with the daughter.'

'With the daughter.'

'Yes, Jen, my friend. The one with the long hair and the big tits.'

'Big—'

'Tits. I knew you'd noticed them. So, anyway, you know how Jen's divorced?'

'Um, about going—'

'And then she started dating other men. Remember how there was no shortage of men? There was that Geoff and that weirdo, what was his name? James. So what I'm saying, Morris. Morris, are you listening to me? Morris.'

'Yes, yes, I'm listening.'

'Okay, so what I'm saying is Jen didn't introduce a single one of those men to her daughter, even though Shelly isn't even two years old.'

'Two years old.'

'Not even. So Jen didn't let any of them get to know Shelly because . . . here's what I'm saying, Morris. The thing is, Jen didn't know if any of those guys would work out. She didn't know if any of them would be permanent.'

'She didn't want too many changes for her daughter.'

'That's it. Morris. That's the thing. But then she met Brian, and after they'd been together for months she thought he would be permanent and then, only then, did she introduce him to Shelly.'

'She must have been nearly three by then.'

'I guess. But anyway, you get my point.'

'Your point?'

'My point is that I'm, well, I'm permanent.'

'You're permanent.'

205

'I'm permanent. You can't hide me away from your mother any longer. She'll be expecting your fiancée to visit her. Well, maybe not expecting, but still, still I think I should, don't you?'

And so Morris thought he could risk taking her the next Saturday. If she was going to leave him, let it be before the wedding rather than after.

'We'll go together to my mother on Saturday.'

Sadie was beautiful when she smiled.

It was cramped and hot in Pearl's little room.

Morris stood when he introduced Sadie. 'You remember, Mum, that Joan told you I'd got engaged?' He kept standing as he tried to explain that Sadie came from a good family, a Jewish family. 'They were travelling, Sadie and her sister. Then they got here and, well, I guess they decided to stay.'

Pearl's good eye was fixed on something behind Morris's head.

From the next room came the sound of a children's television programme.

Sadie shifted her chair close to Pearl's. She leaned forwards and stroked Pearl's bad hand. Then she started chatting about how lovely the English countryside was at that time of year.

Pearl's eye might have shifted a bit. She might have turned slightly towards Sadie when she related how she and her sister stained their clothes when picking mulberries.

At last Sadie stopped talking and Morris stood up to pull down the wireless.

When it was time to go, Sadie suggested to Morris that he leave the radio on. He shook his head, wondering whether she'd argue the point, but she just bent down and gave Pearl's good hand a little squeeze.

Morris walked some way down the corridor before

noticing that Sadie was not beside him. She was pinned against the wall by a cleaner with a trolley piled high with sheets.

Not so very sweet, thought Morris, to put your mother in a place like this.

Sadie gave him a wave from behind the cleaner's trolley and pretended to steal a sheet. Morris wanted her to stop. She shouldn't be joking in this place. Or running. Or clutching him in a tight hug and saying, 'Let's get the hell out of here.'

He tried to smile. 'Watch out. You'll knock me over.'

Sadie looked around her. 'D'you see how some people seem to be moving in slow motion while others are all speeded up?'

'We'd better go. Joan will be waiting.'

'Compare that old man, the one holding on to the rail, with that woman, the visitor on her way out. She looks like she's moving at about twenty-five times his speed. She can't wait to get out of here while he, poor old thing, he's taking all the time in the world to go nowhere. He's like an old cassette that's been played too often and now it drags along so that every note takes fifteen seconds to play out.'

Twenty-five times his speed. Could it be that much? Morris looked at the old man, then at the woman and back to the man. Three times his speed at most.

He made an effort to slow down. He wouldn't want Sadie to think he was rushing out of there.

Outside in the fresh cold air, she said she thought the visit went well and asked about the radio. When Morris told her about the manager, he saw her burn.

'Oh, that makes me so angry. For crying out loud, Morris, who does that woman think she is? Your mother can't read. She can hardly see. The radio's pretty much her only pleasure. The manager said she would confiscate it? Supervised use only? Bullshit. Pearl needs it for the company.'

Sadie insisted that Morris find a solution to this problem. 'Fix the radio so that she can't change the settings. It will be easy for you. You know about electronics and stuff. Make a plan.' Insisted that he discuss the matter with Norman and Joan. 'Come on, Morris, you can do it sensitively so that Joan doesn't take it as a personal affront.'

But Morris blundered and explained it all wrong, and left Joan sniffing that she supposed it was worth trying to fix the settings but there was always music playing in the lounge and it was good for Pearl to go there rather than sitting in her room all day.

Sadie said, 'Joan's right. It is important for your mother to go to the lounge,' and she patted Morris's back.

Norman put a dog on Joan's lap. 'And Morris is right. She should be able to listen to the wireless.'

Later, when Joan and Sadie were in the kitchen, Norman handed Morris a roll of masking tape. 'Stick this over the knobs. That ought to do it.' He fiddled with a pen in his pocket. 'The sad thing is that Pearl's hands have got weaker. Joanie feels bad about it.'

Joan came in with a cake and Norman said, 'Now, Morris, don't you worry about explaining to the management. Joan and I will see to that. Won't we, Joanie?'

'We only want what's best for her.'

The masking tape worked and Pearl did seem to listen to the radio, but from then on, when Morris went to visit his mother, he had to turn the radio off on his arrival rather than on. And that meant trying to find things to say to her.

Every Saturday, setting out with Sadie, and later the children, to visit Levin.

Well, in the beginning it was every Saturday but then you stopped going so often. At some point you became resistant. Why did you become resistant?

I never became resistant.

You became resistant. And you had a good excuse. You had a good wife.

A good wife.

A good wife. Who visited your mother on your behalf. Even though she didn't have a clue who I was.

You used to laugh about her.

So sue me for laughing about your ibberbuttle mother. I never did it to her face. And I wasn't the only one. Joan of Arc laughed too. It was a way of letting off steam.

Steam?

Especially for Joan. She took a lot of strain, you know, looking after your mother. Not even her own sister. So we laughed a bit. So sue me.

Joan didn't mind looking after my mother. She said she didn't mind.

Of course she did.

Did say it or did mind?

Both. Neither. Anyway, what happened to make you resist going?

Nothing happened.

For crying out loud, Morris. You used to go every Saturday. Even after the children were born. You always visited your mother. Then you became all resistant and then you stopped.

I never stopped.

David must have been about three when you stopped visiting your mother.

I never stopped.

What happened, Morris?

Joan was standing at her front door like she always did.

Always so happy to see them, so full of presents for David and kisses for Rachel and I knew you were coming so I baked a cake. The doggies missed David. Did David say hello to the doggies?

David wanted to open his presents and Sadie had news to share with Joan, so Norman said, 'Why don't Morris and I drive to the home together and leave you girls for a bit of a gander?'

'Good idea,' said Sadie. 'You know how Joanie and I love a bit of a gander.'

'And I love being called a girl,' said Joan, 'though really Morris should go on his own today. Norman on his own tomorrow. That way Pearl will feel like she has lots of visitors. She'll feel busy.'

'But if I go today,' was Norman's line, 'I get to have time with my nephew.'

All the way to the home Norman asked questions. How's the new business going? Is the partnership working out well? Is Sadie planning on going back to work? How are you managing financially? Did you see Joanie's dogs in the newspaper?

Fine, fine, soon, fine, no but Sadie did.

On the way back they were silent. Morris focused on the road. Norman ran his hands up and down the lines of his corduroy pants.

On their return both went straight to the bathroom.

Morris wondered whether Norman was also going to wash his hands, whether they felt as grubby as his own, whether he always washed his hands on returning from the home. Did Joan do it too?

Something happened. What happened?
Nothing happened.
What happened?

The door of Pearl's room was ajar. On the radio someone was being interviewed about disco music.

'Knock knock,' called Norman. 'Are you decent, Pearl? We're coming in.'

At first Morris thought she was trying to pick something up from the floor. It must have been something important, because she was leaning so far forward she was at risk of toppling over. He stepped forward to help her, to catch her from falling, and saw that she was dozing and that there was no risk of her falling for she was strapped in.

It wasn't a chair she was sitting on. It was a commode.

Her mouth hung open. She was drooling.

Morris was afraid of her.

Norman said, 'How can they leave her sitting here on her own? She's strapped in, for goodness sake. I'll find someone to deal with this,' and he left the room.

Scared of your own mother. What do you think she's going to do to you? Strapped in the seat as she is? Morris took a step back, but the smell followed him and his mother's head moved. Her eyes flickered and she seemed to be peering over the top of her eyes at him, running through names in her head.

'I'll just . . .' He took another step back. Pearl's head jerked upwards and her hand lifted as if to beckon to him, as if he could help her.

How long did he stand at the door, too scared to approach (think of her dignity and she's not really calling you. She doesn't know who you are, who she is, where she is)? Too ashamed to walk away.

How long before he heard Norman saying that he'd like to discuss this with the manager? Wasn't there a policy about sitting with people while they were on the commode? How long had she been there? She was half-naked asleep, for goodness' sake.

How long before he could call across the room to his mother, 'They're on their way. You'll be fine'?

The nurse chivvied Morris out of the doorway and into the passage. She closed the door behind her. Pearl Goldberg, said the little sign on the door. Room 25. Morris and Norman stood in the passage and breathed the smell of the place and were silent.

Pearl's circle had been stirred away.

You know you're supposed to wash your hands when you leave a cemetery.

A cemetery?

I'm just saying.

Morris focused on the road, Norman ran his hands up and down the lines of his corduroy pants, and when they got home both went directly to the bathroom. In the tiny spare bathroom, Morris washed his hands, dried them, washed them again. There was a little wooden step in front of the toilet. Norman had made it for David to help him reach the bowl. Sadie would have stood next to David. She would have helped him on to the little step, good boy, clever boy. Joan, come and see what a clever boy David is.

Morris washed his hands again. From outside the door he heard David calling, 'Normie said he'd bring me a lolly.'

He dried his hands and went to join his family in the kitchen.

It was like walking into a diorama.

Once, on a school trip, Morris had visited a museum which had dioramas showing how families lived in different eras. From the early settlers through to Modern Auckland, they sat in their living rooms, mother with her tea cup forever poised, father always stern, always gazing at his watch.

Morris's classmates rushed around the museum, tearing

212

from exhibit to exhibit, pointing out the funny clothes, the silly toys. 'Look at that girl's skirt. How did she go to the toilet?'

Morris wasn't interested in the clothes or toys. He was interested in the expressions on the dolls' faces—faces that were still for long enough for him to really look at them. That face is stern. You can see by the frown and the way the mouth is turned down. That little girl is happy. She's smiling and holding her head to the side so that her hair falls over her shoulders. She wouldn't do that if she wasn't happy.

The dioramas had names: *Prosperous Settler Family. A Victorian Mother and Her Daughter Visit the Apothecary.* They told you what to expect, what it all meant. Morris liked that.

The sign on Joan's kitchen door would have read: *Levin: Three Generations Enjoy a Warm Drink Together.* There would have been a red rope across the kitchen door. Morris could have stood on the other side of the rope and worked out their faces. He wouldn't have had to walk in.

'Enter Valentino,' called Sadie.

Joan said, 'You naughty girl,' and pulled her mug up to her face.

'I beg your pardon?' said Morris.

'Valentino. The great lover. Joan was telling me about your first conquest.'

'My what?'

Joan put her cup down. 'I'll see how Norman is doing.'

Morris tried to laugh. 'What were you two talking about?'

'Oh nothing. How's your mother? Nothing really.'

Two Generations of Women Discuss Their Husbands, the plaque might have read. *They are Interrupted.*

I told you on the way home what we were talking about. We were talking about the first time you were with a girl. Junebug Joan said that she was to blame for it.

To blame?

You know what I mean.

But why were you talking about it? Why to her? Give me one good reason.

I don't know. We just got on to it. Jesus Christ, Morris, there are about a million reasons why Junebug and I would be talking about your first girlfriend.

A million.

About a million. And she introduced you two. She told me. It started with her.

It started with Joan. She had a friend who lived abroad whose daughter was visiting New Zealand and was desperate to go tramping. The girl would be staying with Norman's friends in Christchurch, the ones who'd been so kind to Morris when he first went to Canterbury, the ones who'd invited him for Friday night dinners and made sure he had somewhere to go on Jewish holidays.

Joan phoned Pearl. Pearl phoned Morris at the university residence. When Morris heard it was his mother on the phone, he thought someone must have died.

Pearl said, 'Have you got a pen on you? Never mind. I'll put it all in a letter to you, to confirm. Now, Morris, Joan's friend is coming and you're to take her tramping. The girl's name is Natalie. That's N-a-t-a-l-i-e without an h.'

Pearl gave details of the girl's arrival time. She used the letters E. T. A. Morris tried to interrupt her when she dictated the phone number of Norman's friends.

'Mum, I've got their number, but . . .'

'. . . 584. Joan has told Natalie that you'll make contact with her directly. You can arrange everything with her. I'll put it all in a letter.'

Pearl had finished her speech. Morris could almost hear her notes rustling.

'Arrange everything. But I can't. I've got assignments due. Exams are coming up. I'm too busy.'

'It's all organised and it's only one day.'

'A whole day. I can't do it. I'm sorry but I just can't.'

Pearl departed from her notes, put on her I'm-counting-to-five voice. Morris was to stop being petulant and fussing over nothing. It was the least he could do for Joan and Norman. They'd been so good to him.

'But I . . .'

'Anyway, I've already said yes. Phone the number. Make the arrangements. How bad can it be?'

Oh Mum, thought Morris, you have no idea.

Morris knew what Natalie without an h would be like. She'd be blond like that horrible little niece of Joan's—what was her name? Becky. She'd lisp and simper. She'd think she was going for a stroll in the park and be completely under-prepared. She'd keep asking questions about the names of trees. She'd want to chat.

'And one other thing, Morris. She doesn't speak any English.'

'You mean . . .'

'Not a word. Not one word.'

'I can't. Tell them I can't.'

'I'll send you a letter with all the details, to confirm,' said Pearl, and she put down the phone.

Morris returned to his room, kicked—actually kicked—the door open. His shoe left a dark mark which would later give him a warm, bubbling feeling in his stomach but which, as he made it, only increased his anger.

It was a sunny day. Students were lying on the grass outside. Girls had their skirts hiked up. Some guys had taken their shirts off. Any one of those shirtless men would have leapt at the opportunity to take a foreign girl out on her own. Morris could conduct statistical research and ask them one by one: You have just been asked by an aunt to take a female student from Europe tramping for a day. Do you (a) leap at the opportunity, (b) plead exams to get out of it, or (c)—

He wouldn't even get beyond (b). Are you kidding me? What kind of choice is that? Where's the catch? Wait, no, don't bother telling me about the catch. I'll take her anyway. She's alone in a foreign country and wants company, warmth, loving. I'll take her anywhere. She'll take me. Hey, Mike, come and listen to the terribly bloody difficult choice Morris has to make. They'd make ribald jokes and boast about where they'd be taking her, where she'd be taking them, how some things land on your lap, don't they just?

And Morris would study the numbers on his clipboard and wonder what the hell was wrong with him. How could his mother do it to him?

Well, as things turned out, there was nothing wrong with you, was there? You were just a bit shy. Nothing to be ashamed of. Quite cute actually.

Cute. Cute?

And as for your mother doing that to you, well it's obvious why she made you do it. It was a way of helping to repay her debt.

Her debt.

The debt she felt she owed Brother Norman. And Joan. For helping her out.

Helping her out?

Financially.

They never helped financially. My mother had a job.

Sure and her part-time job as a doctor's receptionist kept the two of you in a three-bedroomed house in Kelburn, paid for all

216

those extra lessons you had, not to mention the expense of sending you to university so far away. A part-time job. It's not like women were well paid in those days. How much did she work? Maybe three hours a day? Fifteen hours a week as a doctor's receptionist. That wouldn't get you very far.

It must have been more than fifteen hours a week. She must have worked full time. Why else would Morris have had to accompany her to work so often? Why else would he have spent endless hours in the waiting room with the sick old men and the sniffling babies?

Every time they went to the surgery Morris begged to be allowed to wait in the car, and every time his mother ignored his pleas. The car was cold, the waiting room was warm. There were magazines in the waiting room. He could do his homework in the waiting room. She could keep an eye on him there. If he sat quietly and waited patiently, she'd give him one of the lollipops which the doctor kept for his patients.

Morris hated the doctor's lollipops. No matter how carefully he opened them there were always little bits of plastic sticking to the sweet. One lick made the stick soggy and the lolly crumbly. Some of the lolly crumbs had sharp edges. Morris would feel them in his mouth and wonder whether a splinter could go down his throat. Whether you could die from that.

Worse even than the lollipops was the doctor. 'Call me Doc, everyone else does. Doc Doc Doc Doc.' He'd come booming out of his surgery to greet young Morris, my most regular patient. Sitting so quietly, so patiently. Morris, my most patient patient. Have you had a lollipop? Such a good boy deserves two. Pearl, give him an extra lolly from me. Open your mouth wide, Morris, say 'ah' for Doc Doc Doc Doc. No, no, I'm only joking, you're not sick are you? Look healthy as an ox to me. Eating well? Treating your mother well? How's school? Who's your teacher? Pretty, is she? Such a good boy doing his homework. Give him two lollipops. No, three. From me. Doc. Doc Doc Doc.

Morris would try to peer around the doctor's bulk to catch his mother's eye. Mum, help me. But she'd be talking on the phone, 'Four o'clock this afternoon,' or writing in a book, or might have her back turned completely away from him to open the filing cabinet. Sometimes Morris wondered whether she was ignoring him on purpose.

Once, when Morris was about fifteen, the doctor gave him a job painting the outside wall of the surgery. It took Morris the whole school holiday and every day, around mid-morning, the doctor would come and sit outside with him, lean back in the sun and say something like, 'So, my boy, tell the doc how things are with you.' Morris complained about the doctor's questions to his mother and was surprised when she raised her voice in anger. It seemed he ought to be thanking the doctor, not complaining about him.

So the job was important. The doctor was good to his mother. But still, fifteen hours was only fifteen hours and women weren't paid much in those days. There must have been another source.

Like I said, Morris, there must have been another source.

My father could have left money. You haven't considered that possibility, have you? He must have made plans for us. A nest egg for us. Just in case.

Or Norman helped.

Or my father left money.

Okay, okay, let's think about it. Picture your father. You're sitting next to him in the front seat of his car. Watch him carefully. Take your time. He's speeding along a busy road, driving in time to the music, weaving when the music soars, going even faster

when the drums roll. He's singing and beeping his horn. Is this a
man who saves a little nest egg, just in case? Is this a just-in-case
man?

He wasn't always like that.

Granted. Okay, here's another picture of him. He's sitting in
the lounge. In the dark. He's kind of curled up, folded in half in
his chair . . .

You don't know anything.

Okay, try this one: he's not there. You're only just five and
your mother's sick and who's there? Not your father.

Shortly after Morris's fifth birthday he woke up early one
morning to find Uncle Norman asleep on the sofa in the
lounge.

'Your mum's gone to the hospital. Nothing to worry
about, but for a few days it's going to be just you and me.
That'll be fun, won't it? What do you like for breakfast? I
make a brilliant scrambled egg.'

A few days later his mother came home.

A few days after that, his father.

You're five years old and your father isn't there.

All right. I get it. My father wasn't there. Norman was.

And your mother was in hospital. Why was your mother in
hospital?

I don't know. I was only about four years old at the time. How
was I supposed to know?

Five. And your father wasn't there.

Okay, all right. Maybe my father didn't leave a nest egg. I
don't know. It doesn't matter.

Oh Morris, of course it matters. And if Norman was helping
to support you, that matters too. All of it matters.

I did what my mother asked. I took the girl tramping.

And that certainly mattered, didn't it?

I guess.

You guess? Okay, so, you've agreed to take the girl, that Natalie without an h, tramping. You've organised to fetch her. You get there and she's already waiting outside.

Waiting outside at 6 a.m. because that's what time Morris told her to be ready. She was sitting on the step in the dark. When his car headlights caught her, she stood up.

Morris thought, Oh great, she's overweight.

So not a great figure then.

She'd be unfit.

And her pack was way too big for a day's tramp. She'd packed as if she was expecting a week in Antarctica. He'd end up carrying it.

He tried to explain that they should leave some things behind. She nodded and smiled and he thought she'd understood, but when he opened the boot she lifted the pack in and went to wait at the passenger door. He studied the pack for a moment before shutting the boot. It probably held a picnic basket and a bottle of wine wrapped in tea towels.

When they'd been walking for a while, Morris offered to swap packs with her. She smiled and shook her head and kept on walking.

They stopped for lunch near a swimming hole.

Natalie was sweating. She walked a bit away, and when she came back she was wearing a long T-shirt over swimming togs.

Morris hadn't thought to pack swimming shorts. He turned his back to her and stripped down to his underpants. He kept his singlet on.

Oh my God, stop. I'll die laughing.

It's not funny.

Of course it's funny. Hysterical. This was what? 1967, '68? Dammit, Jim. It was the summer of love probably. Of hanging loose and being cool. And there you were, in the prime of your youth, worrying about your underpants and your vest. My God, even my father used to run around naked in those days, and God knows he wasn't in the prime of youth.

You were in England.

Ah, yes, that will be the difference then. England, free love. New Zealand, worrying about the size of a backpack. Oh, and don't forget to keep your singlet on.

When he turned back he couldn't see Natalie. There was silence. Then her face broke through the water and she grinned at him. He followed her in.

Her swimming togs shone blue through the T-shirt.

Morris looked away but she must have seen him noticing because she crossed her arms over her chest and said, 'Brrr.'

He ducked under the water. When he lifted his head she was a flash of blue behind a tree. His penis had shrivelled with cold before she came back, fully clothed, to the bank and he could leave the water.

She started a little fire and put a billy on.

Morris had not thought it necessary to bring a billy on a one-day tramp on a hot day. He was surprised that she owned one.

She had cocoa, powdered milk, a little bag of sugar. She had hard biscuits like the ones Craig took on tramps. His girlfriend baked them for him. Morris tried to ask Natalie where she'd got those biscuits, had she baked them herself? She shrugged and smiled.

He held the biscuit in front of his face, said, 'Tararua biscuit.'

He pointed to the billy and said, 'Billy.'

'Tararua,' she repeated after him. 'Tararua. Billy.' When she turned to get something from her pack he noticed, in the flicker between fringe and forehead, a sprinkling of acne.

It was the acne that did it, wasn't it? More than the weight, or the fact that she didn't expect you to understand. More even than the wet T-shirt. It was the acne. You like a girl who's not quite pretty, don't you?

It's not that I like—

I mean, after all, you liked me

You were pretty, you were—

Too late, Morris. Way too late to tell me that.

Sadie was almost beautiful. Almost but not quite. It was as if God had taken all the features which make up a beautiful person—the high cheekbones, white teeth, clear skin, little snub nose, even the pouting lips—and messed with them. They were all there, and in some lights, at some angles, they could come together with a symmetry that almost took your breath away. But they were for the most part almost but not quite right.

Morris would notice people looking at Sadie, looking away, then looking back, as if to trick themselves into seeing her correctly. Sometimes he thought he could see their disappointment, could hear them thinking, I don't know why I thought she was pretty. She's quite plain really.

There was something cruel about God doing that to a person. And something grand too. Witness Sadie, proof that God has all the know-how to create a real beauty and all the spite to twist it into nothing, into worse than nothing, into ordinary. Proof that God can always mess with you. Proof that a miss really is as good as a mile.

A miss is as good as a mile—Sadie's words, those.

They've just kissed for the first time. Morris is glowing with surprise. Stop grinning. Say something nice. About her eyes.

'I like your eyes.'

'Oi, don't get me started on my looks. Nice eyes, sure, but they refuse to sit on top of the cheekbones. Not that there's anything wrong with my cheekbones, but they're so damn close to the nose. Do you see how one is closer to the nose than the other? Do you see that? And as for the nose. Of course the nose is well and good, but why does it sit to the left of the mouth? I mean, up and left, not on the side and left, but not in the middle, not symmetrical. And the mouth—well, not bad, you might say, but can you see how it tilts, as if to draw attention to the wonkiness of the nose?'

Kiss her, Morris, lean in and kiss her.

'Sure there's nothing wrong with my mouth. It's a lovely mouth. Lovely. But why won't it stay underneath the nose?'

Tell her she's beautiful and kiss her.

'I think you're . . .'

'Almost beautiful. But let's face it, when it comes to beauty, a miss is as good as a mile.'

Morris never mentioned her looks again.

So now it's my fault you couldn't say something nice.

Well, you wouldn't let me. You—

Always my fault. You couldn't say anything nice but, let's face it, you didn't waste any time in getting my clothes off me.

It was the T-shirt I wanted off.

You certainly did.

No, I mean—you're taking it out of context.

Out of context. What are you? Some doddery politician complaining about the media? You want context? Here goes: You have finished your final year at Canterbury. Your mother is safely tucked away in the old-aged home in Levin. You return to Wellington without even attending your graduation.

Morris moved back to Wellington soon after his final exam. He had a job lined up. He'd written to the Wellington Tramping Club. They'd said they'd be glad to have him join. He didn't stay for graduation.

Years later he attended David's graduation and found the ceremony surprisingly moving. He enjoyed its orchestrated movement, its repetition and sense of history. David said it was boring, but he was wrong. David thought that predictable and boring were the same thing. He didn't understand that it's consoling to do what others have done before, what others will do in future.

Morris was sorry then that he hadn't listened to Joan when she said he should attend his graduation. He was sorry that all he had to look back on was a dinner with his aunt and uncle.

Even if it did turn out to be a pretty important dinner. Let's not forget it was a pretty important dinner.

Norman insisted that they take him out for a celebratory dinner. They were so proud of him—their nephew with the degree and the letters after his name. Their nephew who had secured a job before the final results were even published. Joan started crying when she told how proud his mother would have been . . . was . . . is.

Norman said, 'Now Joanie, this is a happy day. Morris has made us all so happy.' He handed her his handkerchief.

She said, 'So happy. So proud. Oh Morris, you have made us all so very proud.'

'Joanie wanted to tell the whole world. She wrote to her family in Australia and to all her friends. There's no one she hasn't told. Even Natalie's mother in France has been advised.'

'I'm so proud,' Joan sniffed. 'Natalie's mother says she still talks about the lovely day you two had together. You were so nice to her.'

It was enough to make one feel proud of oneself. Enough to make one smile, maybe even direct a smile at the English waitress in the ugly T-shirt.

Again with the T-shirt. What ugly T-shirt?
It had lips on it. And a huge tongue.
I know. I know. It was my Rolling Stones T-shirt. I loved that T-shirt.
It was awful.
It was a Rolling Stones T-shirt. The most recognised image of our generation. Probably.
It was awful.

Joan flirted with the waitress. Turned out she was can you believe it? Jewish! And travelling, all alone. Well, with her sister. Come all the way from England! What brave girls! What bold girls! What almost pretty Jewish girls.

Joan invited Sadie to join them at the table. 'This is an important occasion. Morris here has just returned from university. He's graduated! He's an electrical engineer, which is not the same as an electrician. We're celebrating. And he's got a good job already.'

Sadie apologised. Much as she'd love to join them, her boss would go mad if she sat at the table with a customer.

'Well, never mind, you can stand and tell us about yourself. Have you attended synagogue since you got here? Where are you staying? There's not much of a Jewish community, you know. And it's Pesach coming up. Where are you going for the Seder? Please, you must come and join our Seder. You and your sister both.'

Morris listened, horrified and hopeful, wanting the waitress to accept, terrified that she would. If he kept looking at her T-shirt she'd think he was looking at her breasts.

He was both relieved and disappointed when it transpired that she couldn't make Pesach. She'd met up with some other young people. They were having a Seder at someone's flat. Joan knew the parents of some of the Seder kids. They were good kids. Morris might know some of them.

'Didn't you used to be friends with the Kahn boy? I'm sure you used to be friends with the Kahn boy.'

Morris didn't remember any Kahn boy. The English waitress was looking at him like there was something wrong with him. Like he had a huge tongue sticking out from his chest.

'Get her number,' Joan urged him when the waitress went off to serve some other table. 'Ask her out. You can bring her to our place for lunch. This Sunday.'

'Can't,' said Morris, 'I'm going tramping this weekend.'

'Well then, next weekend.'

Norman put his hand on his wife's.

'So, Mr University Graduate,' he said, 'how does it feel to be finished with your studies? How many letters is that after your name?'

'Should I get her number?' Joan whispered on their way out of the restaurant, with Norman out of earshot.

Morris pretended not to have heard her.

As it turned out, Morris didn't need Joan's help. About a week later he found himself being hailed in the street by two girls in summer dresses.

'I know you,' one of them said, bold as brass. She turned to the other one and said, loud enough so that Morris could hear, 'This is the guy I was telling you about. From the restaurant.'

The restaurant—it was the waitress. Wearing a swirling dress. The other one must be her sister.

'Wendy, this is . . . what's your name again?' Sadie said.

'Morris.'

'Morris, Wendy. Wendy, Morris. Morris has just graduated. He's Jewish. And his mother is such a sweetie.'

'My mother . . .'

'And your father is the kindest man.'

'My father? No, no, those weren't my . . .'

'Your dad left me a tip. First one I've got at that restaurant.'

Then she asked how Morris had spent his week and he said he'd gone tramping. She nudged her sister and said, still loud enough for him to hear, 'What's the bet he went with some girl?' and Morris, flustered and blushing, admitted that he'd gone alone.

This seemed to impress her.

'Isn't it scary to be all on your own in the wilderness like that?'

'I have to go. Sorry.'

'I'll walk with you. Wends, you do your shopping and I'll meet you back here in ten minutes.'

And so Morris Goldberg, recently graduated and newly employed, found himself walking down Cuba Street with a girl in a summer dress at his side. She gave him her phone number before they parted and he asked her to go with him to a movie.

It would be childish to phone Joan and brag that he didn't need her to find his girlfriends for him. He'd organised a date all on his own. It had been easy.

He bought a new shirt and checked the times for the cinema in town.

It was a pity that Sadie and Wendy had been invited to a party that Saturday and Wendy didn't want to go alone. A pity that the host didn't mind if Sadie took Morris—there's no limit to the number of people you can fit in a student flat. A pity that the place was dark and noisy and Morris didn't know any of the music. A pity that Sadie wore that T-shirt which leered and smirked, reminding him of the hairy hippies on campus. Wanton like them.

Or maybe it was not such a pity.

Morris could have refused to go to the party. He could have done it in a way which didn't seem cowardly. He could have said something cool like, Big parties do my head in. And it's *you* I want to get to know.

He went to the party and pretended to smile and drank too much, and after his third cigarette looked at that awful tongue and thought he might be sick. 'I'm sorry,' he muttered. 'I don't feel well. Have to get out of here.'

Sadie took his hand and led him out into the cool night and didn't even say goodbye to their hosts.

She took him to her flat, which was quiet and clean. She gave him sweet tea and asked again about the tramping, about being alone, all alone, in that wild wilderness.

Morris told her, and she leaned in, quiet as a spy, and kissed him.

Stop grinning. Say something nice. About her eyes.

'I like your eyes.'

She didn't like her eyes and she didn't like her nose so he thought he'd better look at her T-shirt, but that was too ugly. He had to get it off her.

She was beautiful.

When Morris told Joan he'd gone to a party with Sadie there flickered across her face something like disappointment. Morris drew himself tall, ready to defend himself for dating a waitress, but Joan wasn't disappointed at their dating. She was thrilled about it. Thrilled! Such a lovely girl and Jewish too. And so far from home. Her parents were in England, weren't they? Were they planning on coming over? Was Sadie planning on settling here for good? Oh Morris, I'm so happy for you. Wow.

Why then, Morris wondered, the flicker of disappointment? Had Joan realised that Sadie wasn't beautiful?

Oh, don't you see, Morris, she was disappointed at having no part in it. She wanted to be the one to set us up. She wanted to do that for you.

Why? Why should she?

Well, she set up your first date, didn't she? Your first time with a girl. What about her? That Natalie? Did you tell her she was beautiful? Her of the acne? Did you gaze at her over the billy and tell her she was beautiful? Did you?

It wasn't necessary to take a billy on a day hike, but it was nice.

When they made love he brushed her fringe from her forehead.

Rewind. Rewind.

Rewind?

Yes, rewind. Give me more details on what came before. Who leaned in first? How did it feel, that first time? Did you tell her she was beautiful?

I can't remember. That's all I remember.

The tuawhatsit biscuits and the billy you remember, but how it felt to make love for the first time—forgotten. Do me a favour.

Why didn't you ask Joan? She seemed to know everything.

Tell me something, Morris.

What now?

Did your father tell your mother she was beautiful? Did they touch each other? Were they intimate together?

I was six years old when my father died and you want me to describe their sex life.

Not sex, Morris, touching. How many times do I have to tell you?

I was six years old. I don't remember.

Are you sure you don't remember? Don't remember Joe coming crashing into the house with a bunch of flowers for the most beautiful woman in the whole wide world, and an angel on top of it. Don't remember him pulling Pearl up and twirling her around in the kitchen, singing, 'Lawdy Lawdy Miss Clawdy . . . you sure look good to me'?

Don't remember her holding on to the table and telling him to slow down, it's dinner time and the boy is in the room? Don't remember her smoothing down her skirt, smoothing down the tablecloth which got snagged in his cuff link? Her hanging up the tablecloth, wet from the vase which toppled with flowers too heavy? You don't remember any of that?

What about the slow times? When his mother, fetching him from school, would bend down to straighten his jacket and say, 'Your father's at home today. I want you to keep quiet. He's not feeling well.' And he would want to fall into her, for who knew how long the slow time would last?

Does Morris remember none of this?

There is one memory. Morris's marble memory—the marble he kept in the pocket of his shorts, the one with the fire-red filament that shone when held up to the light.

Morris is four years old. All three of them have gone camping. Morris is in the tent, swaddled in his sleeping bag. His parents are still at the fire. Morris wants to shine his torch over the ceiling of the tent but his mother has already come in once to tell him not to waste the batteries. He can hear insects and water. He thinks about the boy at kindergarten who is collected every day by his father, not his mother.

That afternoon Joe collected Morris from school, but that was because they were going camping and his mother was waiting in the car. Joe had lifted him up on to his shoulders, there in the classroom, and Morris had looked down on the children as if to say, See here. This is my father. He has an axe in his backpack.

Morris considers putting the torch on again, just for a second in his sleeping bag, so that he can look at the new marble his father has given him. The marble came in a bag with nineteen others. Morris and Joe counted them out together. Three steelies, three oilies, four spiders and ten cats' eyes.

'One, two, three . . . Good boy . . . four, five, six . . . Clever thing . . . seven, eight, nine . . . that's right . . . twenty. There you go. Counting up to twenty. Nineteen, twenty my plate is empty.'

Morris had assumed that the marbles would be coming camping with him, but when his mother found the bag on top of his pile of camping clothes she put it back on his shelf. Morris appealed to his father. Joe said the marbles must stay behind, and turned back to fiddle with the billy. He must not have noticed that his son was almost in tears.

Why did his father even buy the marbles if they couldn't come camping? Joe was unfair and Pearl was unfair. What was the point if the marbles had to stay at home? Morris eyed the bag. If he pushed it in amongst his clothes no one would know he'd taken it. It would serve them right.

He felt the bag in his hand. It was heavy. He put it down quickly. They'd find a big bag like that. But they wouldn't find one marble. No one would know if he took just one.

He chose the cat's eye with the reddish-orange centre. It looked like fire.

Perhaps if he digs right down to the bottom of his sleeping bag, his mother won't see the torch and he can look at his marble. But if he does that he might get stuck. He might suffocate. No one would hear him die. And when they found him they'd see the marble in his hand.

He lifts the flap of the tent just an inch and peers out.

The fire is oranger than his marble. His mother is bent towards it. She has her arms reaching forwards, open palms towards the fire. Morris can see her profile as she turns slightly to his father who has taken her hands and is pulling her to her feet. Joe's face is orange, glowing. Is he smiling? Yes, yes, he's smiling. He's smiling and pulling her up.

She stands, dusts down her skirt, puts her arms around his waist and leans into him.

Morris watches as his mother rests her head on his father's shoulder.

They sway around the fire as if on a dance floor.

That was the last time she went camping with you, wasn't it?
Because she got sick. She went to hospital.
Ah yes. Pearl got sick and Norman made scrambled eggs.

Norman's scrambled eggs were brilliant, like he said they'd be. They ate directly from the pan, because Norman said that was the best way to eat scrambled eggs. And there was less washing up.

After breakfast they went in the tram to visit Pearl at the hospital. Norman told Morris he was going to ask Joan to marry him. He said, 'I feel sure she'll say yes,' then he leaned in close and whispered into Morris's ear, 'After all, she's crazy about animals,' and he growled and tickled, and then they were at the hospital and it was time to be quiet.

Pearl was in a big room with lots of beds in rows. She started crying when she saw them and she kept saying, 'I've lost. I've lost . . .' till Norman took Morris out and left him with a nurse. The nurse gave him a crayon and paper, and said, 'You'll be a comfort to your mother. Such a nice quiet boy as you. At least she has you.'

When Norman came back, the nurse said, 'Your wife will be fine. I'm sorry for your loss,' and Norman explained that he wasn't Pearl's husband. Pearl's husband was unavoidably out of town.

'Well, at least they have the boy,' said the nurse. 'That's something.'

It was all over when Joe came back.

Pearl was home from the hospital. Norman had left.

Joe phoned Norman, and when he put the phone down he started whistling a squeaky tune.

Pearl asked him to stop whistling. It was giving her a headache. She put her hands over her ears and said that he'd be the death of her.

He kept on whistling—whistling and shaking and jiggling his keys in his pocket. Hopping and dancing. Spilling all over the house. He couldn't keep himself together. His threads were too thin. He was fraying at the edges, coming apart at the seams.

There were creases in Morris's father's face, and for all his smiling and whistling and spilling they keep getting deeper, like starched linen that's been folded so often in the same place that no amount of smoothing can remove the scars left by the folds.

Your father's friends had creases too, and cracks in their faces. You remember your father's friends, don't you? You remember them, Morris.

Uncle Jack and Owen with one hand, and that man who always wore a hat. Talking too loud and tossing him too high and sometimes sitting silent at the kitchen table while Joe fussed with the kettle.

Pearl was seldom there to make tea for her husband's friends. She'd disappear into her bedroom and emerge only when they'd all left for the pub. Joe let her know they were going by calling loud farewells. His friends shouted their thanks down the passage.

Sometimes when Morris woke up in the morning he'd find an empty bottle on the kitchen table, a full ashtray beside it, and he'd know that one of them had visited, that his father would still be asleep when he left for kindergarten, might still be asleep when he came home, that his mother would be grumpy and muttering when she saw the ashtray.

Once he tried emptying the ashtray before his mother

saw it, but it was too full and he spilled ash on the tablecloth. The harder he tried to rub it off the bigger the smudge became. He put the bread bin on top of it.

Pearl must have lifted the bread bin and seen the mess he'd made, because she hardly helped him get dressed that day and she hardly spoke to him all the way to kindergarten. When he looked out of the window he saw her coat whipping about behind her, still cross with him.

Those stains never come out, I guess. Like the creases on a soldier's pants.

After the hospital, Joe stopped going up north to visit Uncle Jack and Owen with one hand, and that man who always wore a hat. They started coming south to visit him.

Joe said, 'Are you never satisfied?'

Pearl said, 'Who's looking after their wives while they're in Wellington, while you're all out drinking?' She said, 'What if one of their wives loses her baby? Who's with her? Who's looking after their children? What if one of their wives ends up in hospital and there's blood everywhere?'

Joe said, 'Pearl Pearl Pearl.'

Pearl said, 'I'm exhausted,' and she started crying.

Joe said, 'I'll tell you what. I'll make it up to you. I'll take Morris tramping. Only the two of us. You can have some time on your own. To relax. I'll take Morris.'

'Listen to you—promising to take him tramping like you promised to take him last time. But did you take him? No, you did not. You upped and changed your mind and left me to deal with his disappointment.'

Joe said nothing. He lifted his fists, held them up for a moment, then dropped them flapping at his side. When he turned, he saw Morris standing at the door. 'We'll go tramping together, you and me. Father and son.'

So it was to be only the two of you going tramping. Only the boys. This time he's not going to leave you behind. He's taken you shopping for shorts and he's packed your gear and you're leaving tomorrow morning. You're leaving early. Only you can't sleep and your new shorts are uncomfortable.

Leave it alone. Please, Sadie. I was six years old.

And something's gotta give. Something's gotta give. Something's gotta give.

There's something soft rubbing against Morris's face.

He's lying on David's sofa. There's a pink blanket pulled up over his chin. The blanket makes him feel sad, as if he's playing a part in one of the European movies Sadie used to like. Old man asleep on a sofa. A kind family member comes in, covers him with a child's blanket and leaves. He doesn't stir but later, when the kind person has gone, he feels something soft against his face and he gazes about as though looking for someone.

On the table next to him is a telephone. The old man looks at it before bringing it to his ear to check for messages. He receives only a dull dial tone.

He picks up a flier that has fallen to the floor beside him.

If Morris were the old man in the movie he'd slip the flier under his pillow. The camera would come closer, focus on his eyes as they shut. Or perhaps the movie would cut then, to Rachel alone. Behind her would be . . . would be . . . just sky. There's only sky behind her because she's on a mountain top. She's on high ground, far removed from the raging rivers. She's put up her tent and she's wrapped up in her sleeping bag. Outside might be cold and dark and sliding land, but Rachel is safe on her mountain top. She has good gear. A billy and a mug of something sweet and hot. She has made wise decisions.

They'd never show that in a movie, thinks Morris. Not unless it was at the very end or they had something horrible coming next. If they did show Rachel, it would be ambiguous, unclear, impossible to place. Maybe they'd just show her face. Let her be sleeping, Morris thinks. If you show her face, let her be sleeping.

Then they'd cut back to the old man and you'd see, from the way he lets the flier fall to the ground, that he is blaming himself.

It's his fault for having insisted on wearing the shorts.

It's ridiculous to sleep in tramping clothes. Ridiculous to think that his father will go without him. He is six years old and should know better. He shouldn't have nagged his mother. He shouldn't have slept in the shorts. They're scratchy. Maybe he should go to his parents and tell them he's sorry. His father will ruffle his head and tell him that he wouldn't dream of going without him, and his mother will take him back to bed and tuck him in and tomorrow he'll go tramping with his father. Only the two of them. Man and man.

He climbs out of bed. Goes down the passage. To his parents' door which is closed.

He knocks on the door.

His father opens the door. 'Hello, young man. Awake, are you? And tomorrow's our big day. Come along, I'll take you back to bed. Quietly, don't disturb your mother.'

He takes Morris's hand and leads him down the passage, whispering about what fun they'll have, what fun.

Then Joe starts whistling—cheerfully at first, but still Morris wants him to stop. The whistling will wake his mother and give her a headache, and it's getting louder and louder, less cheerful, more jarring. Morris tries to pull his hand from his father's. Because after whistling comes grabbing Morris and spinning him round, faster and faster, laughing and whistling till everything's a blur.

'Dad?'

Morris sits up.

'Are you awake?'

'Yes, yes. I am. Awake.'

David is standing in the doorway. He's wearing boxer shorts with pictures of Bart Simpson on them. Morris averts his eyes from his son's bare torso.

David says, 'Sorry, I didn't mean to wake you. I thought I heard you talking. I thought maybe there'd been a call.'

Morris apologises and David doesn't ask what for. He says, 'I'll just . . .' and is gone before Morris can ask whether it was he who brought the blanket.

Pink blankets. Why are you thinking about that blanket? The blanket is not what you should be asking David about. You need to ask him your Miss Robson Question.

My Miss Robson Question. But I don't know what it is. I don't know what I'm supposed to be asking.

Oh, I think you do.

David is back in the room. He's pulling a sweater over his head and his voice is muffled. 'Since I'm awake now, I thought I'd check the weather.'

Morris glances towards the window.

'On the internet,' David says.

'On the internet. I know.'

David is heading out of the room.

Bart's grin is mocking, shifting, a cartoon figure that can't tell Morris anything.

For God's sake, Morris. You need to ask David. Ask him. Ask him what?

Come on, Morris. This is important.

'David?'

David almost trips over the carpet when he turns. He puts a hand on the back of the sofa to steady himself.

'Yes, Dad?'

'Why don't you sit for a minute?'

The hand moves along the sofa to his father's shoulder.

'Sure, Dad. Just for a minute, then I'll check the weather.'

He pushes the pink blanket aside to sit next to Morris, not opposite him. Together they stare at the dark television.

He won't sit there for ever, Morris. Jesus Christ, ask him before I do.

Before you do?

Just ask.

'David, I want to ask you something.'

David turns to look at his father. Is that eagerness on his face? 'Sure, Dad, anything.'

'Well, um, I haven't seen Rachel for a while, you know? At least a week or two.'

'You're busy. And she's not exactly easy to pin down. We'd never get to see her if Debbie hadn't signed up at that gym.'

'But you . . . you see her sometimes. You saw her shortly before she left.'

'Wednesday night last week. Debbie bumped into her at the gym and convinced her to come for dinner. See what I mean about only seeing her because Debbie joined the gym?'

'How was she? How did you find her?'

'How I found her? She was fine. She seemed fine.'

'Fine.'

'Fine. Like I told Wendy, even keel.'

'Not upset or anything?'

'The thing is, Dad, we didn't know about Strobe . . . about Stewart then. Debs only found out after—'

'Fine. Not tired? It must be tiring for her teaching all those classes. And being, I don't know . . .'

'Bouncy. Being bouncy at the gym all the time. Yeah, I guess it is tiring. But she didn't seem tired. She seemed fine. Maybe if we'd known about Stewart we would have paid more attention but you know, Dad, she really did seem fine.'

'About being bouncy. Um, she wasn't maybe . . . maybe happier than usual? Exuberant?'

David snorts. 'Exuberant? Rachel? I don't think she's ever exubed in her life. Bouncy at work is one thing, but exuberant? Rachel? No. She seemed the same as always. Fine.' David pauses. 'Even keel.'

'Even keel.'

'Even keel. Like I told Tim.'

'You told the cop.'

'And I told Search and Rescue.'

'You told Search and Rescue.'

'They have to know about the mental state of the person they're looking for. Search and Rescue have to know what they're dealing with, whether the lost person could have gone off the rails, or maybe tried to . . . you know, and apparently they often get old people going missing. Because of dementia.'

'Rachel doesn't have dementia.'

'Of course she doesn't. But they ask about the mental state of everyone. They have to.'

And you had to answer, thinks Morris, and he remembers David mumbling into the telephone and walking around so that he can't overhear. Gossiping with a policeman when Morris is out of the room.

Don't get all uppity about that. David was trying to protect you.

To protect me.

You know how protective he is.

Protect me from what?

Well, what do you think?

They keep looking at the dead television for a while, then David says, 'I'll tell you if there's been any change in the weather.'

Don't let him go. Call him back. Ask him if she's happy. Ask him if she's lonely.

He said even keel.

At the door David turns back. 'Dad, there is one thing. I guess Debbie and I were wondering about something—'

'Um, you were wondering about something?'

'Well, Debbie wondered, and I did too, whether it's quite normal for Rachel to . . . I mean, what type of person goes tramping alone? I mean, don't get me wrong, I don't think there's anything wrong with it, and Tim said it's fairly common. We just wondered. I mean three days is a long time to be alone and isn't the whole point of going tramping that you get to have time with someone else? Chatting under the stars, sharing the beauty of nature, that sort of thing.'

Miss Robson gave Morris tips on answering exam papers.

'The first and most important thing . . . Are you listening?'

He nodded and her head seemed to go up and down. He thought scarves were completely stupid. They could get caught in doors or . . .

'The first and most important thing is to Read. The. Question. What must you do, Morris?'

'Um, you must—'

'Read the question. That's right. Read it carefully. Ask yourself what is being asked of you. Find the key word. Are you being asked to explain something? To give an example? To describe it?'

If a scarf was really long, a woman could trip on it. She might fall over. Wasn't there an actress who . . .

'What must you ask yourself, Morris?'

'Um, I must ask myself—'

'That's right. You must ask yourself what is being asked of you. Now David, for example, he is asking you to do what?'

'To describe something.'

'That's right, Morris. Good boy. David is asking you to describe the person who goes tramping alone.'

When Miss Robson leaned back out of the light, she didn't look bald any more.

Describe—the key word is describe. David is asking for a description. But how can Morris describe this person? It could be anyone. Anyone who's alone.

Morris says, 'I don't know. Normal people. Like the policeman said, it's fairly common.'

He doesn't say, except in the Tararuas. The Tararuas are not for tramping alone. The Tararuas are my mulberries.

David says, 'I guess so,' and he's gone to check the weather.

You could have described your father.
My father.
Your father used to tramp alone.

There's a window seat in the bay window. Six-year-old Morris lies flat on his stomach on the cushion with the green flowers, and kicks his feet. He screams, 'I want to go too. I want to go with him. He promised.'

His mother stands beside him. 'Morris, Morris, stop screaming.'

'But he promised,' Morris wails.

'Morris, listen to me. Stop crying and . . . and . . . I know what we'll do. We'll go and see Joan's new little puppy. That will be fun—to play with the puppy. We can take something nice for tea. You'll like that.'

'Don't want Joan's puppy. I want . . . I want.'

Pearl talks to the window. 'It's out of my hands. Maybe next time. Try to understand.'

Morris will not understand. He is six years old and cannot imagine a next time.

He is burning.

Pearl stands up, smooths down her skirt. 'That's enough, Morris. I'm leaving now.' At the door she turns back. 'Morris, please.'

'He promised.'

'Joe Goldberg's promises,' she mutters. 'The sooner you learn . . .' and she is gone from the room.

Morris peeps over the edge of the bay window. His father is facing the boot of the car. He has his back to the house. Pearl walks towards him, then stops at a bit of a distance and watches him. Joe turns to her, and she looks away to inspect a plant. She pulls something off a leaf and stamps on it.

He says something and takes a step towards her. Then he walks past her to go into the house.

'I want to go with. I want to go too.'

'Morris,' Joe says softly.

'You promised I could go. I packed my bag.'

'Morris,' louder.

'I want—'

'Morris,' angry now, 'I'm leaving. Are you going to say goodbye to me?'

'You prom—'

'Oh, for goodness sakes. This is ridiculous. I'll be back in two days. Stop bawling and I'll bring you something. Just stop bawling, will you?'

'But, but, I want to go—'

'I said. Stop bawling. Just stop.'

Joe's hand is lifted. His face is red. He bangs his hands on the side of his pants, turns and walks from the room. Morris gasps, holds his breath and hears his father asking the walls if it's any bloody wonder he needs time on his own? God, he needs a bit of peace and quiet. Two bloody days, is that too much to ask?

A bit of peace and quiet. That's all Rachel wanted. She works too hard and her job is tiring with its loud music and exclamation marks. Its passion. Its bouncing. All that bouncing will take it out of you. Not to mention the flashing lights. She'd need some peace and quiet.

A bit of peace and quiet. That's all his father wanted. But there's no peace and quiet when your wife is complaining about your friends and your ridiculous son wants to sleep in his clothes. It's enough to make you wish you'd never bought the damn shorts. To make you wish you'd never invited him to come along.

It is ridiculous to sleep in tramping clothes. It is ridiculous to think that his father will go without him. He is six years old and should know better. He shouldn't have nagged his mother. He shouldn't have slept in the shorts. They're scratchy. Maybe he should go to his parents and tell them he's sorry. His father will ruffle his head and tell him that he wouldn't dream of going without him, and his mother will take him back to bed and tuck him in and tomorrow he'll go tramping with his father. Only the two of them. Man and man.

He climbs out of bed. Goes down the passage. To his parents' door which is closed.

He pauses at the door.

Open the door, Morris.

He's not supposed to go into his parents' room.

Open the fucking door.

He puts his hand on the handle, turns it, opens the door.

What's the wording on a Jewish telegram?

A what?

A Jewish telegram. It's a joke. What's the wording on a Jewish telegram?

A joke?

Start worrying. Stop. Details to follow. Stop.

Morris looks at his watch. It's six o'clock. He must have fallen asleep. David must have come and gone with his news of the weather. There's light coming through the curtains. Footsteps coming down the passage.

Wendy comes in. She's wearing a white bathrobe, like she's in a hotel. Her hair is wet. Morris looks down to her feet, half-expecting to see a pool of water. Her toenails are painted bright red.

She says, 'Jeez, you look terrible.'

So terrible that she can't bear to look at him, for she's covered her face with a towel. When she starts rubbing at her head, he looks away.

Sadie used to rub at her hair like that. He liked watching it. First she'd cover her whole head with a towel—face too. Then she'd . . . well, attack herself. Morris would watch the towel pummelling away at her head and marvel. How did she come to be so secure, so confident?

From beneath her towel she'd keep talking to him. 'So I bumped into that woman who used to work at the pharmacy today and she said that . . .' and he'd be wondering whether she wasn't hurting herself.

When she lifted the towel, her face would be glowing

and her hair puffed out around her like iron filings exposed to a magnet.

Until she rubbed it off entirely.

She enjoyed rubbing at her hair, Morris thinks. She would have missed it.

'At least it's getting light,' Wendy says. 'That will make the searching easier.' She turns to open the curtains, then turns back. 'About what I said last night, about Sadie and the touching . . .'

Morris says, 'We were both stressed,' and is surprised to see a flash of anger burn across her face.

'Of course we were stressed. We still are stressed. But that doesn't make it . . . it doesn't make it wrong what I said. It's still right, what I said.'

She wants to start the fight again. She's still burning with it. All that stuff about Steve was just a layer of ash hiding the coals which are, right now, going to flare up again. Morris doesn't think he can bear it. He needs to stop her.

'You were right,' he says. 'There is something the matter with me.'

She takes a step forwards.

'Sadie knew there was something the matter with me. She always knew.'

Still she advances.

'She knew. She understood. It's just . . . it's like . . . in some things I need instructions. Sometimes I need instructions.'

Wendy stands still, fiddles with the towel, is quiet for a while before saying, 'You know, if there was one thing Sadie loved, it was giving instructions. Sadie Bossy Boots. Used to drive me nuts when we were kids. And did she take as good as she gave? No she did not. She hated being given advice.' Her voice is drenched. The burn is gone. She is damp again. 'My sister managed to avoid advice-givers for most of her adult life only to find herself completely at the mercy of do-

250

gooder nurses and know-it-all doctors. How unfair is that?'

'How unfair—'

'Grossly unfair. Anyway, I'd better get dressed,' and she is gone from the room.

She has forgotten to open the curtains.

Drink this. Swallow that. Try not to think of the pain. The nurse knows what's good for you. The doctor knows better. The visiting specialist knows best of all.

They pared away at Sadie with their instructions, down to bald bone.

She just lifted a languid hand, lay back and was told.

They left her with only one thing to instruct Morris on: what to do when she died.

She chose early morning to give Morris his what-to-do-when-I-die instructions. Before the day wore her down.

'Don't be squeamish, Morris. Write down what I say. In your notebook. Humour a dying woman.'

Morris took some time in finding the right page in his notebook. Sadie didn't complain. She lay back and breathed, and he was reminded of the evenings when they used to sit together after dinner, Sadie turning a glass of wine by its stem, Morris writing down what time he should collect the children, what bills to pay when he went to the bank, who would be coming to David's birthday party. They were comfortable those evenings. Sadie sat still and his notebook filled with the knowledge of what he needed to do.

Later, when he re-read Sadie's death list, he wondered whether she'd noticed that he didn't feel uncomfortable about being instructed on her death. Had she seen that he felt relief? Had she known that he'd considered and reluctantly rejected the possibility of writing his own list?

He couldn't write his own list. Someone might see it and ask questions. But if Sadie insisted, that was different. He would humour her.

First she had instructions on how to deal with the instructions. 'When we're done I want you to tear these notes out of your notebook. Put them somewhere you'll remember. Next to the phone.'

She paused to breathe, and he wondered whether she was expecting him to make a note that he was to rip the pages out. She knew that he hated ripping pages from his notebooks.

'If you don't rip the pages out, you might not be able to find your notes. I'll be rotting away while you flip frantically through your gazillion notebooks . . . gazillion notebooks . . . looking for the one that contains the bloody instructions.'

Did she have to use so many words? When every one was tiring. 'Bloody', for example.

'Sadie, I . . .'

'Okay, I'm exaggerating, but let's not forget that you will be overwrought and . . .'

Should he be timing her pauses, remembering how many words she managed per breath? Would the nurse want to know that?

'. . . overwrought will be the appropriate emotion. Your wife will just have died.'

'Sadie . . .'

'Don't fight with me, Morris. I don't want you alone with my body. That's all.'

But it wasn't all. There were three instructions. 'First you phone the Chevra Kadisha—you know, the people at the shul.'

How do you spell Chevra Kadisha? Where do I find the number of the shul?

'Then you phone Wendy and the children. Then go and sit in the front room and wait.'

Only three.

Sadie closed her eyes and sighed, and the nurse came in and said it was almost time for the patient's painkillers, and what a funny angle she was lying at. It couldn't be comfortable.

That evening, when Morris went to answer the phone, he saw that there was already a note above the phone. Wendy had written the number of the Chevra Kadisha on a Post-it and stuck it on the wall. When Morris tried to pull it off, he discovered she'd stuck Blu-Tack on the back of it. If he pulled it off he might damage the paint. Why did she use a Post-it if she was going to stick a great wad of Blu-Tack on the back of it? And why that particular Post-it? The one with the estate agent's logo on it and those words—We Go Beyond.

Sadie and Wendy probably thought it was funny. 'I wonder how far beyond the Chevra Kadisha will go with me? To hell maybe?'

'You should be so lucky, darling. It's off to heaven for you. You're an angel.'

Morris was alone in the house when Sadie died, just as she'd known he would be. Early in the morning, after the night nurse had left, before Wendy arrived. Before the visitors or the children or anyone.

He didn't flip through a gazillion notebooks and he didn't need to check Sadie's list. He'd learned it off by heart. It was that short. Phone the Chevra Kadisha. Then the children and Wendy. Then sit in the front room and wait.

Rachel was at the house within ten minutes. Still in her gym clothes.

One of the men from Chevra Kadisha looked at her skimpy shorts as if to say what kind of a daughter? What kind?

The kind of daughter who finds her father sitting in the front room and doesn't try to stop him when he says he'd like to see the body before they wrap it up. The kind of daughter who walks behind him down the passage and doesn't try to hug him when he stands outside the spare-room door unable to turn the handle, who doesn't take his hand or burst into the room and disturb the men who have closed the door behind them. The kind of daughter who walks away from the door so that he follows, then sits opposite him and says nothing.

The men were finished when Wendy arrived. David got there soon after.

'We will drive away slowly,' said the older of the two Chevra Kadisha men. 'You, her family, you walk behind us. Down the road, till the end of the road. You accompany her on this last journey.'

Wendy took David's hand and put her arm around Rachel. Morris pulled back to walk behind them. At the end of the road the car sped up and merged with the morning traffic.

I wonder if the Chevra Kadisha was involved when your father—

When my father.

I wonder who followed your father down the road? Do they even do that when someone—

Who would have washed and wrapped his father's body? Not the careful man who had actually met Sadie at someone's birthday party and remembered her laugh, who was sorry for their loss and wished them long life. Not his younger partner who knew someone who'd been taught by Sadie and was silent and respectful and kept his eyes down.

It was a well-matched pair who took Sadie away. Balanced and synchronised. They eased her smoothly from the world. They went further.

And the two who took Joe away? A hunchback banging his club foot behind him, the box balanced precariously on his bent back. Holding the other end of the box, an impossibly tall, horribly thin pale man who stops every now and then to wipe his bulging forehead. When he stops he puts his end of the box down but doesn't tell the hunchback, and the box is dragged along for a few clumping seconds before the hunchback realises and throws his end down, spits, shouts something guttural. Raising dust. Always raising dust.

Who followed the car down the road? Did anyone lead the spirit out of the world or was it still bouncing about in the house, banging doors and creasing tablecloths? Spilling out. Always spilling out.

Morris should have been there, walking behind his father. He should not have gone rushing off to hide at Norman's, to sleep on the floor on Joan's side of the bed. Boy oh boy a Lincoln Toy.

David hasn't come back to report on the weather. It's probably bad news. David doesn't like giving bad news. He left it to Rachel to phone people when Sadie died.

It must be bad news.

Morris listens for noises in the house. He should go and look for David. He should open the curtains, fold the pink blanket, brush his teeth, put the kettle on. He should get up from the sofa.

Or you could have described yourself.

Described myself?

When David asked you what kind of person tramps alone, you could have described yourself. You'd just come back from tramping on your own when we met—well, when we met properly and I chased you down the road. I thought it was sad and sweet and sorry for you to have gone on holiday on your own. I pictured you walking down a long dusty road trailing a suitcase.

A suitcase on a tramping trip?

Forget the suitcase. The point is that you'd gone tramping alone. It made me sad that you went alone. You'd been gone for four days. Four days all alone.

It had to be at least four days. Four days was Morris's minimum for tramping alone. The first day was for making the transition. That morning he would have woken in a bed, eaten at a table, looked in the mirror and turned a tap. He might have spoken to people and still be full of their words. On the first day he repeated phrases in his head—advertising jingles and snatches of equations whose only value was that they fitted the rhythm of his footsteps. He ran through his plans in his mind, repeating rivers and mountains, track names and times over and over. He looked at his hands and feet on the first day, getting his bearings. Sometimes he fell into counting footsteps.

The second day was for looking up at where he was going and looking down at where he'd come from. Once, on the second day, Morris crawled out of his tent and saw the sun shining off a river. Beyond the river was the mountain he would climb. It had sprinklings of snow on top. Everything was sparkling and silent. He stamped his feet—I am here, alone in this world—then let out a great whoop. Mouth stretched, eyes closed, Morris Goldberg cleared his throat.

The second day was for elation. At the end of the second day he looked down at where he'd come from and thought, I am closer to God and there's nothing wrong with it.

The third day was for coming down and being tired. The third day said you're right. You are insignificant. You're nothing and that's the way it's supposed to be. The bush closed behind him and forgot he was ever there. Morris liked the third day best.

But on the third night he'd start thinking about what he was going back to. When the tent was up and the fire was made, he'd start thinking. And telling himself not to think. Telling himself there was still a full night and most of a day to go.

The fourth day was for walking out safely, for making it out.

It made me sad to think of you alone for four days. And then you stopped.

It made you sad and then I stopped.

Not because it made me sad. Because you got the malaise.

The malaise?

The tramping-alone malaise—that uneasiness when you're
tramping. Like the Craglet said.

The Craglet?

Craglet Craig, almighty president of the Canterbury Tramping
Club. Father figure to university students far from home. The
Craglet who you haven't thought of for years and now keep
thinking about.

Only because you make me.

I make you?

Morris did not get the malaise, though his experience
was similar to the one Craig described. It started, as Craig
had said it would, with general uneasiness and murmurings
of anxiety in the air around his skull.

He'd done what Craig had said he'd do: 'At first you don't
realise that it's in your head so you do a kind of tally on your
body and on your surroundings. You check that everything
is where it should be. You try to focus on some real pain
like the blister on your heel that bothers you every time
you put your foot down. You tell yourself to feel the pain
but you can't feel the blister and you don't recognise your
surroundings and there's this sucking-in feeling telling you
it's stupid to keep on going.'

They were sitting around the fire when Craig told his
story—Murray, Morris, Craig and a friend of Craig's who'd
joined them for the tramp. The friend handed Craig a hip
flask. Craig took it but didn't drink. They all gazed into the
fire.

At last Craig said, 'You tell yourself to be cool. It's just the
weather, you tell yourself. It's just a funny feeling that will
blow away, you tell yourself.'

When stories are told round the fire there are long
silences, draws on the hip flask, time to pause and think
about what has been said. When stories are told round the

fire you can keep up with them.

Craig held the hip flask towards the fire, turned it and pulled it closer to study the engraving. 'Maybe you'll be lucky and it will blow away. I wasn't. It got worse and then I thought, What the hell am I doing here?'

It was unlike Craig to use strong language.

'I knew the area well. I'd done that route often, but I suddenly looked round and thought, Where the hell am I and what the hell am I doing? I didn't recognise my surroundings at all and everything seemed completely pointless. It's like there were voices in my head telling me I shouldn't bother to keep walking. I should sit down where I was. Just sit down. Just stop.'

The fire was as red as the inside of a marble.

Murray said, 'What happened? What did you do?'

'I did what one does in those situations. I picked myself up. I put one foot in front of the other.'

Craig called it trampers' malaise.

It made Morris think of the voice of an old man wishing him Mazel Tov in an accent so strong he had to lean forwards to catch the words. The noise of a classroom when you're trying to concentrate. A boy saying, 'so they can . . . wait for it . . . breathe!' All your father needs is a bit of peace and quiet. Here's a backpack filled with food. Nothing is too much for Morris.

Craig said, 'It can happen to anyone. Any time. But people don't want to talk about it. They hold it in and they hold it in, and then they stop tramping and they become miserable buggers. I'm not saying it will happen to you, but it could. Chances are it will. And when it does, you have to talk about it. Tell someone as soon as you get back. Tell as many people as you can.'

It started exactly as Craig had said it would, and yet it took Morris a while to consider that he might be suffering from trampers' malaise. It wasn't until he found himself unable to recognise the track he'd walked on many times that he remembered Craig's story.

Morris considered but quickly rejected the idea that he was suffering from the malaise. For it to be the malaise it would have to be something out of the ordinary, and for Morris there was nothing extraordinary in feeling lost. Feelings of unease and futility might have been unusual for Craig but for Morris they were all too familiar.

Morris Goldberg moving beyond the title page of tramping hardly warrants a fireside story.

How easy it would be to lie down on the edge of the ravine, to let himself go, to fall down.

But you didn't. You didn't. You picked yourself up. Put one foot in front of the other.

Plodded my way through my failures.

Plodded your way—oh Morris. Did you tell someone when you got back? You didn't tell me.

He didn't have to rush off and talk about it. It wasn't like it was anything unusual. Morris couldn't sustain the myth that he was good at something. Morris was surrounded by anxiety and uselessness. Morris was true to character—you couldn't share a hip flask over that.

He was thinking of giving the tramping a break anyway. Sadie was pregnant and shouldn't be on her own.

Aha, so you're blaming David for the fact that you stopped tramping.

David? How does David come into this?

Well, I was pregnant with him at the time.

—

Okay, so maybe that's a long shot. Anyway, the point is, you made the malaise worse 'cause you didn't follow Craig's advice.

I didn't follow his advice because it wasn't the malaise.

You didn't tell anyone. You bottled it in like a miserable bugger. And you didn't get back in the saddle.

Morris might never have tramped again had Rachel not one day said, 'There's a boy at school who's going camping with his father. He keeps boasting about it.'

So what did you tell Rachel about the malaise?

Tell Rachel?

About the malaise. How did you explain it to her? When did you explain it to her?

I—

You never explained it to her. Oh Morris.

The pink blanket still needs to be folded. The gym flier is lying on the floor next to the sofa. The curtains have yet to be opened. Morris Goldberg did not tell his daughter about the malaise.

Or about the other dangers of tramping alone.

Other dangers?

You know, how people push themselves too hard. It was another one of the El Presidente's lessons.

El Presidente.

El Presidente. Craglet. You know—Craig. He must have had a lesson about tramping alone. Doesn't sound like the sort of man to let that one slip, our beloved Presidente.

They were on a tramp near Blenheim when they encountered the red deer—Morris, Craig and a group of beginners who were, to a man, completely thrilled by the deer. Craig said the deer were destroying the bush, but that didn't dampen their excitement.

When they stopped for lunch, Craig told how he'd once come across a red deer feeding right on the track. He got so close he could almost touch it. He'd been alone at the time and was moving quietly. 'Not like you lot, charging about like bulls in a china shop.'

And that's how he'd got on to talking about what it's like to tramp alone, and how it had both advantages and disadvantages.

'The advantages,' said Craig, 'are self-explanatory,' and Morris thought, Of course they are. They're obvious. It's the disadvantages that needed explaining—what could be bad about being alone in the bush?

For some months the idea of tramping alone had been tapping at his thoughts. Imagine if you didn't have to talk at all, if you could go at completely your own pace, only you and your thoughts. No distractions. Imagine if you were all alone. It wouldn't be risky if you planned it properly.

Craig said, 'The biggest disadvantage is that it's definitely more dangerous. Whatever anyone tells you, it's more dangerous.'

Morris said, 'D'you think it's always more dangerous? What if the person is really careful and doesn't take chances?'

Craig leaned back on his backpack. 'That's a reasonable question. What if it was a careful, risk-averse kind of person?'

Someone like me, thought Morris.

'The problem,' said Craig, 'is that even the most cautious person turns quite reckless when they're alone in the bush. I've seen it happen often.'

One of the beginners said, 'If they're alone, how could you have—'

'People alone take more risks. They push themselves too hard. If there's more than one person, you can test ideas on each other. You can make sure that no one does anything rash. But when you're on your own you become . . . you become literally your own worst enemy.'

Your own worst enemy.

'It's like you're competing against yourself, and that's no good. That's when people do stupid things.'

The pink blanket still needs to be folded. The flier is still waiting to be returned to the coffee table. The curtains have yet to be opened. Morris Goldberg did not warn his daughter about becoming her own worst enemy.

You have to go there.
I have to go there.

Morris is calling, 'David, David'. He's breathing hard. He wants to bang on doors. 'David. David. I have to . . .'

David sticks his head through a door and Morris says, 'We have to go there. To where Rachel is.'

David says, 'Okay. Give me five minutes.' His head goes back in, then out again. 'Tell Wendy what's happening.'

It's that simple.

Wendy's in the kitchen. She says, 'Didn't that cop say we should stay put?' Then she says, 'The cop's an idiot. If you feel you need to be there you should be there. David too. It's not like you're going to interfere with their rescue plans. I'll stay here by the phone. If Molly calls I'll tell her you're on your way. Or maybe I won't. That cop doesn't scare me.'

She bangs the kettle on the table. 'I'll make a flask of coffee.'

Morris is awash with relief. And with something else that could be affection for Wendy. He says, 'Thanks for . . . for . . .'

She says, 'Take a quick shower. Ten minutes won't make a difference.'

David rests his hand on Morris's shoulder when he comes into the room. 'Man, I'm pleased you made that suggestion. I've been thinking but didn't want to—'

Wendy is firing instructions and questions.

To David: 'Good. You're here. Is your phone charged?'

To Morris: 'Jump in the shower.'

To David: 'Phone Debbie and tell her what's happening.'

To the kettle: 'God it feels better that we're actually doing something. I'll make a flask of coffee.'

Her voice propels Morris to the kitchen door. He is

almost out of the room when he thinks, And when we get there? What will we do then?

Behind him, David says to Wendy, 'I have no idea what we'll do once we get there.'

She says, 'Once you're there you'll find out.' She says, 'Sometimes you have to go somewhere to find out what you're doing there.'

David says, 'Sometimes you talk a lot of crap.'

'Morris, go already. Take the shower,' says Wendy.

It starts raining as soon as they get on to the highway. Hard. As if God is saying, You want to go there and see what's to see? You want to wring your hands and experience something of what Rachel's going through? Well, I'll give you something to see. I'll give you something to wring about. Hell, I might even give you floods. That'd be good for a laugh. And snow. Snowy floods. I like that. And I'll tell you something, you gabbling turkeys—you won't experience even an inkling of what she's going through. I can lay on hell and high waters and you still won't have the faintest idea what Rachel is going through.

God is quieter in the tunnel. The windscreen wipers drag noisily against the glass. David switches them off with a flick of irritation, says, 'Just because it's raining here doesn't mean it's raining there too. Could be the contrary. Could be that the rain is heading south.'

'Could be.'

They listen to the news, which is full of two teenaged boys convicted of killing a neighbour. Morris listens for mention of the Arctic ice but it seems that teenaged murderers are more important than opening sea routes. He wonders whether the teenagers really are more important, then quickly corrects his own priorities. A murder must be more important than a bit of melting ice, surely. One committed by teenagers, definitely. Think what the families of the deceased must be going through.

David says, 'God, it must be awful for the families of those teenagers.'

Morris's priorities take another shift.

The weather report offers little. There's rain in Wellington and rain in Kapiti but no special mention of the Tararuas. David turns the radio off and says, 'Molly would know what the weather's like. D'you think we should call her and ask?'

'Um—'

'No, no, you're right. There's no point in worrying her.'

David's cell phone rings. He says, 'Maybe that's her. Speak of the devil. You answer it, Dad,' and he hands the phone to Morris.

Morris hesitates before taking the phone. Why should he be the one who has to tell Molly where they're heading?

He's relieved to hear Wendy's voice, even if she does say, 'That was a worried-sounding hello. You thought I was Molly. You thought you were in trouble, didn't you? Didn't you?'

'Um—'

'Anyway, this is no time for jokes.'

'I wasn't . . . wasn't—'

'Some guy from Search and Rescue just called. They found Rachel's phone.'

'Found Rachel's phone.'

'They couldn't get any information from it. It was too wet. It had been in the river. Washed up on some rocks.'

'Washed up.'

They're putting extra searchers on the ground.'

'Does that mean—?'

'I don't know what it means, Morris. I don't know if it's good or bad. I don't know how many extra people and I don't know why. The guy wasn't one for chatting. He just said, "We've found her phone and I've been told to let you know that we're putting extra searchers on the ground," and he hung up.'

'Hung up.'

'Okay, so he said goodbye and then he hung up.' As if to

demonstrate, Wendy says, 'Goodbye,' and the phone goes dead.

Morris repeats the information to David quickly, without pause for David to ask, What? What? What does it mean?

David doesn't ask what it means. He just frowns like it was unfair of Morris to give him such news.

Downstream and wet and caught on a rock.

Focus on a fixed point, Morris tells himself. If you focus on something steady and still you won't be sick. He puts his hand on the dashboard. Focus on that.

After a while David says, 'I wish they could have got some information from the phone. Like who she called last. Like whether she tried calling for help.'

Your hand on the dashboard. Keep looking at it.

'Wouldn't you be able to retrieve the information?' David says. 'Isn't that what you do?' Then he says, 'No, I guess not. Especially if the electronics are shot. Water does that to cell phones. Still, I wish the phone could have given us more information.'

Morris manages to speak. 'Just finding it is information. It would tell the searchers a lot, just finding it.'

Don't ask what it would tell the searchers, thinks Morris. Don't make us think about where they found it. Downstream and wet and caught on a rock.

'I guess them finding it is what you'd call the metadata.'

Not quite, thinks Morris, but he says, 'I guess it is.'

Extra searchers, says God. Ha—like a few more ants will make a difference in the landslides I am this very minute letting loose. Ha!

The windscreen wipers are furious. David aims the car at the rain like a soldier with a bayonet. Like he's running into no man's land. They are submerged.

God says, And as for you two—you toy soldiers in your dinky car. I might cover you both in ice. For ever.

Debbie calls. Morris holds the phone up to David's ear so he can talk to Emma. David raises his voice to be heard above the noise of the rain. 'Sweetheart,' he says, 'Babyface,' and, 'Give your mum a giant kiss for me. A giant sloppy wet kiss.'

Morris repeats the words to himself like a prayer.

David has to say, 'I'm done,' three times before his father takes the phone away from his ear and snaps it shut.

After a while the rain drops off. It's quieter, and David sits back in his seat. He takes one hand off the wheel to rub his shoulder. 'How about some of that coffee Wendy packed? Can you reach it?'

Morris reaches to the back seat to get the thermos flask, steadies himself and carefully pours a few mouthfuls of coffee into the wide plastic cup.

Sadie always poured just a few mouthfuls. Enough so it was satisfying but not so much that it could do any damage if it spilled. Not that it ever spilled. She wouldn't let that happen. She kept a hand hovering, ready to take the cup on the slightest signal. Like a pianist's page-turner playing along in her head.

Sadie's car coffee tasted of plastic, but Morris liked it anyway.

In all the years of their driving together they didn't spill a single drop.

He says, 'Your mother always liked having a flask of something in the car when we went on a journey.'

'I know.' David sips on his coffee.

Morris lifts a hand so David will know that he's ready to take the cup.

'You know how people have car-journey memories?' says David. 'I'll tell you mine. You're driving. Mum is screwing the lid off a thermos flask. She's got a school lunchbox on her lap with sandwiches in it.'

'Cheese and jam sandwiches.'

'Jam and peanut butter.'

'We used to have coffee after the sandwich.'

'Rachel and I had those square school water bottles with the plastic lids. Mum used to pass the sandwiches back and let us choose.'

'Sometimes she packed fruit.'

'Unless we were going to Levin. If we were going to Levin we used to stop for fruit on the way.'

'Going to Levin.'

'To see Aunty Joanie and Uncle Norman.'

'You don't remember going to Levin to see Joan and Norman.'

'Sure I do. I loved those visits.'

'But you must've been, what, four or five when they left.'

'I guess, but not so young that I can't remember being spoiled rotten. Cakes, presents, lollies. What's to forget?'

Morris says nothing.

'Cakes, presents, lollies and puppies.' David continues. 'Joanie really knew the way to a kid's heart. What kid isn't won over by cakes, presents, lollies and puppies? I remember sleeping over there. Norman made scrambled eggs.'

'Scrambled eggs out of the frying pan.'

'Hey, that's right. They *were* out of the frying pan. How did you know? And Joanie read a story that went on and on and on.'

Morris is emboldened by his success with the frying pan. 'Was it about a princess frozen under ice?'

'A princess frozen under ice? Could have been. I can't remember.'

David hands Morris his coffee cup.

When everyone had eaten, Sadie used to rest her head against the car door. She could be quiet for ages on a car trip, gazing out the window.

There is nothing but rain and wind outside the window. Morris closes his eyes.

'Joanie used to read to us for hours,' says David. 'I remember thinking that parents' stories were short but aunts' stories were really long. Isn't it funny how you can have insights as a five-year-old and not even know they're insights? Parents' stories are short and aunts' stories are long. Aunts don't skip bits when they're reading to you.'

Joe's stories weren't short. Joe's stories went on for as long as Morris stayed awake, as long as Pearl would allow. Sometimes beyond. Joe's stories could go on for days.

Joe's stories had hunters who lived for weeks in the bush without seeing another human being, without taking a bath, without shaving. Their beards grew wild and full of twigs. Their whiskers almost covered their eyes. Joe's stories had giant birds that taunted the hunters and lived in secret places. They ran ahead of the men, luring them deeper and deeper into the bush, further and further into the dark. Joe's stories had flooded rivers and thrashing rain and horses which galloped faster than their jockey who fell in a pile in the bedclothes. Sometimes his stories had pretty girls whose kicking legs cut through the sky like scissors.

Joe's stories didn't stop even when Pearl said, 'You'll frighten the boy.' They didn't stop when she removed Morris from his father and took him to bed, muttering about getting the child all worked up before bedtime and how was she supposed to get him to sleep when he'd been over-excited? Hadn't she already told Joe it was supposed to be Morris's quiet time?

Joe had a story about a soldier who travelled across the world to fight a terrible monster. Everywhere he went he heard tales of the monster's teeth as large as chimneys, and of the ashes and smoke which trailed behind it. There were holes in the earth where the monster had taken bites, cracks in the land, burning crevices. Whole towns collapsed into ash.

The soldier ran across the burning land, searching for his enemy, but the monster was always ahead of him, always out of reach. He encountered some of the monster's henchmen and fought them in bloody battles. With each victory he became braver and prouder. I am invincible, he told himself. I'm not scared of a stupid strutting monster. Come and get me with your terrible teeth.

Until the day when the monster turned around and looked him full in the face and the soldier saw that it wasn't the teeth he had to fear. It was the eyes. In that moment he lost all his bravery. He stepped backwards without checking what was behind him. He was so scared that . . . so scared that . . .

Pearl swooped on her son, lifted him from his father's knee.

'You'll give him nightmares with stories like that. He's only six years old. And anyway, anyway, it's time for bed. You two have an early start tomorrow. Come on, Morris, we need to get you out of those shorts and into pyjamas.'

Joe shifted in his chair and kept on telling his story. To himself.

Knock knock
  Who's there?
  Gee, I've got you well trained.
  Gee, I've got you well trained who?
  No, no, I meant . . . forget it. Knock knock.
  What now?
  Oh, forget it. You were standing outside your parents' room.
  Outside my parents' room.
  You were about to open the door.

It wasn't the shorts which woke Morris. It was a nightmare about a monster with smoking teeth.

The nightmare has woken him and the shorts have scratched him and he has walked down the passage to his parents' room. To his parents' door which is closed.

He pauses at the door.

Open the door, Morris.

He's not supposed to go into his parents' room.

Open the door Morris.

But he's six years old and alone and reckless. His own worst enemy. He turns the handle and opens the door.

My God, all this drama. Sometimes you can be so dramatic, Morris.

Me? Dramatic? But you're the one who—

Oh no you don't. Don't turn this on me. We're talking about you now. You with your hand on the door like a kid in an old-fashioned horror movie. Get on with it.

But you keep—

Just get on with it.

At six years old Morris climbed out of bed and went down the passage to his parents' door which was closed.

He paused at the door.

He was not supposed to go into his parents' room and yet he put his hand on the handle, turned it and opened the door.

Morris's mother had her back to him. She was wearing a long nightie and she had a bright red scarf over her head.

'Mum, Mum.'

She was talking into the telephone and all around her there was mess. Piles of clothes all over the floor. A chair knocked over. Drawers leaking. Clothes spilling out of the wardrobe. A chest of drawers with a gaping mouth where a drawer should be. Papers thrown around, some of them crumpled, and there, on the floor at Morris's feet, a map. Morris looked around the room for his father. He looked at the bed and saw a pile and thought, There he is, he's still here, he hasn't gone without me. But he knew that he was looking at a pile of clothes. He knew that his father had gone, had left for the tramp without him.

And he knew whose fault it was.

His mother was supposed to have woken him. She should have run down the passage and shaken him from his bed and said, 'Quickly, Morris. Jump out of bed. Off you go. Your father is leaving. Run, Morris, run.' She should have stopped Joe. She should have stood at the door and said,

'Wait, wait for the boy. He's been so looking forward to this. He'll be there in a minute. Wait for him. Wait.' She should not have been talking on the telephone.

Morris looks at his mother's back. It's all her fault and Morris is burning and screaming and banging on her legs. He's shouting and crying. He's pulling her nightie, shouting that she shouldn't have let him go. It's all her fault. All her fault. And now she's turning and facing him. She's bending down towards him. Her face is white and blank. Her eyes are red and her mouth is red and opening and shouting that he shouldn't have opened the door. He should have knocked. Who does he think he is? She's shouting that he's just like his father, can't control himself. Can't do as he's supposed to do. Can't for once just do the right thing. She's holding him by the shoulders and shaking him. She's yelling, 'Upped and left. He's upped and left. Taken his backpack. Taken his clothes and gone.' She's shouting, 'Good riddance. Bad rubbish.' And holding Morris's shoulders, putting her face close to his. There's spit in her voice. Her head is swollen and bumpy under its scarf. She's a screaming monster with leaking eyes, shouting, 'Stop your crying. Just stop. Your shrieking and your crying. Stop. Stop.' Hurting his shoulders with her fingernails, and shaking him and shouting, 'Shut up. Shut up. Just shut up.'

Morris closes his eyes and is terrified.

He squeezes his eyes so the crying will stop, holds his breath so the crying will stop, and hears, from somewhere behind his mother's whimpering, a small voice saying, 'Morris, Morris is that you?'

The phone is dangling off the table. Norman's voice is both tiny and shouting. 'Morris, Morris, is that you? Morris, come and pick up the receiver. Talk to me.'

Morris opens his eyes. His mother drops her hands and sags into a pile on the floor. Her scarf has slipped. There are small spikes on her head. She's melting into a pile of clothes on the floor and Norman's tiny voice is shouting through the receiver, 'Morris, come here straight away. Come and talk to me before you do a-ny-thing else.'

So Morris picks up the receiver. He tries to say, 'Hello, this is Morris talking,' but he's hiccupping and sucking in air. The receiver is wet.

There is a deep sigh from the other end. 'Oh thank God.' Another sigh. 'Okay Morris, I need you to be a big boy now and listen to me very, very carefully.'

'Norman.'

'Don't worry, big boy. I'm here. I need you to be a brave boy and stop crying. Stop crying and tell me what you see.'

'Mummy's on the floor.'

'Good boy. What else?'

'Norman, she . . . Norman.'

'I know big boy. I know. Tell me what else you see.'

'Her head is all bumpy. There are prickles.'

'That's right. You clever boy. Now listen to me very, very carefully. Keep on listening to me. Take a deep breath, hold your tears and listen to me.'

And so Norman, sweet Uncle Norman of the pen-stained pockets, talked Morris through the process of fetching his mother a glass of water. 'She didn't mean to shout at you. She's just upset. Those aren't prickles on her head, they're curlers. They can't hurt you or her, I promise. Don't worry about the clothes on the floor. We'll tidy up later.'

Comforted him when his mother stirred, 'She's not cross with you, big boy. She just got a little fright when the door opened. Just a little fright. That's all.'

Talked him through giving her water and helping her to straighten a chair and sit in it. 'Wasn't your mummy silly to shout like that just because of a little fright? Aren't adults silly making such a mess in the room?'

Told him that he was an excellent young man, that he should give the receiver back to his mother and go back to sleep. Told him not to worry about where his father was or whether they'd go tramping tomorrow. Told him not to think about the tramping, rather to think about Mrs Pierce from next door who would be there any minute now.

Norman, sweet Norman who step by step, instruction by instruction, talked Morris into some kind of order, gave his mind something to hold on to. Conjured up Mrs Pierce from down the road in her dressing gown and slippers.

Norman, sweet Norman who said, 'Morris, big boy, best not to mention your father. Or tramping. It'll only upset your mother again, and we don't want to do that, do we?'

And Joan, dear Joan who laid a mattress for Morris on the floor beside her bed, who read him an endless story about a princess asleep beneath a sheet of ice. And about the tall prince who kissed her. The prince wore a heavy coat and fur-covered boots. His long beard kept out the cold. His boat pushed through the snow to the land where all was ice. 'And the prince's horse went galloping, galloping, melting the ice and bringing spring.'

The next day she bought him toys and cooked his favourite foods. 'Your mother is upset because your father's gone away for a while. But she'll be better soon and your dad will come home soon and then you'll go home. And in the meantime you and your mummy will stay here with me and Uncle Norman. Because we love you. And Morris, don't ask your mother about your father. Don't ask her anything. She's fragile, your mother. Like a delicate glass. She can break easily.'

When Pearl was well enough to go home, Joan spent the morning helping her move the furniture around while Morris played with his new toy car.

They swapped the bedroom and the lounge. They

separated the two single beds and put one in the basement. Morris didn't ask where his father would sleep when he came back.

Dear Uncle Norman whose voice was on the other end of the phone, saying, 'Morris, big boy, when I'm finished talking I want you to put the phone back on the receiver and go to your room. Go back to sleep. I know you're not going to start crying again because you're a big brave boy. I know you're not going to mention your father or the tramping because you're a good boy who doesn't want to upset his mother. A good boy doesn't upset his mother.'

Norman who put a blanket around his mother and bent over her while he led her to his car, as if she was his child.

Norman who ruffled Morris's head, and said, 'Your Aunty Joan and I have had a lovely idea. Why don't you and your mum come and stay with us for a few days? Joanie's got some great new toy cars for you. Boy oh boy a Lincoln Toy.'

Morris wanted to tell Norman that he couldn't go to Levin, he had to wait at home. He had to be there when his father came home. They were going tramping. Only the two of them. Man and man. He was dressed and ready to go. His father had an axe. But if he tried to speak he'd start crying again, and Norman didn't want that. And there was a monster ready to turn and face him and there was a marble stuck in his throat. He didn't know where his father was and the marble was growing and growing and could explode in his brain.

Norman who took him home to Aunty Joan, gave him hot chocolate to drink, knelt down in front of him and said, 'Morris, brave boy, take off the shorts.'

Norman who lied to Morris. Lied about his mother being fine and lied about his father coming back soon, about him just needing a bit of a break and coming back soon. Lied about all that. Even though Morris let Mrs Pierce into the house like Norman said, even though he went back to bed like Norman said, and closed his eyes when Mrs Pierce told him to. Even though he didn't mention his father. Or tramping. Even though he was a good boy who didn't cry or upset his mother any more.

And that, as they say in the classics, was that.
Classics?
Bedroom tidied. Rooms changed. Bed in the basement. Just you and your mother. Listening to the radio and sometimes spending a day in Levin. And I suppose that some time, somewhere along the line, you stopped waiting for your father to come home.

Morris and his mother listened to the radio and sometimes spent the day in Levin with Norman and Joan.

And some time, somewhere along the line, Morris stopped waiting for his father to come home. Stopped thinking, If I hold my breath, tie my shoes right, hold my pencil properly, draw in the lines, listen to the teacher, finish my food. If I keep my clothes clean he'll come home. If I don't cry, remember everything on this list, pass this test he'll come home. Stopped waiting and started thinking, Maybe he's dead. Started thinking what it would be like if he was dead. Tipping his mind towards wishing that he was before wrenching it back, telling himself you don't think those thoughts. Even if you want an explanation, a proper explanation, for why he isn't there.

After a while all the waiting and thinking and wishing stopped, and it was just Morris and his mother, and that was okay.

Okay? How can it be okay? Your father's gone and it was all okay?
It was me and my mother and that was okay.

279

What about after he died? Was it still okay then?
After he—
Died. Died. When your father died, what then?
—

After they sat you down and explained that he was gone.
What then?
—

After they told you he was never coming back. In heaven with
God, six feet under, pushing up daisies, finito completo, dead and
buried, gone.
Finito completo.
Finito completo, gone for ever, never coming back. After the
funeral. What then?
—

Come on, Morris, didn't things change after the funeral?
I never . . . they never . . . there wasn't—
A funeral. Morris Goldberg, do you mean to tell me—?
—

Jesus Christ, Morris, you do mean to tell me there was no
funeral. No sit down because we have sad news for you. Do you
mean to tell me they didn't give you a ritual?
A ritual?
Jesus Christ, Morris, we did it for a cat. For a cat we had a
fucking funeral. But for a son whose lost his father—nothing.
They didn't even tell you he had died. Did they, Morris? Did
they?
—

My God, Morris, I could smack your mother. And Norman.
And Joan. And you. I could smack you too. You should have
asked them. You should have insisted on being told. You should
have asked for details of his death. When you were a teenager. An
impertinent up-yourself teenager.
I was never an impertinent up-myself teenager. Neither were
you. We've been through this.

So when then? When did you know that your father had died? Jesus Christ, Morris, when did you know that your father had died?

I guess . . . I guess I always knew.

But for sure. When did you know for sure?

For sure?

Think, Morris, think.

When I saw the backpack in my bedroom.

The backpack in your bedroom. For God's sake, Morris, speak sense. What backpack? What bedroom?

The backpack was waiting for Morris when he came home from university on his first Easter break. Waiting for him on the floor in his bedroom. He circled it a few times before kneeling down to study it. It was khaki canvas. It smelt damp. A Trapper Nelson. It looked familiar to Morris, as though he'd seen it in a picture.

When he thanked his mother for it, she said it had been in the basement gathering dust.

He said, 'Where did you get it from?'

'It needs a clean.'

'But it's a really good backpack. Really, really good. Where did you get it? Was it—?'

'If you want it, take it outside and clean it. If you don't want it, put it outside and I'll get rid of it. And please Morris, please, stop asking me questions.'

'But—'

'Morris, please.' She turned back to the socks she was darning for him. 'Please Morris. Please. Stop asking questions.'

But you didn't stop asking questions. You asked Norman. You asked Joan. You asked your mother again.

—

Norman? Joan? Someone?

—

Oh Morris, sweetheart. You didn't ask.

He was dead. There was no point in pushing it.

Yeah, well, I would've insisted on being told. I did insist on being told. I wasn't too shy to broach the topic. I chose Joan 'cause she loved to talk.

Sadie wouldn't have been shy to broach the topic and Joan might have been grateful for her questions. Morris can imagine that she might have been quite relieved, eager even, to share the burden of Morris's father with Sadie.

When did Sadie ask Joan? Was it before they married? Did she marry him in the knowledge? Or was it afterwards, when the children were born and it was too late to do anything about it? Too late to do anything but watch and wait and pray that, whatever it was, the children didn't catch it.

It was probably on one of the Saturday afternoons. They're in Levin. Morris has gone to visit his mother. Sadie is sitting at Joan's kitchen table. She thinks maybe it's time she and Morris considered getting married. She has just one question for Joan. She asks it outright. 'So tell me, Joan, what was the story with Morris's father? Sorry to be blunt, but I need to know what I'd be letting myself in for. I need to know the truth, Joan.'

Or it is another Saturday afternoon, much later? The children are there. Rachel is a toddler. Joan tries to lift her on to her knee but she wriggles away, squirming. Joan makes light of it, but Sadie is ashamed. There's something wrong with a toddler who doesn't want to be hugged. Sadie doesn't understand it, has never seen anything like it. She's worried enough to ask Joan outright: 'This reluctance about being touched is in Morris's family, isn't it? There's something not quite right, isn't there? Come on, Joan, don't be coy with me. I know Morris has something not quite right. Did he get it from his mother? I imagine she could be kind of . . . I don't know . . . not the hugging type. And what about his father? Tell me, Joan, what was the story with Morris's father?'

Well, yes, I asked Joan and she told me.
When did she tell you?
It doesn't matter when she told me. It doesn't matter what I know. What matters is what you knew, what you didn't know. What matters is that they didn't tell you. When it mattered. The details. You didn't know the details and that's what matters.

Even after he'd scrubbed it outside and left it in the sun to dry there were still some watery stains on the backpack. Morris traced a finger round those stains and knew that his father had died somewhere damp. Somewhere damp and overgrown. Where explorers used axes to cut through the jungle. Where vines could rise out of the water, pull you in. Could drag you down and swallow you.

David says, 'Hold on. Hold on.'

Morris opens his eyes. It's raining hard again. The road is awash. The car is shaking from the current. He puts his hands on the dashboard and holds on.

'I do remember a princess frozen under ice. There *was* a story about a sleeping princess—kind of like Sleeping Beauty on Ice. Joanie read it to us when we went to visit them in Australia. Man, Rachel loved that story. She used to get Joanie to read it again and again.' He pauses. 'That was a nice holiday, when we went to Australia.'

David starts talking about ice creams in the park, about peeling noses and water fights. About how embarrassed Joan got when one of her dogs pooed on the beach.

The current is pulling Morris downstream.

David is telling a story about Rachel freaking out when he put a block of ice down her T-shirt.

Morris's feet can't find a hold in the rushing water. He doesn't know up from down.

David remembers what Joan gave them to eat (hot dogs and tinned peaches), how Norman goofed about at the barbecue, how Sadie spent half the holiday in Joan's garden with a book and a cold drink. 'Come to think of it, it was probably a gin and tonic. It was that kind of holiday. It's a pity you weren't there.'

David remembers everything.

But the arguments that preceded their visit to Australia. Does David remember them? Does he remember the cold silence that sat in the car on the way to the airport? Does Rachel?

It's unlikely David would have heard the arguments. When she was really angry, Sadie would wait until the children were asleep before setting her tongue free.

'Norman is over seventy. This could be the last time you get to see him. How can work be more important than that? Some stupid deadline more important than seeing Joan? Of course they want to see you. You're like a son to them. Of course they told you not to worry about it. Of course they told you they understand. Of course they said there'll be a next time. That's what they do. They tell you not to worry. They tell you they understand. They console you with next time. And your job, Morris—your job is to worry. To be a son to them. Jesus Christ, Morris, there might not be a next time.'

The night before they left she pulled a towel over her wet hair and said, 'It's not too late to do the right thing, you know.'

But it was too late. He was too tied up in their argument. She'd immobilised him with her absolute truths.

'They love you like a son.'

At the airport she gave her knots one last pull ('Look how excited David is. He can't wait to see them') before letting go and leaving him spinning and reeling, a child's toy in an empty passage.

That was the last time any of them saw Norman.

Morris saw Joan only once more, at Norman's funeral.

They died within a month of each other. Norman at the hospital, Joan at her niece's house where she stayed after Norman's death.

The only inconvenience was the dogs. Becky didn't want them. They were old and incontinent. She'd put up with them messing on her carpets for long enough. She had them put down. Morris told her it was the right thing to do.

The children came back from that holiday with suntans and toys. Sadie's suitcase was packed with vases, plates, wine glasses Joan had got for her wedding.

Morris said, 'That was nice of her to give those things to us.'

Sadie said, 'To *me*. Joan gave them to me. She didn't send anything for you.'

Morris didn't believe her at first. Sadie could be spiteful when she felt superior. Joan wasn't spiteful and Joan never considered herself superior. Joan was on his side.

Later, alone in his office, he reconsidered. Superior or not, Sadie didn't often lie and Joan might, in the heat of the Australian sun, have finally decided that Morris wasn't worth bothering with. No more presents for Morris.

No more presents for you, he told himself, and grinned. This is no laughing matter, he told himself, but he kept on grinning. No more backpacks filled with chocolate for you.

Morris Goldberg had done something wicked enough to cause his aunt to withhold a gift. He felt like a naughty schoolboy who had got away with a prank.

Only it wasn't a prank. He'd wounded Joan. And he hadn't got away with it. He'd been found out by Sadie who would never forgive him. She told him so that evening, when they were clearing away the dinner dishes.

'To tell you the truth,' she said, 'Joan sent those things for you too. Not that you deserve them.'

Morris turned to wipe the table. 'You shouldn't have—'

'*She* might have forgiven you for not visiting them,' Sadie told the dirty dishes, 'but I haven't. I don't think I ever will.'

Maybe she forgave him when he went over for Norman's

funeral. If she'd seen how he reached over to hug Joan, how long he let her hang on to him, she would surely have relented.

Joan was tiny on her low shiva stool. The dogs circled her like the sea. One of them put his paws on Morris's back when he bent down to be held.

It was probably the same dog which kept Morris up that night, jumping on to and being pushed off the sleeper couch in Becky's spare room.

The next day he came home, bad tempered from lack of sleep.

It was too hot there, too dry.

Norman should not have died in a desert.

It was raining when Joe died.

No one walked through the rain to follow his spirit out of this world.

He was sucked under.

So maybe I was wrong to be unforgiving but, you know, I didn't know the whole real story then.

The whole real—

Story. The full megilah. The whole catastrophe.

The whole catastophe.

The thing is, Morris. Are you listening to me?

Am I?

Listening to me. The thing is, I didn't know there was that whole business of them not telling you when and how your father died. It's no wonder you were pissed off with them. Furious. Angry with them and not knowing why.

I was never—

Pissed off with them. Of course you were. They should have told you.

Morris turns to look at David's profile. 'I think maybe your grandfather committed suicide.'

David doesn't say, 'Bloody hell, Dad, where did that come from?' Or, 'Jesus Christ, I'm trying to drive.' He doesn't say, 'I don't know what the fuck you're talking about.'

He says, 'I've also been thinking about that. I told Tim but it doesn't mean . . . it doesn't mean . . .'

The windscreen wipers shake from side to side. Even the policeman knows.

Morris's window has misted up. He could take his finger and write his Miss Robson Question on the glass. Or he could ask David, 'D'you think Rachel could have . . . you know? These things can be genetic.'

The land slides and the water comes rushing down to

catch the car in its current. David pulls hard on the wheel. Morris braces himself for the skid that doesn't come.

They have pulled over to the side of the road. The windscreen wipers are still. The rain drums on the car roof. David's hands rise to hold on to his father's face.

'Dad, you have to listen to me.'

Morris flinches when David touches him.

'Listen to me, Dad. Listen . . .' His hands cup Morris's cheeks. 'Dad, I'm sorry. It's just . . . It's just . . . you know, Mum and I discussed this. That time when Rachel went tramping and Mum was in hospital. You remember— Rachel and I had a fight and I was pissed off that she was going and you looked so sad. Man, you were so drawn in and sad about it all.'

If David moves his hands, Morris's face will melt away.

'Mum was . . . she was like . . . okay, she was worried you'd be worried that Rachel might be like . . . be like your dad. She was worried you'd be worried that Rachel would just leave one day. Just disappear or . . . or commit, you know. She said Rachel was nothing like your dad. She said your father had post-traumatic stress from being a soldier in Europe during the war and he lost family in the holocaust and your mother was so . . . She said if anything Rachel was more like your mother than your father. Mum said there was something about a miscarriage and a hysterectomy and Joan said your mother never got over it and she blamed him and . . . man, Mum said that Joan said that your mother and father . . .'

David is talking and talking, drowning Morris in words. Until he stops, takes his hands from his father's face, freeing Morris to say, 'Sadie and Joan discussed this. You and Sadie discussed it.'

'Don't be cross with Mum. She had to discuss it with me. She was worried there would be a time like, well, I guess like this, and she wanted me to be able to tell you . . . she wanted you to know that there's nothing wrong with your genes.'

Morris clenches his jaw tight shut. His face will not melt away. He will hold it together with grinding teeth.

'The thing is, Dad, I've been wanting to tell you. It's been worrying me since Rachel . . . since yesterday. I've been wanting to talk to you about it. But you know—'

'I'm hard to talk to.'

'Hard to talk to? No . . . well, maybe a bit. But that's not what stopped me. I didn't want to be the one to raise it. Debs thought it might start you worrying about something you weren't thinking about in the first place.'

And Debbie knows.

David opens the glovebox to reveal a box of tissues. 'You look exhausted. Maybe you should lie down in the back of the car.'

If Morris leaves the car he might keep on walking. He might get swept away in the rain. He might get sucked into the earth. He shakes his head and David understands. 'It's okay, Dad. It's warmer in the front anyway.'

He starts the car, says, 'I don't even know what I just said. My words ran away with me.'

David has nothing left to say. His words have run away without him. They've been evicted by Sadie's words, which are crammed into the car like unwanted hitchhikers. David picked them up when he swerved to the side of the road, but it's not his fault. Sadie's words are good at hitching rides.

Sadie's words send one pretty-girl word out. She stands on a flat stretch of road so you have time to study her as you approach. You notice the tentative angle of her thumb, the way the sun catches her hair. When you get closer you see her smile. Could that be a gap in her teeth? Sadie's pretty-girl word shifts her handbag from one shoulder to the other.

She has nothing to hide. She wouldn't hurt you for the world. She's worrying about taking lifts from strangers. You melt faster than Ahasuerus faced with Queen Esther.

You pull over.

Sadie's pretty-girl word takes a step forwards.

You lean over to open the passenger door.

She smiles and flicks her hair off her face.

You open the door and hear dogs barking.

Words come roaring out of their hiding places on the side of the road. They throw their backpacks in your boot. You try to lock the doors but it's too late. They're crammed into the back seat of your car. One hangs on to the roof, leaning forward over your windscreen so you can see the knife in its mouth. A scarred word leers hungrily at you from the passenger seat. You're too afraid to say this is not what I signed up for.

Your passenger sneers. 'We're here for your own good. Now put your foot on the gas. We've got places to go, you and us.'

It's not David's fault he let Sadie's words into the car. Not David's fault he listened to a pretty girl with a gap-toothed smile saying, Let me tell you about your grandfather. I know a thing or two about your grandmother.

Morris could give Sadie's words a bit of a shaking. He could use some words of his own. He could say to David, That's your mother's story. It wasn't really like that. You know how she used to exaggerate. He could say, Your mother was in pain and on medication. She was rambling. I'm sorry you had to listen to it. He should say, She shouldn't have told you all that. It wasn't fair of her to tell you. Not fair on me and certainly not fair on you. She shouldn't have dumped all that on you.

He says, 'D'you want more coffee?'

David shakes his head.

Sadie's words sprawl out on the back seat and sigh with contentment.

Not fair of me? Not fair? I had to tell him the whole catastrophe.
I couldn't rush off and die without putting things in place.
Putting things in place.
Look, Morris, I'm a talker. I use words. So sue me.
Post-traumatic stress. Hysterectomy. Was there anything you
didn't tell him?
I didn't tell him they never told you when your father died. I
didn't tell him that.
You didn't know. You didn't tell him because you didn't know.
Look, it doesn't matter what I told David. What matters is
that you both know it wasn't genetic.
Wasn't genetic.
Not even slightly.
Fighting in Europe and losing family in the holocaust. I didn't
even know that.
Oh, Morris, of course you did. Just because no one told you
doesn't mean you didn't know it.
No one told me.
But you knew it anyway.
You told David.
Your mother should have discussed it with you. She should have
sat you down when the news came of his death. She should have
explained about post-traumatic stress. She should have explained
that he wasn't coming back. I still can't believe she didn't talk to
you about it.
She wasn't. We weren't . . .
You know, I could smack the woman.
Enough talk of smacking her.

Morris has a sudden image of Sadie advancing on his
mother. 'I'm terribly sorry, Mrs Goldberg, but it seems I'm

going to have to put you over my knee. You know you deserve it.'

Sadie would find the image funny. But Sadie would be wrong. It's wrong to blame Pearl for not discussing it with him. Pearl was quiet. They were quiet together. That's the way they were, Morris and his mother. Quiet.

David turns the radio on in time for the weather report. It's rain, rain, rain.

Some of Sadie's words reach over from the back seat to tap Morris on the shoulder. You may be right about us dumping all that on David, but we meant well. Doesn't it help you now, knowing it was the circumstances which killed your father rather than some ridiculous aberrant gene?

But don't you see, Morris wants to shout into the empty back seat, Rachel's circumstances are not so great either. I too can make a list of awful things for David: Rachel's exhausted. She's lonely. Her fridge is just white. Her boyfriend's girlfriend is pregnant. Her career has exclamation marks, loud music, passion. Her ballet's been replaced by strobe lights and her mother's dead. Honestly, Morris could shout into the empty back seat, something's gotta give.

He looks over and sees that his son is crying.

David cries like he did as a child—quietly, as if he didn't know that his face was crumpled and wet, his nose running. As a child he could cry for hours. Without noise, without drama, his activities uninterrupted.

When Sadie died he cried for days.

Morris hands him the tissue box. David takes a few but doesn't use them. Morris feels a flash of irritation. And fear. Don't you start weeping on me now. I kept my awful list to myself.

293

Sadie used to tell the children stories to distract them from their crying.

'I suppose I should tell you why I hate the Tararuas,' says Morris, 'because really, the mountains are okay. It's not the mountains' fault.'

David is quiet. Morris wants to lean over and wipe his nose.

'Well, I started tramping round Christchurch, when I was at Canterbury . . .'

When the story's done, he looks over to see if his son is still crying. 'That club was my mulberries,' he says, 'like when your mum—'

'Poor Mum. I'll never forget her and those mulberries. It's like she was trying to recapture a childhood she never had in the first place.' David sniffs, then blows his nose.

'Never had in the first place.'

'You know, the storybook English childhood.' He blows again. 'If anyone was carrying nutter genes it was Mum.'

'Nutter genes.'

'You know, nutcases. Like Mum's parents.'

'Sadie's parents.'

'And Wendy's. Talk about nutters.'

'I suppose they were a bit—'

'A bit? A bit! There was nothing "a bit" about Mum's parents. They were raving nutters, by all accounts. I mean, all that stuff about becoming gypsies when they were well into their forties.'

'Buying a caravan.'

'Leaving their house to some hippie friends who turned it into a commune.'

'Wendy coming home from university to find someone living in her bedroom.'

'A smelly druggy living in her bedroom.'

David and Morris are telling Sadie's how-we-came-to-live-in-New Zealand story.

After a while David says, 'It was funny when Mum told it.'

'Well, not really.'

'But it had a happy ending.'

'Happy ending?'

'She met you.'

Morris turns his face to the window.

It's not the full story. There's an addendum to the how-we-came-to-live-in-New Zealand story. Sadie's secret pain. Morris imagined Sadie's pain to be like a pebble—shingle-grey like the beaches of England, with a forked white bolt that looked as if might split the stone in three. It had a sharp point. It could wound her if she handled it too much.

Sadie kept her pebble to herself, but Morris watched her closely. In unexpected moments he'd see the loss of animation, the frown. He'd recognise in her hunched shoulders the movements of someone who is reaching into her pocket to pull out her pain and feel it in her palm.

He kept close to her in those moments. If they were alone he'd take her hand, as if by holding it tight he could stop it from reaching for her ache.

If they were in company he might catch hold of the cuff of her sleeve.

She'd brought the pebble back from a trip to England. She'd gone on her own before they were engaged.

Morris didn't go to work on the day she was due back. He didn't go to the airport either. He stayed close to the telephone. If she didn't call him within twenty-four hours of returning, he'd know it was over. Within forty-eight hours. Twenty-four. Thirty-six.

An hour and a half. From touchdown to telephone. He wanted to weep when he heard her voice.

She said he should come to the flat. He said he'd be right over.

But after he put the phone down he paused and thought their conversation through. She hadn't said she'd missed him, and she'd sounded flat as if steeling herself to give unpleasant news. Morris could guess what that news was: she was going to break up with him. Well, if she wanted to break up with him, let her come to his flat and do it. Let her be the one to close the door behind her and walk away.

Ten minutes later the phone rang. 'I'm so pleased I caught you. Would you mind getting some milk on your way? I could really, really have a cup of tea.'

He took his jacket out of the wardrobe and went to her flat.

She was in her dressing gown. Her eyes were red, her face creased. She smelled of cigarettes and alcohol. She had her hands in her dressing-gown pockets as if they were full of marbles, as if she was rolling them round between her fingers.

He kept his fist closed over the door handle, his hand cramping with the knowledge that she was leaving him. For good.

She'd been gone for two months. Eight weeks. Morris knew how many days. He'd counted them off on his calendar. He'd drawn a little cross to mark the last time she wrote to him.

In the beginning she wrote often. When the first aerogramme arrived, he felt a joy like reaching the top of a mountain. He ran his letter opener through its folds as if opening a present. Her handwriting was clear and consistent. She hadn't written in huge letters to be sure of using up the whole page. Neither had her writing become smaller and smaller as she got near the end.

An aerogramme was more than a dashed-off postcard. More than a long rambling wad of papers (both of which Morris had feared). An aerogramme folded up around itself. An aerogramme said, I know exactly what I want to say to you.

Sadie's letters were surprisingly formal and restrained,

like an itinerary in retrospect. She'd visited an aunt, had lunch with a cousin. She took a bus to friends from teachers' training college but couldn't stay long because she had to get the bus back on the same day. She was invited to a music festival but didn't go ('I've never <u>loved</u> music festivals. Not ever'). She stayed with her mother but not in the house. She was going to Brighton.

'I'll tell you the Brighton story when I see you,' wrote Sadie, and Morris felt a gush of camaraderie.

At the end of that aerogramme, right up close to the folded part, in cramped, tiny script, she'd written, 'Don't worry if you don't hear from me for a while. Things are a bit crazy here.'

The camaraderie was short lived.

A silent week later he woke up certain that she was not returning. She'd met an old boyfriend. Or found a new one. He took her to music festivals which, actually, she'd always loved. Very much. Why else the detour from her itinerary to explain that she didn't like them? Why else the underlining of the word 'loved', the repetitive 'Not ever'? The boyfriend had sideburns and long hair. He rode a motorbike. Maybe they took drugs. They were going to rent a hotel room in Brighton. Across from the pier. They'd lie on the beach and smoke. She was considering how to break the news to Morris. That last aerogramme was just buying time.

She was never coming back.

It took three more aerogramme-less days before he brought himself to phone Wendy.

'Oh Morris, it's good to hear from you. I'm missing her so much.'

'___'

'It's not like her not to write for so long.'

'___'

'Morris. Are you there?'

'I miss her too.'

They continued to call each other every few days, though they didn't have much to say. 'Just checking that you're still there,' Wendy said the first time she called Morris, and he knew he was not the only one looking for reassurance that Sadie would return. He and Wendy had become each other's insurance. She'd never leave Wendy on her own, thought Morris. As long as Wendy is here, she'll come back.

Joan phoned too. 'Has she written? Has she phoned? Remind me when last you heard from her.' Once she said, 'Married women don't go off on their own for weeks on end. Well, they didn't in my day.'

She did come back. She brought pockets full of marbles and a pebble with her.

When Morris saw her in her dressing gown, all weighed down, he gripped the door handle and thought, Tell me now. Don't make me come inside. Don't make me sit down and look at you. Tell me now and close the door behind me.

She took her hands from her pockets and fell into him. 'Oh Morris. I missed you so much.'

'Sadie, will you marry me?'

She slid down as if going on one knee to him.

He pulled her close.

The marbles fell from her pockets and rolled away.

There was just the one pebble after that. When she fell pregnant with David, she threw it away.

The day after Sadie's return, Wendy made one last call to Morris. She said, 'You've made Sadie happy. Hell, you've even made me happy. Well done. Brother-in-law.'

The insurance phone calls were Morris and Wendy's secret.

The pebble was Sadie's secret, though she shared parts of it with both of them. Different parts, Morris suspected.

She had to tell Wendy the facts of it, but he knew she

softened them, protecting her younger sister from the cutting edge that didn't have to be revealed. To Morris she handed the sadder part, the bit that made her cry. She handed a piece of her pebble to each of them, but kept a part, maybe even the largest part, to herself.

Morris is sure that Sadie didn't discuss her pebble with Joan over a hot drink on a Saturday afternoon. She didn't mention it to David or touch on it with Rachel. It was thrown away by the time they were born.

He looks over at David's profile. He could tell him now.

But Sadie wouldn't want it. And Wendy wouldn't want it. And what would it achieve?

If Morris did tell David Sadie's pebble story, he'd keep it short, like parents' stories are. It would go like this. Before your mother and I got engaged she went to England. When she arrived there she was surprised to find that her father (your grandfather) had left the family home and his wife (your grandmother) to go and live with a young girl in Brighton. The girl had twin sons. Your grandfather was playing at being their dad. He said (and these are the words your mother used in the telling of it) that he'd had to 'shrug off the claustrophobia of his first family in order to find out who he really was'. He said (again your mother's words) that he'd been 'stifled and suffocated for all his married life', first by his wife and then by his daughters. He said they were a pack of witches. He said they could all go to hell.

And what about his wife, your grandmother? She was still living in the old family home. The house had been taken over by squatters. She had one little room. The house was filthy. The power had been cut off and there were rats. She said the squatters were her friends.

They weren't so friendly when your mum suggested that they might need to move because she was considering selling the house.

Your mother travelled to Brighton to ask her father for help in getting rid of the squatters and selling the house. He told her she was materialistic and grabbing, and who was it hurting if the crazy old bitch wanted to share with a few friends? Or was Sadie worried about her inheritance? She could go to hell.

Your mother had to deal with lawyers. She had to deal with policemen. She had to sell the house and help her mother move in with a cousin. She had to protect Wendy from the really bad parts. She had to leave her mother and return to New Zealand because 'Wendy and I owe it to ourselves to make our own good, better lives. And to be honest, I can't deal with all that. I'm not strong enough.' She cried about the materialistic, grabbing comment. She felt guilty about leaving her mother, but not guilty enough to go back.

That's how Sadie's pebble would go, if Morris told it to David. But he won't. There's no point and Sadie wouldn't want it. Wendy neither.

Joe was suffering and Pearl was quiet. That's all.

Morris and Pearl were quiet together. That's how they were.

Morris and Rachel could be quiet together for hours.

Or, better still, quiet and not together. But not apart. Somewhere close. In the house. Alone together.

Sadie is teaching one of her Saturday afternoon classes which she really didn't need to take on but, 'Oh Morris, if you saw how those students improve from week to week, you'd know why I do it,' or she's out to lunch with a friend or Wendy, or Wendy and a friend.

David has rushed out in a flurry of sports gear and bus tickets, wheedled money for movies and a bit extra for a friend who's always broke.

Morris is in his study overlooking the washing line.

At the other end of the house, behind her bedroom door, is Rachel.

The front door is complacent in the knowledge that no one will knock.

Morris has pulled the telephone plug out at the wall. This is his secret from Sadie. He does it every time David and she are both out of the house. Rachel once saw him doing it. She nodded and continued on her silent way down the carpeted passage.

Sadie's radio has been turned off. David's tape recorder is silent. The house creaks and Morris wonders whether he should make himself a sandwich.

Rachel's in the kitchen. She looks up and he says, 'I thought maybe a sandwich.'

She's got bread and cheese on a board. Morris cuts the

bread and she fetches a tomato.

They sit at the table and Rachel passes him the newspaper. She keeps the weekend magazine section for herself.

Soon the day will come when Rachel doesn't pass on the newspaper but takes it and her sandwich to her bedroom. Morris won't mind. He can get the news online, and his office is warmer than the kitchen.

Honestly, Sadie, he wants to say. I didn't mind. That's how Rachel and I were . . . are.

And that's when David's phone rings.

The phone is ringing and David's pulling the car over and saying, 'Oh my God. Oh my God.'

He takes hold of Morris's face again. 'They've found her, Dad. She's . . . she's . . . she'll be okay.'

David is crying. His hands drop. Morris's seatbelt pulls tight as he leans to hug him.

There are more phone calls and talk of hypothermia. Rachel's been taken to a hospital in Palmerston North. She'll be discharged in a few hours. Molly says it can take a while to warm up those who have got profoundly cold.

Wendy's voice is both loud and small as she shrieks and sobs through the tiny cell phone.

David laughs and cries, first to Wendy then to Debbie.

Morris hopes they won't discharge her before she's warmed up completely.

It has all been arranged. David will drive to Rachel's car, which has a hidden key in a secret place beneath the bumper that David knows about because he put it there. He will then drive Rachel's car to Palmerston North and fetch her from the hospital.

Morris will drive David's car home. Later he'll go to David's for a celebratory dinner. Debbie will make the chicken dish that everyone loves and Wendy's crocodile man will snap his hands at Emma.

Morris does not say, Maybe Rachel would prefer to be alone.

The cat is at the front door. It weaves round Morris's ankle as he finds the right bunch of keys. Mrs Mac might not have fed it enough. Morris will see to it shortly. But first there is something he must do.

He goes to his bedroom that is exactly as he left it a day ago.

His wardrobe is squat and smug. Hiding something. He opens the door, pushes hangers aside to reveal, pushed flat against the inside wall, Sadie's coat.

'I'll come back for the coat,' Rachel had said. 'It won't fit into these bags. I'll take it separately next time I'm here.'

On Morris's computer a window had flown into a window had flown into a window. Morris had raised his hand. 'See you tomorrow then,' and listened as the dustbin bags heaved their heavy way out of the house.

Rachel forgot to come back for the coat. Morris didn't remind her.

He moves the clothes aside to give the coat more breathing space.

He takes Rachel's notebook from his wallet and slips it into the pocket of Sadie's coat.

Slowly, as gently as if he was easing an ill woman into a sitting position, he lifts the coat from the hanger and up to his face.

Maybe now, Morris thinks, I will cry.

There's a faint whiff of lavender and cloves.